Retribution

Larry Jeram-Croft

Cover Image - HMS Apollo's Wasp. Courtesy of her Flight Commander, Harry Benson, also now a best-selling author - his latest Fleet Air Arm novel, *'Distinguished Service'* is available on Amazon.

Also by Larry Jeram-Croft:

Fiction:

The 'Jon Hunt' series about the modern Royal Navy:

Sea Skimmer
The Caspian Monster
Cocaine
Arapaho
Bog Hammer
Glasnost
Retribution
Formidable
Conspiracy
Swan Song

The 'John Hunt' books about the Royal Navy's Fleet Air Arm in the Second World War:

Better Lucky and Good
and the Pilot can't swim

The Winchester Chronicles:

Book one: The St Cross Mirror

The Caribbean: historical fiction and the 'Jacaranda' Trilogy.

Diamant

Jacaranda
The Guadeloupe Guillotine
Nautilus

Science Fiction:

Siren

Non Fiction:

**The Royal Navy Lynx an Operational History
The Royal Navy Wasp an Operational and Retirement History
The Accidental Aviator**

Prologue

The little village nestled in a wooded valley. It was at the head of a narrow road which only went as far as the village square. There were only a handful of houses around the square with a couple of shops. Further out in the countryside were farms which generated the little wealth that there was in the area. So far the village had been peaceful. That was about to change.

Arianna Kasun felt like weeping with frustration. She had stayed at the university in Sarajevo for as long as she dared but the situation slowly spiralled out of control and eventually, she realised that it was no longer safe. She was lucky, she got out just in time. The city was under siege now and there was no end in sight. The journey to her home in the hills had been almost as dangerous. Luckily, she had been brought up in the region and knew the surrounding countryside like the back of her hand. She had avoided the Serbian army patrols and made the final dash to the village on foot having left her car hidden off the road almost twenty miles away.

Her parents just wouldn't listen to her. She repeatedly explained that the Serbs were coming and would force them out, even kill them but they refused to believe her. The village had inhabitants from many of the former Yugoslavian republics and they had all lived together peacefully for years. They simply couldn't understand that things had changed so much in such a short time.

She was just about to try one last time to get them to take her seriously when she heard shouting outside accompanied by the roar of large vehicle engines. Suddenly their front door was kicked in and with a sickening feeling, she knew she had left it too late.

Chapter 1

'BRITANNIA ROYAL NAVAL COLLEGE,' the shout echoed over the parade ground. 'COLLEGE, HO!'

There was the crisp sound of hundreds of leather boots snapping together. For a second there was silence only broken by the harsh cry of a seagull and the snap of the large white ensign flying from the College flag staff. Commander Jonathon Hunt turned around and faced the Captain of the College and saluted. 'Britannia Royal Naval College mustered and correct Sir. Ready for inspection.'

The Captain returned the salute but instead of proceeding down the steps to inspect the parade himself as he would normally do, he turned to the Admiral to one side of him and saluted and repeated the age old phrase.

The First Sea Lord saluted back and accompanied by the Captain and his aide, made his way down steps to inspect the formed ranks of officers under training who were passing out of the College today.

Jon was at last able to relax slightly. His part in the ceremony was largely over. As the Commander of the college, he was responsible for getting the parade ready but now it was up to the individual squad commanders to greet the inspecting officer as he made his stately way around the parade ground. He suddenly had a flashback to the last time he had attended this ceremony. It was when Helen, his wife, was passing out as one of the first commissioned female officers in the Royal Navy. The memory twisted like a knife in his guts. It might have been three years ago that she had died in that stupid car accident but it still seemed like only yesterday to him. Would he ever be able to put it fully behind him?

'Silly old sod's taking his time. We're going to be standing here for bloody ages.' Brian Pearce, Jon's long time friend and also the Training Commander of the College muttered under his breath.

'Tut, tut, Brian, we're the gamekeepers now. You'll have to give up with the poaching, we have an example to set.'

'Tell that to my aching feet.'

Jon knew exactly what the subtext of Brian's remarks were. After two years in the Embassy in Moscow as the Assistant Naval Attaché, he had been hoping for some reward when he returned to

Retribution

England. After all, there had been the odd moment of excitement even if the Prime Minister, Home secretary, MI6 and only a few Admirals would ever know what had actually happened. And of course, the prestigious appointment as the Commander at Dartmouth was held by many to be exactly that. However, it wasn't a ship or an even air station and Jon had had to be talked into accepting the role. He was offered a carrot and hopefully, in the not too distant future, there would be a command role in the offing. Brian had been in a similar situation and one of the factors that convinced them both to accept their roles was the chance to renew their friendship.

He looked over the sea of faces. The First Sea Lord was almost half way through now so it wouldn't be long. This was the end of his first full year and he was amazed as to how many of the young faces below him he could put a name to. When he was being honest to himself, he would acknowledge the satisfaction that came from taking young men and women, often straight from school or university and starting them on their progress to becoming effective naval officers.

'Four weeks off to look forward to,' he muttered to Brian. 'I can't wait.'

'Mind you, it seems like only yesterday you were giving that rousing speech to the new intake.' Brian replied in kind.

Jon thought back to that day. He had only been in the job a few weeks himself but it was tradition that the Commander welcomed the new intake and said something motivating. He remembered reading a book called 'We Joined the Navy' when he was a teenager and that had started with a speech to the new joiners where the simple brief had been to 'scare them silly'. In some ways it was actually good advice and he had decided to use the concept to some degree.

He remembered standing at a lectern in the quarterdeck just inside the main doors of the College and looking at nearly the same sea of faces as now and choosing his words carefully.

'Ladies and Gentlemen, welcome to the Britannia Royal Naval College, welcome to the Royal Navy. My name is Jon Hunt and I am the College Executive Officer, I also teach certain subjects here and we will be seeing a great deal of each other over the coming months. Later on, the other staff behind me will introduce themselves but I wish to say a few words first. You have all

Retribution

volunteered to be here today, well done. However, be under no illusions, the next year is going to be hard. Unlike the other services, in the Royal Navy we all fight together. It doesn't matter whether you are the Captain or a Junior Seaman, when push comes to shove, we are literally all in the same boat. Think about it. For this reason, although some of you here are already thinking of yourself as Engineers or Supply or Seamen officers, you need to forget that. You are all naval officers first and foremost and will be treated as such while here. Yes, you will all go on to specialise later but first, you have to learn the same core skills together. Look around at each other. There's a good chance that at least one of you today will become an Admiral, even the First Sea Lord at some time in the future. Some of you won't last a week. For those that see it through and hopefully, that will be most of you. Some will have exciting and varied careers, others may find it's not what they expect and leave early at some stage. I can't predict who will become what. What you achieve and how you do it, is totally up to you. Our aim here at the College is to teach you particular skills and to test you to make sure that you know that you're up to the job to come. One final point. Some say that being an officer in the Royal Navy is a job like any other. I disagree. Firstly you won't become rich. The days of prize money are long gone I'm afraid.'

A small ripple of laughter greeted the remark.

'That said, you won't be poor either and there is a degree of security, when the enemy aren't actually shooting at you of course. But that's the point. This is a fighting service with a tradition of success and victory won over hundreds of years and we will try to train you to have the same values. However, you will need to look inside yourselves to find that extra spark for yourself. Call it a vocation or a calling if you wish but without it you won't succeed. I'll now hand you over to Commander Pearce, the Training Commander who will let you know what he has in store for you over the coming months and I'll see some of you in the gym at six tomorrow morning.'

He kept true to his word and when the new intake were all mustered for Early Morning Activities or EMAs at the gym the next morning at six o'clock, he was there to watch. He made a personal effort to follow the courses and get involved as much as his duties allowed which included spending time on the river in the multitude of boats owned by the College. In the process, he rediscovered his love of sailing. It was something he had always promised himself he would do more of when he had the time and being at Dartmouth was exactly the opportunity he needed.

By the end of the year, the wheat had been sorted from the chaff and he felt an almost paternal pride watching the surviving group of young people slowly develop. He had seen them turn from immature youngsters into well-disciplined young men and women who all clearly had the potential to go further.

He was called back to the present by the return of the Captain and Admiral who took their places at the dais ready for the final march past. The Royal Marine band struck up 'Hearts of Oak' and the squads of Midshipmen started to march past and salute the Admiral. Then suddenly, it was all over. The squads conducted the final traditional march up the steps of the College and were then dismissed.

Jon and Brian turned with all the other staff officers, saluted the Admiral and then fell out themselves.

'What are your plans now Jon?' Brian asked. 'Kathy and the girls are looking forward to seeing you later in the summer.'

'Well Training Commander,' Jon responded. 'I'm going to follow your own guidelines and for the first week, I'm off on an Exped. I'm sailing in one of the yachts to France. It was a last minute thing but they were short of a crew and I volunteered. It will also give me the final hours and miles to do my Yachtmaster exam later on.'

'You really have got the bug haven't you?'

'Seems so, and it keeps me busy, which is no bad thing.' Jon replied with a sad note in his voice.

Brian knew exactly what his friend meant but refrained from reacting. He knew Jon was still hurting, even after all these years but it wouldn't help to comment on it. 'Well have a good time and we'll see you in a few weeks.'

Chapter 2

The sudden light as the hood was wrenched off Arianna's head was momentarily blinding. Her mouth was so dry she could barely swallow and the ache in her wrists where they had been tightly bound in front of her was causing her to lose the feeling in her hands. However, none of this got anywhere near the anger and anguish in her heart. The same hands that had pulled off the blind now roughly pulled her to the rear of the truck where she was unceremoniously pushed out to sprawl on the ground as her breath was wrenched from her lungs. Taking whooping gasps of air she tried to sit up and look around. Four other girls had been treated the same way and were in various stages of recovery. She could also see at least four armed men standing around them and grinning at their obvious distress.

Getting to her knees she forced herself to breathe and think. Her last memory before she was grabbed from behind and the hood forced over her head was of the terrified look on her parent's faces as they confronted the three armed men who had burst into their house. What was most horrifying was that one of the men was a neighbour of theirs. She was friends with his daughter and now he was raving at them about bloody Croats ruining the country and how they all should be killed. Before she could react, she had been dragged out and thrown into the back of the lorry she could now see. However, that didn't stop her hearing the screams from behind her. After that, it hadn't been long before the truck started and drove away. In that short time, judging by the screams and noise, it was clear that other houses had been treated the same way. The truck hadn't driven very far and she judged they were still on the valley road that led to the village.

She focused on one of her captors, an angry looking, almost bald man, dressed in military camouflage. 'What did you do to my parents you maniac?'

He looked down at her with a sneering expression. 'None of your business bitch. We're clearing all Croats out of our homeland. Just be grateful that you're still alive.' And with that he backhanded her across the face and she fell onto her back fighting back a cry of pain as she did so. She was damned if she was going to show weakness in front of these murderers.

Another man joined him and grinned down at her. This one was slim with shaggy dark hair and almost feral look in his sharp featured face. He looked at all the captives. 'Now listen ladies. You have been carefully selected by the victorious Serbian army to provide for our comfort and who knows in time maybe bear us fine Serbian sons.' He stopped and let the words sink in.

Arianna couldn't believe what she was hearing. 'This is the twentieth century you animal, you can't do this.'

The man smiled at her. 'Well volunteered. I was thinking of picking you anyway but you've just made the choice simple.' He walked over to her and grabbed a handful of her hair and pulled her to her feet. With her hands securely fastened there was little she could do but even so she managed one decent kick at his groin which was easily avoided and gained her yet another head ringing slap. Through the pain, she vaguely saw the other girls being given similar treatment. She was dragged off the road and into the trees where she was flung down again on to the ground. The man didn't waste any time and reached for the waist of the jeans she was wearing and started to rip them open.

Arianna stopped struggling. She was remembering the advice given to her at university when she had attended self defence classes. Her time would come. Once the man had her naked from the waist down he seemed satisfied and stood over her and stripped off his own trousers. He was clearly ready for rape. Arianna wasn't. However, she didn't resist when he pulled her legs apart and knelt down with his face only inches from hers.

'Prepare for the first but definitely not the last time you will be honoured by a Serbian,' he said as he felt between her legs and attempted to gain entry.

Arianna waited for her moment. The moment when he was totally distracted. She brought her forehead up as hard as she could, crunching into the bridge of his nose with a spray of blood.

She had been anticipating the pain of the contact of their foreheads, even so her sight dimmed for a second. However, the man was caught completely by surprise and he screamed, clutching his face as he rolled off her, presenting her with another opportunity. With all her might, she swung both her legs into his crotch. He was now doubled up in agony. She could hear similar noises from elsewhere in the woods but suspected it was the girls, not the soldiers making them. Still, hopefully, no one would come to investigate for a while. When the man had dropped his trousers she had seen a holster on his belt. Frantically reaching for it she managed to pull out an automatic pistol despite her bound hands. She had absolutely no idea how to fire it but that didn't matter. Holding it by the barrel she repeatedly slammed it down on his head. He struggled for a few moments and then lay quietly as she continued to pound his skull until she realised she could stop. She didn't know whether she had killed him or merely knocked him out and didn't care. She knew she had only a small window of opportunity. Should she try and rescue the other girls or just save herself? She was saved from having to make a decision by the sound of footsteps approaching and a male voice calling out. She saw a knife on her antagonist's waist and managed to grab it awkwardly before also scooping up her jeans and shoes. She slipped quietly away into the woods. The woods she knew like the back of her hand from her childhood and where no one would be able to find her.

Two hours later, with the bonds securing her hands now cut and decently dressed, she looked down from the hill over her village at the scene. It was eerily quiet. There was no sign of military vehicles but smoke was rising from several houses. She cautiously let herself down the slope behind her parent's house. It was one of the ones with smoke pouring out of it. She crept into the back garden and up to the window at the back of the house. She looked in and promptly vomited. Sitting in the middle of the kitchen were two people. Or more correctly two corpses. They had been bound to two chairs back to back. It looked like someone had poured petrol over them and then set them alight. Despite the blackened and charred features, she could still recognise them. Her parents grimaced in the agony of death. It was surprising the whole house hadn't gone up and probably that was what had been intended but maybe there hadn't been time to do a thorough job.

She reached into her waistband and pulled out the pistol. She had worked out how to use it on the way here. She had nothing more to lose and stood and walked boldly onto the road in front of her parent's grave. The place she had spent a wonderful childhood growing up in. There was no one about, it was eerily quiet. Three doors down was the house of the village butcher, the house of the man who had accompanied the soldiers. The house of the man she thought was a friend. When she got there she didn't waste any time and kicked the door hard. It held firm but the noise was clearly heard from inside and it swiftly opened. He confronted her, initially with annoyance and then he recognised who it was. He then saw the pistol and blanched.

Arianna didn't speak, she didn't ask for explanations, she didn't ask for apologies. Levelling the pistol, she took considered aim and even as he started to stutter and beg, calmly pulled the trigger. Although the noise was deafening and the pistol kicked hard in her hand, she noticed neither. What she did notice was the small hole appear in his forehead and the spray of blood and brains over the door frame behind him.

Without a word, she turned and walked through the village and out of her old life. Curtains twitched in several of the houses but no one confronted her. She had one thought and one only. She knew that not only was there a Serbian army on the rampage but there was also a Croatian one and she was going to sign up.

Chapter 3

Jon was wet, tired and to a small degree a little apprehensive. He was in one of the College's Contessa 38 yachts named Pegasus. The weather was meant to be good in July but the trip over the English Channel from Dartmouth had been rough and now they were looking for their landfall and just when he needed it, the visibility had reduced enormously. By just how much it was hard to tell as with the sun now setting, judging distances was just about impossible. He was scanning the horizon with the yacht's binoculars but all he could see was grey. The yacht did boast a DECCA radio navigation system but as he was meant to be navigating this leg as part of his training for qualification as a skipper he wasn't allowed to use it. For the last twelve hours, he had had to rely on the old fashioned methods of dead reckoning and estimating his position based on tidal data. Luckily, before the weather had closed in, he had managed to get a fix off the light house on the infamous Roche Douvres just off the coast and knew reasonably well where he was. The real problem was the tide. It ripped along the north Brittany coast at up to four knots and could seriously upset a person's ability to judge position as well as making landfall bloody dangerous.

He turned to the yacht's actual skipper and an old colleague of his, Lieutenant Commander Geoff Gregory, who had been his training officer when he commanded 844 Squadron some years ago and was now a divisional officer at the College. GG, as he was universally known was an experienced yachtsman and despite the disparity in rank, was the man in charge.

'Bloody hell GG, should we really be trying to get in, in these conditions?'

'Your decision Jon. How certain are you of our positon?'

'Hmm, fairly sure, to within half a mile or so. I guess we can press on a little more but I would feel happier if we dispensed with the Genoa and just continued under the main and engine, that way we can turn clear of any last minute rocks much faster.' Jon was worried that with the wind behind them a sudden need for a major change of course could result in an accidental jibe which could easily damage their rigging or even hurt one of the crew.

Retribution

'Good call Jon,' GG replied. 'I'll get a couple of the lads to get the Gennie down and you start the engine.' He called down to the saloon where the three midshipmen who were also on the trip were temporarily sheltering. Jon turned the key and the engine caught straight away and soon the foresail was neatly stowed on deck. He felt far more comfortable and in control now. Also, with the big foresail down, his forward vision was much improved.

'Mike, Pete and Jenny, can you please stay on deck now. We need all eyes looking out. What we're looking for is a rocky island on the port bow called the Isle de Brehaut and then land on the starboard side. In the centre of the estuary are several red and green can buoys so look out for them as well. Once we've identified a buoy or a point of land we'll then buoy hop up the estuary.'

They continued on in tense silence for several minutes. Jon had the chart of the estuary on the cockpit table in front of him and GG was steering. However, until they could identify exactly where they were, the chart was next to useless.

'We could always try the six pack method of navigation,' said GG.

''What on earth's that?' Jon asked. 'Not heard that mentioned before.'

GG gave a short laugh. 'No, it's not in the book but we used to use it in my racing days. When approaching the coast of France you have the chart and a six pack of beer to hand. Rather than charge on into the coast, you find a French fishing boat and give him the chart and the beer, he then returns the chart with your position marked on it. Don't laugh, we did it several times quite successfully especially in the days before DECCA.'

'And that of course, assumes that the Frenchman actually knows where he is,' Jon snorted. 'Who knows, with these new American satellites likely to become available, even to civilians soon, being lost might become a thing of the past.'

GG snorted with derision. 'That's all well and good right up until your system goes tits up and then it's back to the old fashioned methods. Which is why we're practicing it now, even though we've got a DECCA set below.'

Jon thought for a moment. He knew GG had taken a sneak peek at the DECCA a few minutes ago and hadn't said anything so hopefully that meant his position couldn't be that far out. 'You

Retribution

know, driving a frigate is much easier than this. This is real back to basics.'

'Which is why it's so much fun,' GG grinned back at Jon. He was just about to say something when Jenny, their female midshipman called out. 'Sirs, I can see a red flashing light just on the starboard bow. Hang on, it's one flash every five seconds.'

Jon looked at the chart and immediately identified it as probably being the light on a buoy marking the main channel up the river. 'Come to starboard GG please and aim to let it pass down the port side so we can confirm its name.'

GG did as instructed and within a minute Jon knew exactly where they were.

'Not bad Navigation Jon,' GG observed wryly. 'I assume that was the one you were aiming for?'

Jon grinned back, 'you'll never know now, will you.'

It took them almost another hour to get up the Lezardrieux River on the last of the flood tide. The pilot book had been quite emphatic about not arriving at half tide as the current in the river could be very fierce. The channel was extremely well marked with buoys and poles on the shore and even with the poor visibility, they had no trouble tying up in the small marina in the village of Lezardrieux in good time. Because they were not sure of the facilities ashore and GG warned that many French restaurants shut on a Monday, Mike had volunteered to make supper as they ghosted up the river. So by the time they tied up, a good old fashioned sailing 'spag boll' was ready for them all.

With a full stomach and at last beginning to warm up, Jon was starting to feel quite sleepy. The two glasses of red wine might have helped as well. The three Midshipmen were made of sterner stuff and asked to be allowed to go ashore and check out the village and were given the blessing of the two older men once they had done the washing up of course.

When they had disappeared up the main saloon hatch, GG reached inside the saloon table and produced a bottle of scotch. He poured two generous measures and they both sat back in amiable silence for a few minutes.

'Well Jon, that's sailing. Even a shitty trip like that seems wonderful once you're tied up and warm again.'

Retribution

Jon laughed, 'like banging your head against a wall. It's so nice when it stops. I have to say I was impressed by our three officers under training they took it all in their stride.'

'Yes, they're all in my division,' GG said. 'And they've all done well this past year. The girl in particular. She's definitely a future star. In some ways she reminds me of Helen.'

He immediately saw the look on Jon's face. 'Shit, sorry Jon. I didn't mean to rake things up.'

'No GG, we can't pretend things didn't happen. I'll never be over her but I've come to accept it now and not talking about it just bottles things up. So, you see her doing well, I hope you've steered her towards the Air Arm then?'

GG laughed ruefully. 'Tried and failed I'm afraid. She wants to be a warfare officer for some unaccountable reason and despite my best efforts won't change her mind. Maybe you can talk to her over the next few days and get her to change her mind.'

'I'll give it a go but from what you've said I probably won't succeed.' Jon tossed down the last of his whisky. 'Anyway, if you don't mind, I'm knackered and my pit is calling me. I'll go and get my head down.'

The rest of the week was a great improvement. The sun came out and the temperature soared. They sailed every day and visited several of the pretty little fishing villages along the Brittany coast before heading north to stop off at the Channel Islands before heading home. Jon got to know the three young trainees quite well and as predicted by GG failed utterly to convince Jenny to become an aviator and that was despite the three of them pumping him unmercifully about his past escapades, those that he was allowed to talk about of course.

Their final evening was spent in Bray harbour in Alderney. It would be an early start the next morning but that didn't put off the three youngsters heading off in the yacht's dinghy for a final run ashore, once again leaving the two older men to share the remains of the whisky bottle.

This time, they were sitting in the cockpit watching the sun go down. 'The bloody Germans built most of this you know,' GG observed pointing to the harbour facilities. 'They even had four bloody concentration camps on the island at one stage. They say that after the war no bird sang on the island for almost ten years.'

'What happened to the residents then?' Jon asked.

'Oh, I think they were shipped off to Guernsey but nearly all came back when they could. Anyway, what are you up to when we get back Jon? We've got almost a month of summer leave still to go.'

'Good question, I'm going to spend a few days with my parents and I'll stay with Brian and the kids sometime. Nothing really important.'

GG could hear the melancholy in Jon's voice but hoped there was something he could do about it. On top of awarding Jon his skipper's ticket, which was clearly well deserved. He and Brian had been keeping quiet for some time but he had been able to get to a phone the previous day and spoken to Brian who had confirmed that it was all sorted out.

'Jon, do you ever miss flying?' he asked innocently.

The question caught Jon out for a second. He thought carefully before he answered. 'Between you and me GG it's the one thing I dislike about the navy. The bloody Crabs let their senior officers fly. They even insist on it for many of their posts. Station Commanders are expected to be current on all aircraft on their stations. Don't get me wrong, driving a ship is up there with the best but I joined the navy to fly and now I can't.'

GG gave Jon a strange look. 'It's not up to me to tell you about this but when you get back, pop in and see Brian, I think he may have a surprise for you.'

Despite several attempts by Jon to get more out of GG, he was unsuccessful and then the rest of the crew arrived back from the pub and there was never time to investigate further.

Chapter 4

'Come on sunshine, where the hell are we going?' Jon asked, intrigued.

Brian just laughed as he turned the car off the road at the top of the long hill that leads down the town of Dartmouth below. He came to a halt in front of two large metal gates that were secured with a big padlock.

Jon immediately recognised where they were. 'Hang on, this is the old Dartmouth Flight airfield. We used to have an aircraft here to give air experience flights to the students and teach them about the Fleet Air Arm. Bloody hell, this is where I first flew in a naval aircraft but it's been closed down for years. Come on, what are we doing here?'

Brian ducked the question. 'You're right there Jon, some supermarket chain is trying to buy it and build a shop but that won't happen until at least next year and meanwhile, although it's shut down, as the Training Commander it's all on my slop chit until then. More importantly, I've got the keys. I don't think any of my predecessors ever bothered to come over and check it out but I did a couple of months ago. I think you might be interested to see what I found.'

Jon realised he wasn't going to drag anything more out of his friend who was clearly relishing making him squirm so decided to keep his mouth firmly shut. Whatever the big surprise was, he would find out pretty soon.

With the main gates open, Brian drove in and closed them behind them before parking the car next to the aircraft hangar. He led Jon to a door in a small building built on the side of the hangar and opened it with another key. Inside, it was depressingly deserted and smelled musty from disuse.

Jon looked around at the almost empty room. 'I hate seeing places like these. I remember how busy and exciting it was. It always seems a crime to shut these places down. They've closed Daedalus and are even talking about doing the same to Portland you know.'

'I had heard,' Brian replied. 'Of course you can take some of the blame.'

'Eh, how do you work that one out?'

Retribution

'How does the quote go? Oh yes, that's it 'Mikhael Gorbachev, my part in his downfall.' Maybe if you hadn't been so successful in Moscow we would still have an Evil Empire to confront.' Brian observed with a friendly grin.

Jon chuckled ruefully, 'got me there and I don't suppose the bloody politicians will do anything else but use it all as an excuse to keep cutting us more and more. Maybe we need another Falklands. No, forget I said that but you know what I mean.'

While he had been talking, Brian had been fiddling with his large bunch of keys and opened an inner door that led into the hangar. 'Righty ho, Jon, happy birthday.' He said happily and ushered Jon past him into the gloom of the large building.

'Hang on its not my birthday,' Jon started to say and stopped dead. 'Oh come on Brian, that old thing was here when the last King died.'

They were both looking at the carcass of an old Dragonfly helicopter that had been used as a training aid and had obviously been left behind as nothing more than scrap. Brian laughed, turned to the wall and pushed up a lever on a metal box. The lights in the hangar sprang into life and Jon immediately saw that the Dragonfly was not the only aircraft in the hanger. Parked behind it and partially obscured, he could still immediately recognise what it was.

'You have got to be kidding. Why the hell is that still here?' he asked as he strode towards the smaller machine. 'Bloody hell Brian, it looks immaculate. Has someone been cleaning it?'

'Yup, GG and I gave it a once over, although it was covered in an old tarpaulin when I found her. What do you think?'

Jon stood back amazed as he examined the Wasp. It was indeed spotless, with the College crest still emblazoned on the front doors and the white callsign numbers across the nose. He walked towards it and opened the pilot side door and looked in. It was as clean inside as out and everything appeared to be in place. He walked around the airframe, noting the tyres seemed to have full pressure. The rotor blades were spread as there was plenty of room in the hangar and the engine and gearbox looked brand new. He turned to Brian. 'How on earth is this still here? It should have been taken away years ago.'

'That was my first question,' Brian replied. 'It seems that when they closed the Flight down it was meant to have been collected,

Retribution

along with all its spares. They had already re-appointed the Flight Commander so there was no one to fly it out. The low loader never appeared and no one questioned why. I suppose everyone was too busy and forgot about it. Even if someone looked casually in, it was covered up and very hard to see unless you know where the light switch is. I checked with the various Admiral's staffs but as it was part of the College and not part of an operational or training command, then no one knew anything about it and anyway, anyone who did will have moved on long ago. So, I had a go at the engineers in London and once again they were all given new jobs once the aircraft left service and nobody can remember a thing.'

'Jesus, how can something like this just get lost? It beggars the imagination.'

'That was my first reaction but there were loads of Wasps around towards the end of the life of the fleet and I don't suppose the people who were meant to be keeping a record were that motivated. It literally just slipped through the cracks. Luckily, all the paperwork is also still here and I've checked it out. She's almost brand new with only about six hundred hours on the airframe and the engine and gearbox were replaced only about fifty hours ago. Not only that, come over here and have a look.' Brian indicated to the rear of the hangar where there was a large pile of crates and boxes. 'There are two absolutely brand new engines as well as heaps of other spares, enough to keep her flying for years if anyone wanted to.'

Jon stopped dead and looked at his friend. 'So you and GG have known about this for some time and even gone to the effort of cleaning her up. What's going on Brian? She belongs to the Crown so what's the point?'

'Er, actually that bit about belonging to the Crown isn't quite true, at least not anymore. You see, I contacted Defence Sales in London. Any surplus equipment automatically reverts to them when no longer required by the service who used it. Their job is to dispose of all sorts of stuff including helicopters. They sold quite a few Wasps off when the fleet was decommissioned but none were in a serviceable condition, not like this one anyway. So, I sort of made them an offer and they accepted. I bought it last week. It's mine.'

'What! Brian have you gone fucking mad, what's the point? It can't fly and even if it could, you can't fly either. Jesus, how much did you pay for it?'

Retribution

Brian burst out laughing at his friend's reaction. 'Calm down Jon. It didn't cost much at all, in fact, if you really want to know, I paid only three thousand pounds for the aircraft and all the spares. Defence Sales were actually rather embarrassed and just wanted to get rid of the thing. As for flying it, the Civil Aviation Authority rules say it has to be inspected by an airworthiness inspector and then it can fly under a special permit to fly. That inspection happened last week. I'm waiting for the paperwork now to say that it's on the civilian register. And you're right, I can't fly it, at the moment that is. But you can. You flew Wasps on your first tour didn't you? All you need to do is get a civilian qualified instructor with experience on type and there are several around, to check you out. You will have to do some of the civilian exams as well but they should be very straightforward and then you will have a private pilot's licence on helicopters as well as be qualified on type.'

Jon was completely bowled over and just didn't know what to say. The sudden prospect of being able to fly again was almost overwhelming. He had thought about doing some private flying in the past but the prospect had never seemed to excite him. Now, looking at this little naval helicopter, the one he had cut his operational teeth on many years ago, all his old enthusiasm and excitement returned in a rush.

'Hang on a second, what was that about not been able to fly it yet? Have you been taking flying lessons or something?'

'No need to sound so surprised Jon. In my spare time I've been down to Roborough where they do the Elementary Flying Training selection and managed to scrounge a few hours on Chipmunks over the last few months. I should have my private pilot's licence within a few weeks and then you can teach me how to fly this little beast. I will need to do formal helicopter training as well to get my own licence but by flying with you I can cut the requirement down to the minimum.'

'Bloody hell Brian you really have been busy. But where are we going to keep her and how will we maintain it? Neither of us are engineers after all.'

'Good question Jon. GG came up with the answer to that one. The Historic Flight at Yeovilton have said they are prepared to hangar and maintain it for us as long as we can do a number of flying displays in the summer months.'

Once again, Jon felt completely overwhelmed. 'I really don't know what to say Brian. Does Kathy know about this?'

'Sort of, she knows I've been having flying lessons and have some cunning plan to get you involved but she doesn't know the detail.'

'The detail being the amount of money you spent on it I'm guessing?'

'Something like that, but I'll talk her round, don't worry.'

'No, I've got a better idea. I like your plan. I like it enormously but I would like to suggest one change. Let me buy the aircraft from you or at least half a share. That way you won't have to face the wrath of your wife when she finds out. You may be over six foot tall and she may be barely five foot but I wouldn't want to be in your shoes if she finds out you spent that much money on an old helicopter.'

'Thank you Jon, I was rather hoping you would suggest that,' Brian replied smiling but looking relieved at the same time.

They spent the rest of the morning examining the aircraft in detail, the pile of spares and the paperwork. At one point, Jon jumped into the pilot's seat and looked carefully around the cockpit trying to remember the start-up checks. He was quite surprised how much came back to him when he was back in the environment he was most comfortable in.

While Jon was playing at being a pilot again, Brian felt a swell of happiness. Not because he would no longer have to face an angry wife but because for the first time in a long time he could see the true light of excitement and happiness in Jon's eyes.

Chapter 5

Arianna was dog tired, cold and wet. She had been walking now for two days and living rough in the woods. The skills she had learned as a child with her father on summer holidays long past were serving her well, particularly her ability to light a fire but without even the most basic of equipment she knew she couldn't last long like this. The real problem was she didn't really know where to go. Although she had been brought up in the Republic of Yugoslavia she knew that it was in fact a conglomeration of countries forced to together after the Second World War and that now it was fragmenting along the old borders. She just wished she had paid more attention at school because she had no real idea where those borders were. She knew that Serbia to the east of her was the original protagonist and that Croatia was opposing them by allying with Bosnia Herzegovina where most of the actual fighting was taking place. Her village had been on that eastern border with Serbia so she knew she would have to travel westwards to find people who could help her and who she wanted to support. That could mean heading back towards Sarajevo but that was the last place she wanted to visit. It had been bad enough just getting out. So she tried to make a path to the north west which would keep her clear of the old capital and angle her towards Croatia. A good plan maybe but one that really needed the aid of a map and compass.

It was early morning now and she had risen with the sun. Not having eaten anything except for some berries she had found yesterday, her stomach was complaining but she forced herself to trudge on. Maybe she could find a friendly village and beg help.

It was her nose that first alerted her to something ahead. A mixture of wood smoke and cooking meat. It was quite enticing. Suddenly the woods opened and she was looking down the side of a gentle slope to a cluster of buildings and farm stockades. There were cows lying in an enclosure next to what must be the main farmhouse but no sign of life outside. When she looked at her watch and realised just how early it really was, she wasn't surprised. Even so, she sat and watched for a while but nothing moved.

Carefully keeping to the edge of the trees which reached down to the left of the buildings, she was able to approach quite closely and

Retribution

remain concealed. As she started to be able to see past the farmhouse, it was clear where the smell of smoke was originating from. She surmised it must have once been the main barn but it was now a smouldering ruin of blackened timbers. With a mental lurch, she then had a dreadful feeling she knew what the other smell was. Taking great care, she approached the wrecked building. She was only halfway towards it when she saw something sticking out of the side. It was a human child's foot and surprisingly intact with a small pink shoe. The leg above it was charred bone.

She stopped and vomited the meagre contents of her stomach. The horror and unreality of the last few days closed in on her like a black cloud. She found herself kneeling on the ground sobbing uncontrollably. She knew she shouldn't stay there in plain sight but suddenly she didn't care. What had her modern civilised world come to, where rape and the murder of children were suddenly commonplace, where whole families could be wiped out? Part of her was telling her to go into the house and call the police, surely this couldn't be allowed to go on? But she knew that if they came, all it would result in was her being taken to some camp and subjected to God knew what brutality.

And then all the hate and anger that had sustained her over the last few days drained away. What was the point? Why did she think she could make a difference? She sat there, numb in the early morning sunshine, lost in misery and despair. So she didn't hear the footsteps behind her until almost too late.

At the last moment, she spun around but it wasn't in time to stop the man falling on her. In her panic, she fought to push him off. Her apathy disappearing in an adrenalin fuelled rush of anger and hate. He fell sideways and she felt something sticky and slippery on her hands. She realised it was blood and the man hadn't attacked. He had collapsed on top of her. Pushing herself clear, she knelt down to the now unconscious form lying on the ground. He was wearing some sort of workman's clothes and looked quite young, probably about her age. His face was grey and blood was soaking through the back of his shirt. She ripped it open and saw a large wound, possibly the exit wound from a gunshot. She had seen them before when she had been hunting with her father and they had shot a deer. But this was no deer. With nothing else to hand, she continued to rip his shirt and make a pad which she pressed into the wound. Slowly, the bleeding stopped as she applied pressure and the man's breathing eased. Looking around she realised the predicament she was in. This was probably a member of the murdered family and he had somehow escaped or been away when they were attacked but had managed to get himself shot in the process. Looking at him, she realised there was little chance she could move him far and anyway she needed to tie something around him to hold her pad in place. With no other option, she took off her shirt and tore it into strips which she fastened around his chest. Then, with all her strength, she was able to pull him in towards the main farm building and prop him against the wall next to the front door.

Leaving him, she found the front door open went inside. The house was a mess. It had clearly been looted. Ignoring the chaos, she looked for a bathroom and found one on the first floor. Unlike most of the rooms, it had been left alone and to her relief, she found a first aid cabinet. Clutching some large bandages and antiseptic she ran back down to find the man was now conscious and staring over towards the burned out barn. Tears were streaming down his face and he was grunting with the effort of trying to stand up and not succeeding.

She gently pushed him back. 'You must be still, I have to put a proper dressing on your wound. What happened here?' she asked as she started to bind the wound with bandages. She left the original pad in place, reasoning that trying to pull it clear would result in the man losing even more blood.

He didn't answer her question. 'Who are you? Why are you helping me? Did they kill everyone else?' his voice was a croak.

'I don't know, I only just got here myself. It was the Serbians?' she asked.

'Soldiers, I only saw them from a distance. I had been out in the fields and returning when I heard shouting and saw the smoke. As I ran back someone must have shot me. Where is everyone?'

'I don't know. I'm afraid they might all be dead in the barn. Were they your family?'

'No, I just work here but they were like my family. I live in the house. I've been here several years.' His eyes shut briefly and he choked a sob. 'Is that a child's foot I can see? That was little Marie, why did they do that, what's this all about?'

Arianna settled him back. She had also brought a bottle of water she had found in the bathroom and made him drink while she explained what she thought was going on. She also told him of her experiences over the last few days and what she was now trying to do. 'It's being called ethnic cleansing in the press. The Serbs are killing or removing anyone who is not one of them.' She finished. 'Oh God, you're not a Serb are you?'

He looked confused by the question. 'I'm not sure what that means. I thought this was my home, my country but I suppose to a Serbian I must be an enemy. They shot me after all. But what do we do now?'

She hadn't thought of the future for several minutes now and the precariousness of their position suddenly hit her. 'I was hoping to find some food and a map but what we really need is some form of transport. Do you know how far it is to the Croatian border?'

She found she was talking to an unconscious man. She carefully let his head rest back on the wall of the house. She had no idea how long they had before someone came and whether when they did, they would be friendly. She couldn't take the risk. Running back into the house she found the kitchen. It was as bad a mess as the rest of the house but there was plenty of food even though most of it was strewn over the floor. She found a shopping bag and managed to fill it with some bread and large sausage as well as several cartons of milk. It would have to do. With her mouth full of some of the sausage she quickly went back outside.

The man was awake again. 'Here, drink some this,' she said as she tore open a milk carton.

As he gulped some down she continued. 'My name is Arianna, what's yours?'

'Goran,' he replied with milk dribbling down his chin.

'Good, now Goran, is there be any form of transport around? Anything, a car, a truck even a tractor?'

He looked around and frowned. 'They kept all the vehicles in the barn so I guess they are all destroyed, that or they were taken away. There was a pick up truck and tractor there. Hang on, can you go around the barn and look the other side, see if there is another small barn. It's very old and looks like it's almost falling down.'

She ran across the yard, giving the smoking ruin a large berth and looked past it, then ran back. Breathlessly she spoke. 'Yes, I can see it. It's such a wreck I guess they must have ignored it. Why what's there?'

'The old man was a bit of an enthusiast for old cars. He used to collect them but never did anything more. He was always going to do them up but never did. There should be about five in there. Maybe we can get one to work.'

Realising she had no other options, she was about to run back but Goran stopped her. 'No, go into the hallway. There should be an old desk halfway down. He used to keep the keys for them in there.'

Nodding, she went back inside. The desk was there but the drawer had been pulled out and the contents were strewn all over the floor. Scrabbling around in the half-light, she found several sets of keys. When she had as many as she could find, she went to the old barn. The door was rickety but padlocked. Without hesitation, she raised her foot and kicked it hard. The door flew open and she realised she could see inside because of the light leaking through the gaps in the roof. She stood for a second taking in the scene and then despite all the tribulations of the last few days, she began to laugh.

Chapter 6

Rupert Thomas was sitting at his desk lost in thought. He had been back from Moscow for some time now but the novelty of the new job he had been given still hadn't worn off. On getting back to England after the exciting days of the Gorbachev revolution, he did wonder whether life would ever be as exciting again.

What he hadn't been expecting was the interview with the head of MI6 that he had been invited to attend almost as soon as his feet touched the ground. It had been a private meeting in a very secure room within the bowels of the MI6 building in London. Rupert had been surprised there were only the two of them present but it soon became clear why that was necessary. The need for absolute secrecy while working for an organisation that lived on secrets had been a bit of a surprise but once it was explained, he fully supported the requirement.

The Berlin Wall may have fallen and there may well have been an outbreak of democracy across Eastern Europe and the remains of the Russian Empire but that didn't mean that traitors were still not in the British system. Of course, if there were, there was precious little of their ideology left in the world but that didn't mean that they were either harmless or shouldn't still be rooted out. In the past, various attempts had been made to track spies and traitors within the system and with some success. Of course, there had also been the obvious failures such as Kim Philby. However, there was evidence to suggest there was still at least one if not two high-level soviet sympathisers within the government. Rupert's task was quite simple, find them and bring them to justice. Simple it may have sounded but achieving it was another matter. In the past, teams had been set up, meetings had been held and all of them had leaked one way or another. This time only two men would know the truth until enough evidence could be gathered. Rupert was given a cover story which seemed to satisfy his peers who all thought he was conducting an internal process review. This not only made him fairly unpopular with everyone who thought he might be a threat to their jobs but it also gave him virtually unrestricted access to areas he would normally not be allowed to go near. Unfortunately, despite tantalising hints, getting anything concrete proved harder than he had expected. Eventually, he had had to go back to his boss and say he needed help. The sheer volume of data that needed to be analysed was beyond him and he knew somebody whom he could not only trust but had the skills needed. His boss had needed some convincing but in the end agreed that Ruth could work as his assistant. In the end, it was the fact that she was Rupert's sister which gave him sufficient confidence that she could be trusted.

The reason that Rupert was so lost in thought at this particular moment was lying on the desk in front of him. It looked like a simple list of names which in fact is what it was. However, it wasn't the list that was the issue it was the purpose that was causing him concern. Ruth had requested it from GCHQ a few days ago as part of her routine data gathering. It didn't take her long to realise that some of the names on the list should not have really been there and one in particular stood out.

'Why the hell had somebody requested that the telephone of Commander Jonathan Hunt be routinely monitored. Not only that but the request was fairly recent, about the time that Jon got back from Moscow.' Rupert thought. It was proving surprisingly difficult to find out any more facts. It appeared that GCHQ did not keep records of individuals authorising watch lists. As long as the request came from an authorised organisation with the correct authentication, then the name was added. It had taken some time to track down the ministry that had made the request and to Rupert and Ruth's surprise, it wasn't the MOD but rather the Department of Trade and Industry. This put Rupert in a quandary. If he was to start asking questions directly of the Department it would immediately alert who it was who had decided that Jon needed watching. However, Ruth had suggested an idea that might resolve the problem quite quickly.

Making a decision, Rupert reached across his desk and picked up the telephone. The person he spoke to at the Dartmouth Naval College told him that Jon was on leave but could probably be contacted at the air station at Yeovilton. Slightly surprised, Rupert spent another half an hour trying to contact Jon and eventually tracked him down at the wardroom at Yeovilton. He kept the conversation to casual reminiscences of their previous work together but also suggested that Jon might like to come up to London in a few day's time for a party that he was organising. Initially, Jon was

Retribution

reluctant. He explained that he had acquired a helicopter, of all things and was undergoing some refresher training at Yeovilton. Although Rupert thought it highly unlikely that GCHQ would or even could be monitoring a call from MI6 to a military base he wasn't prepared to bet on it. In the end, Rupert finished the call by saying, 'well Jon we would love to see you if you decide you can make it. It'll be like old times, just like when you worked out that I wasn't a Royal Marine because my hair was too long.'

There was a few seconds silence at the end of the line and then Jon agreed that maybe they ought to meet to talk over old times. Rupert gave him his London address and said he was looking forward to them getting together next Thursday.

Jon was intrigued, it was clear that Rupert wanted to meet personally and it would seem that the last thing they would be doing was reminiscing over the past. Both of them knew full well that during the Falklands war Jon had worked out that Rupert was definitely not a Royal Marine because his hair was so short that it had left a tide mark around his neck. No, this was Rupert saying that they needed to meet face to face.

Two days later, Jon was standing outside a rather elegant, white painted town house in St John's Wood. He looked down at the piece of paper with Rupert's address written on it to check he was really in the right place. This just didn't seem like the residence of a spy. He went up to the door and knocked on it with the large brass knocker. A few seconds later the door opened and there was his friend.

'Bloody hell Rupert, how much do MI6 pay you?' asked Jon as he admired the four story house.

Rupert laughed. 'Not enough to buy this place. It was left to me and my sister by our parents. We share it. She also has a small place in Sussex courtesy of a previous marriage so I'm here on my own most of the time. You'll meet Ruth today though as she's up for a couple of weeks.' And then seeing the look on Jon's face. 'Don't worry, she knows what I do she's even helping me out at the moment. We are both in the same line of work.'

Rupert opened the door and ushered Jon in. He led the way up a surprisingly steep and narrow set of stairs to a light, airy living room with a large bay window overlooking the street.

'You know these houses were built over two hundred years ago now, when it really was a wood. Apparently, they were funded by members of the aristocracy as residences for their various mistresses. It was far enough out of town to be discreet but close enough so that they could nip down here for a quickie when they felt the urge.'

Jon laughed and took the large whisky that Rupert had handed him while he spoke. 'So after all these years, I've found out that you live in an historic knocking shop. I'm impressed.'

Rupert grimaced. 'Something like that.' He went over to the window and drew the curtains. 'Right Jon, grab a seat. If we can't talk here, we can't talk anywhere.'

'Well, you've got me mystified Rupert. Why on earth do we need to talk with such secrecy? I take it that your cryptic remark on the telephone was designed to get me here without anyone knowing. But that could only mean that you thought there was the possibility of someone overhearing our conversation, which I have to say, scares me slightly.'

'Yes, I'm sorry about that Jon and actually I can't really tell you everything that is going on but I thought you needed to hear this. Before I tell you my news, can I ask if anything unusual has happened since you returned from Moscow?'

Jon frowned, 'I'm sorry Rupert, what do you mean by unusual?'

'Anything out of the ordinary, anything at all.'

'You mean apart from acquiring my own personal helicopter?' Jon smiled. 'No I don't suppose that's what you were thinking of. Let me think. Things have been pretty routine and I've been very busy working at the College. Oh hang, on I did get a strange telephone call two weeks ago. You might remember that after Helen's inquest I was bundled out of the country in a bit of a hurry. The Coroner released all the evidence after the inquest but as I was abroad by then most of it is still in the police stores in Truro. However, the wreck of the Triumph was taken into storage by the company who had originally built it. They're somewhere in Somerset I believe. I had the owner of the company ring me. He explained that the car was a complete wreck and they had put it into the back of an old barn on their premises and promptly forgot about it. They had originally meant to contact me to ask what I wanted to do with it. However, two weeks ago they had a fire and the barn burned down. Apparently, it was extremely hot and several cars were completely destroyed including mine. The fire brigade investigation could not come up with an explanation as to why the fire had started. The man thought I ought to know, although of course, there's nothing that can be done now. Mind you, he did suggest I might like to pay him some money for the storage charges up until then, which I did. Apart from that, I can't think of anything else.'

Rupert was about to say something when they both heard the front door open and then close. Footsteps could then be heard coming up the stairs. 'Ah, that sounds like Ruth getting in. I had better introduce you.'

Jon got to his feet and studied Rupert's sister as she came into the room. She was younger than her brother and looked to be in her mid thirties but there was a clear family resemblance. She was quite small, with dark wavy hair and piercing brown eyes that held a lively intelligence. She was wearing a track suit and held a cycling helmet in her hand. Her slim figure was clearly visible through the tight fitting sports gear.

'Ruth, this is Jon Hunt, who I told you I was going to talk to about 'you know what''. Jon, this is Ruth, my sister.'

She smiled at Jon and held out her hand. Jon shook it, noticing how light it felt in his own and how nice her smile was.

'Hello Jon, I've heard a great deal about you from Rupert. It seems every time you two get together something interesting happens, to say the least.'

Jon smiled back ruefully at Ruth, 'you've got a point there. Hopefully nothing untoward will happen this time.'

Rupert broke in, 'Ruth used to work full time for MI6 Jon but after her divorce she decided to go part time. Nowadays, she works as a consultant analyst on specialist projects and one of those projects is the one that I'm running.'

While Rupert was speaking, Ruth flopped into one of the chairs and helped herself to a whisky and then realising her bad manners, offered the bottle to the two men. They both nodded and she pulled them both a good measure and they all sat back down.

'So come on Rupert, what's this all about?' Jon said firmly after taking another healthy swig of scotch.

Retribution

Rupert looked at Ruth. 'I think Ruth could explain it better Jon. She was the one who stumbled across the information.'

'Yes Jon,' Ruth said. 'Rupert and I have been working on a project for the last few weeks and I have been analysing reams and reams of data. It's my specialisation. A little while ago, I was looking at a list of names and telephone numbers that GCHQ were tasked to keep an eye on. One of the names was yours. Do you have any idea why that might be the case?'

Jon looked completely nonplussed and not a little angry. 'Are you saying that the spooks in Cheltenham have been monitoring my telephones? What the hell for?'

'That's exactly what we want to know Jon,' Rupert said. 'What's more the request came from someone in the Department of Trade and Industry which we can't understand at all. Look, I can't tell you what my current work is about and I don't know if this has anything to do with it but I can't ignore it. However, there is a good chance you can help us sort this out very quickly. I have here, the names of all the employees at that department at the time the request was made starting at the top. Could you cast your eye down the list and see if there's anyone there you recognise.' He handed Jon several sheets of paper.

Jon started to scan the list. He hadn't been at it very long when frowning, he stopped at the first page. He then quickly flicked through the other pages before returning to the first one. 'I'm guessing that whoever did this must have been fairly senior and there's only one name on this list that I recognise and you should too Rupert.'

He pointed to a name near the top of the page.

Chapter 7

Arianna pulled herself together. This wasn't any time for levity and in fact maybe tears would be a better reaction. All the cars she could see were wrecks. She couldn't really recognise any of them they were so dilapidated and rusty. All had flat tyres and clearly none would ever run. Maybe in years to come some would be valuable restorations. She could see a couple that looked quite old but that was of no use to her now. Then she looked to the far right and saw something sheltering under a tarpaulin. With little hope of salvation but with no better idea, she pulled it off and revealed a little car in what looked like quite good condition. There was certainly no rust. For a moment, she had no idea what she was looking at. It was boxy in shape and painted a rather sickening green but seemed to be intact. At least the tyres seemed to have air in them. Then she suddenly remembered where she had seen one before. It was on the television when they were showing the collapse of East Germany. Many of the people fleeing to the West were driving them. She had no idea what it was called but she didn't care. Her only hope was that it would start.

She opened the driver's door and sat in. Clearly, some form of rodent had had the same idea in the past as both front seats were considerably chewed up. Praying that she wasn't about to sit on a nest of rats, she got behind the wheel. At first, she couldn't see where to put a key and then found it hidden on the side of the steering column. Fumbling with the keys she had found in the house and praying that one was the right one she tried them all in turn.

'*Why is it always the last bloody key you try that's the right one,*' she cursed to herself as she finally got one to fit and turn in the lock. With delight, she saw several lights illuminate on the dash and as she continued to turn the key she was rewarded with the sound of the engine slowly cranking over but it resolutely failed to start. She stopped before the battery was fully flat and looked around the driver's position again. There was little enough to see, just one speedometer and a few switches. Then she spotted a little lever almost hidden below the dash. Praying that it was the choke, she pulled it out and tried to restart the engine. It immediately roared into life with an odd clattering sound and clouds of black smoke from the exhaust. The door to the shed was off to her right but with a slight grinding of gears, she managed to get the little machine moving out into the daylight and drive it around to the front of the house.

When she got to Goran she was relieved to see he was still conscious. She parked up beside him on the passenger door side and went round to help him get in. It wasn't easy but between them they managed it.

Once back in, she looked at what she assumed was the petrol gauge. It was reading almost empty. 'Goran did they keep any fuel around here?' she asked, suddenly seeing all their escape plans about to come crashing down.

Gasping with pain as he tried to find a comfortable position, he answered her. 'Behind the house is a large red tank its full of diesel for the heating and the tractors but there should be some cans of petrol there as well. Just drive around.' And he sat back with his eyes shut.

Arianna did as he said and sure enough there were half a dozen cans sat underneath an old rusty tank. She shook them but only two were heavy enough to have anything in them. She prised open the tops and smelled the contents and was gratified to confirm it was petrol. She then looked around the car for the fuel filler. After a complete circuit of the little machine, she was totally confused. There was no sign of a fuel tank anywhere. She managed to open the boot but there was no sign of a tank or filler. This was crazy. After yet another check around the car, there was still no sign of how you got fuel into the damned thing. She suddenly realised there was one place she hadn't looked. The bonnet opened on a little catch and she lifted it up to look at the engine. There at the back of the compartment was what looked like a tank with a filler cap in the middle. Twisting it open she immediately smelled petrol.

'What morons designed a car with the fuel tank over a hot exhaust,' she wondered but only for a moment as she started to carefully tip in the contents of the first can. It didn't take long to brim the comparatively small tank and she put the other can, still half full, in the boot as a precaution and then jumped back in. The fuel gauge stubbornly stayed on empty it must be broken but at least she knew they could get a fair distance. Hopefully, far enough to get over the Croatian border. As the little car sped away down the rough

Retribution

track that led to the main road, the two cans of oil next to the fuel cans lay undisturbed.

Once on the main road which was in fact little more than a narrow two car width lane, Arianna forced herself to think. She had a rough idea of where they were but really needed a road sign to confirm her guess. She looked over at Goran who was now lolling against the door with his eyes shut and breathing very slowly. She realised he would be no help and he needed expert care soon or he would die. However, there was no way she was taking him to a Serbian hospital. He would have to take his chances with her. A T junction loomed ahead and she saw she would soon be on a main road. Not only that but a signpost pointed to the right for the town of Prnjavor and she knew where that was. It also meant that her navigation through the woods hadn't been as accurate as she had thought but it was good not bad news because she knew if she turned north from there it was only about twenty five kilometres to the Croatian border.

The little car was utterly gutless but nevertheless she got them up to a reasonable speed as soon as they were on the main road which she discovered was the R474. This was part of the country she knew reasonably well. She had travelled this way with her father in happier times. The family had come here camping and fishing in her teen years. The only problem was that if there were any roadblocks or troops in her way there was no way to get off the road now. The right hand side was lined with deep forest and the middle of the two lane highway had a large Armco central barrier. Her luck held. In fact, there was hardly any traffic and despite the state of the car no one seemed to take any notice. This far north and west she was hoping that they were leaving any Serbian forces behind them. She just prayed that it was not wishful thinking. They were soon approaching Prnjavor but she knew if she just stayed on this road it would take them to the village of Srbac which was literally on the border. There was no official crossing, that was further on at Gradiska but the last thing they needed was the possibility of hostile troops barring their way. Anyway, she knew a cart track that would take them to a ford on the Sara River and this time of year the water level should allow the little car to cross and then they were in Croatia. The town of Pleternica would not be far away and she should be able to get medical help there. She looked over to Goran who was starting to look very white. She just prayed he would last.

Retribution

They had just cleared Prnjavor when she looked up and checked her rear view mirror. Her heart leapt into her mouth. They were on a straight section of road and in the distance behind her she could see several, green clad vehicles, all with their headlights ablaze. The leading one looked like a large truck but there was clearly a machine gun mounted on top of the cab although there didn't seem to be anyone manning it.

She slammed the throttle down as far as it would go, not that it made much difference. She had no idea of their speed as the speedometer needle was flicking up and down so much she couldn't read it. It felt fast but in reality, she suspected that the little wreck wasn't capable of much more than one hundred kilometres per hour and that was when it was new. As it was, the steering wheel was starting to vibrate terribly in her hands and the whole car felt unstable. It couldn't be far now and she could turn off into the forest, hopefully before they were seen doing so. The lights didn't seem to be gaining, she had probably only seen them because the road was so straight. Then, they rounded a gentle curve and the rear view mirror was empty again. Breathing a sigh of relief even though she knew the soldiers were still there, she started looking for any sign of how much further they would have to go. And then the engine started to make a new noise. It started as a ticking but rapidly grew until it sounded like someone shaking a metal bucket full of old nails. At the same time as the noise grew the car started to slow down. Sobbing with frustration and knowing there was absolutely nothing she could do, she kept her foot down and prayed that it would keep going. At the same time she desperately looked for somewhere they could pull off the road and hide but the forest was unforgiving and the Armco barrier solidly intact. After a few minutes they had slowed so much she had to drop a gear just to get the engine to keep pulling and then the headlights reappeared in the rear view mirror and this time there was definitely someone manning the gun on its roof and it was pointing directly at them.

With a sickening bang, the engine let go and the car shuddered to a halt with smoke starting to pour out from under the bonnet. She felt totally defeated. There was nothing else she could do. She just sat there in the smoking wreck as the truck halted directly behind them and soldiers started to pour out.

Retribution

Her door was wrenched open and she knew she was either going to be raped or shot or more likely, both.

To her utter surprise, the officer was polite and asked her if she needed help. For a second she was completely disorientated, then she saw with flood of relief that the shoulder flashes on his uniform were different to those of the soldiers at her village. Also, his accent was totally different.

'Are you Croatian?' she asked desperately.

He smiled at her. 'Of course I am. We are only a few miles from my country. We've been hunting Serbs.'

She didn't know what to say and simply broke down in tears. Between sobs, she asked if they had any medical staff and Goran was soon being taken care of by a competent looking man with a large bag of medical supplies.

The officer questioned her a little more and she gave him the outlines of her story. When she told him about her village and the massacre at the farm his eyes narrowed with anger.

'You are not the first person to tell this sort of story but I will need you to come back with us. It will be very useful intelligence and we should get you to talk to the press as well.'

Arianna nodded. 'And then I want to sign up. This is my war now.'

The officer didn't respond to that but he did look at the front of the car which had now stopped steaming.

'I take it you found this car at the farm you mentioned?'

'Yes, why do you ask? I found it in an old barn.'

The officer didn't answer straight away. He lifted the bonnet and looked at the wrecked engine. Bits of metal were everywhere which had clearly come from the exploded crankcase.

'I think you have no idea how lucky you've been my dear. That young man of yours would probably not have survived much longer without medical help and you are rather a long way away from any, apart from ours that is. I take it you thought we were Serbs and were trying to run away.'

'I'm sorry, I don't understand.'

'You refuelled at the farm you said?'

'Yes, there was some fuel stored there.'

'Did you put any oil in the fuel?'

Completely baffled, she shook her head.

Retribution

'Ah well, this is an East German Trabant and the engine is a two stroke. Without any oil, I'm surprised it lasted as long as it did.'

She had no idea what he was talking about but neither did she care.

Chapter 8

Jon was having trouble keeping a straight face and not letting the sound of laughter affect his voice. Brian was muttering and swearing under his breath and clearly unhappy with his performance. This was because he was trying to learn to hover 'Wanda the Wasp' as one of his children had quaintly named it some weeks previously. He wasn't having much success.

'For crying out loud Jon, how the bloody hell do you do this?' He said through gritted teeth as the little aircraft wandered out of his control yet again.

Jon laughed, 'it'll come Brian, don't worry, stop trying to fight the aircraft just guide it and remember every control input you make has an effect which has to be counted by yet another control input but for God's sake don't think about it, let it come naturally. Let me have control again and I will put us back in the hover. Don't worry, you'll get the knack soon.'

Jon was thoroughly enjoying himself. When he had contacted the CAA six weeks ago they had given him several names for instructors who could clear him to fly the Wasp. It was with some amazement that he recognised one of the names as the instructor who had taught him to fly the aircraft all those years ago. He immediately rang Peter Adams and after quite a few minutes reminiscing about the old days got his agreement to test fly the machine and then fly it from Dartmouth to Yeovilton and then spend a week getting Jon back up to speed and through the necessary ground exams. Jon was now the proud owner of a private pilot's licence (Helicopters). At the same time, Brian had managed to get his own licence for fixed wing aircraft. So now, as promised, Jon was attempting to teach his friend the wonders of rotary wing flying.

Brian took control once again and this time although they still wobbled around a little, he suddenly found that he felt he was in control. Jon kept quiet and let his friend slowly get the hang of it. Within minutes Brian was holding a reasonable hover although Jon could see he was still having to concentrate hard to keep the little machine under control.

Eventually, he took pity on his friend. 'Alright Brian, let me take her now. Let's go and do some normal flying.' And then over the radio he called, 'tower this is Wasp seven two, request departure from current position to operate in the local area to the west, over.'

The tower quickly responded with approval. Jon took control and pushed the nose forwards, at the same time pulling a little more on the collective. The Wasp accelerated forwards and as soon as they were at sixty knots he eased it into a climb. Within minutes, they were at a thousand feet heading west towards the distant Bristol Channel.

They both relaxed as Jon levelled out at two thousand feet. The local area was well known to both of them from years of flying from Yeovilton. Jon took Brian through the effects of controls which were little different from a fixed wing aircraft with the exception that you had to hold the machine into a manoeuvre unlike its conventional counterpart where you banked the aircraft and then neutralised the controls. He decided that flying with the autostabilisation system switched out could wait until another day.

'So Brian, you have control and give it a go. Use the aircraft's attitude to control airspeed and the collective like a throttle to maintain height.'

Brian very soon picked it up and Jon let him experiment for a while. He was still surprised at how well the little machine performed compared to the ones he had flown many years ago as a first tour pilot.

'You should have flown these with the flotation gear attached Brian,' Jon observed. 'I had it taken off as you know. It's a different aircraft without the drag of those bloody great clamshell containers and Forth Road Bridge girders supporting it either side.'

'Never quite understood those,' Brian replied. 'Surely, being mounted so high, the aircraft would have floated with the poor bloody aircrew underwater?'

'Yup but we flew without the front doors fitted so would have been able to get out anyway. The drag from the gear was ridiculous. She's a totally different machine without it. Look, we're doing a hundred knots with ease. With it fitted, we'd barely be able to make that with full power applied. My cynical mind thinks it was really only there to make sure the aircraft could be salvaged. Some of us wanted it removed but whoever would listen to front line pilots in those days?'

'Different now thank goodness. Look at all the things we got changed on our Sea Kings and the Lynx in the Gulf. Most of that was from feedback from the front line. Oh, by the way, I haven't thanked you properly for buying Wanda from me.'

'No problem, you've got two kids and a Kathy to support. I don't have anything to spend my money on these days so it was a no brainer, besides I seem to go around saving people's lives yours included old chap.'

'Eh, how'd you work that one out?'

'Simple, I know what would have happened if your loving wife had found out.' Jon replied with grin.

Brian acknowledged the truth of the remark. 'Hell hath no fury like a wife who finds her husband has spent all the holiday money.'

'True, now let's get back to flying. Turn us around and we'll head back.' Once they were settled on course for Yeovilton again, Jon looked at his friend. 'Seems you have the knack Brian, why on earth didn't you actually join up as a pilot? I've never really asked before but you could easily have made the grade.'

Brian, who had now relaxed, snorted in amusement. 'Typical bloody pilot's attitude there Jon. Not all Observers are failed pilots you know. As you know, I joined as a career officer but never really wanted to be pilot. To me, the action was in controlling the battle and fighting the fight. I've always thought that being behind the controls was a secondary activity. Mind you, it is fun isn't it?'

Jon pondered Brian's words. They both had had their share of fighting over the years but he could see his point. 'Oh well, you're having a go now old chap and there's no fight to have, unless you count keeping this old crate in the air. Now you've been having it far too easy, let's go back to the field and try a few autorotations.'

An hour later and they had pushed Wanda back into her hangar and checked her over before signing off the paperwork. One of the Historic Flight maintainers had taken them through the pre and post flight checks although any deeper maintenance would be done by them. They had also refuelled the helicopter before putting her away.

'Just in time for Sunday lunch at the pub Brian if we're quick,' Jon said as they drove out the air station gate. 'Oh and I need to talk to you about something that came up recently.'

Retribution

Mystified, Brian couldn't get any more out of Jon until they were sat in a quiet corner of their old haunt, the Ewe and Duck, a well known Fleet Air Arm pub between the airfield and the nearest town of Ilchester. With two plates of roast beef and Yorkshire pudding well on the way to disappearing, Brian looked over at his friend. 'Right, what's this all about Jon? I really hate it when you go all mysterious on me.'

'Hmm, remember that little fracas I had in the ministry a few years back when you were swanning around in Prometheus?'

Brian snorted in amusement. 'Not quite how I'd describe that period of my service career. But yes, it would be hard not to forget what you got up to, it was plastered all over the tabloids for days. You and Rupert nabbed a naval Lieutenant who had been dipping into secret files and passing them on to the Soviets. Don't suppose anyone is that interested these days, what with the wall coming down and democracy breaking out in Russia.'

'Yes and I thought that was all done and dusted in the past but something's come up. I can't go into too much detail but our mutual chum Rupert is working on some mysterious 'eat before reading' task and discovered something that links directly back to that incident in a rather ominous way.'

'Should you be telling this to me Jon? It all sounds highly classified.' Brian observed looking worried.

'If I can't talk to you Brian, then who can I? I really need a second opinion on this. Look Rupert discovered that someone had put my name on a phone watch list after I got back from Moscow. They couldn't discover exactly who it was but the request came from a government department and the only name I recognised was an ex-Air Marshall who had gone outside and was working in the Department of Trade and Industry as the senior military advisor. You'll know him, he was the one who married Inga.'

Brian nodded. Jon had told him about it at the time.

'What you don't know is that he was the head of the MOD department that I worked in and had that spy in it. At one point he was even suspected but in the end, it turned out to be the Lieutenant who ran the classified registry.'

'So what are you saying Jon? That he was the one who requested the phone watch on you?'

'Well, Rupert and I can't seem to find any other connections. He's moved on now, working for some consultancy firm.'

Brian had a thoughtful look. 'Jon, what job was it that you were going to after you left us in Prometheus? You know, before they gave you a pierhead jump to Moscow?'

'I never found out.' Jon replied. 'I had a letter from the appointer before I left the ship but as we had been away in the States for some time, I never heard any more. The letter was actually pretty cagey on the subject, just saying to get in touch when we returned. Why do you ask?'

'Well, it seems to me that if the good Air Marshall had some sinister motive to keep tabs on you when you returned, it might have been because you could have been some sort of threat to him. How sure are you that he wasn't part of the conspiracy you talk about?'

'Don't think we haven't already thought about that Brian. Rupert is doing some very discreet digging at the moment but your point about my appointment that didn't happen is a good one. I'll see what I can find out.'

Chapter 9

Arianna lay prone behind a large bush. She had been there most of the day and it had been raining non-stop. She was cold, wet but far from miserable. From her vantage point, she could see everything that was going on below her. The column of Serbian vehicles had been halted on the road for nearly the whole day. She wasn't quite sure what they were doing but that didn't matter because the man she was waiting for had finally turned up.

'*About bloody time*,' she thought to herself as she took careful sight through the telescopic sight on her rifle.

She had been training for this moment for what seemed to have been an age. At first, the Croatian military seemed to have very little interest in her or Goran for that matter. But while he was recovering in hospital, she simply made a nuisance of herself. Things changed once she managed to explain what her skills were to one of the officers. Having been brought up by a father who was a keen huntsman and having spent many a happy hour alongside him hunting deer and the occasional wild boar in the forests, she knew she was a natural shot. She also explained how she had come to have left home and the burning desire inside her for revenge. They had passed her on to an old Sergeant who had served in the previous war. The grizzled old veteran was more than happy to teach the skills of a sniper. She soon learned there was a lot more to it than just shooting accurately. The art of camouflage and of making sure her exit and entry routes were clear at all times was not something you learned in an afternoon. They hadn't made life easy for her either, treating her just the same as several men who were also being trained for the same role. However, nothing was going to get in the way of her being able to exact the revenge that she needed. It hadn't just been sniper training either, they took her through the full gamut of military training including the use of all their weapons, not just a rifle.

It hadn't taken long for Goran to recover. His injuries hadn't been as bad as first thought, the bullet had missed any vital organs and once he had been patched up, he was soon back on his feet. Whenever she could, Arianna would be by his bedside. She felt responsible for him in more ways than one. So it wasn't surprising that once he was back on his feet they became lovers. Their shared experience and mutual desire for revenge was part of it but there was also the simple attraction to young people cast adrift together in a dangerous world. As soon as he was well, he insisted on joining Arianna in her training. The military didn't seem to mind even though he was one of the worst shots they had ever seen. However, in many ways their skills complemented each other. Despite his inability to hit a barn door from ten feet, he had enormously good field craft and the ability to move silently in almost any environment a legacy of his childhood. His job was to get Arianna to where she would be needed, protect her while she did her job and then get them both out safely. It hadn't taken long for the military to recognise what a strong team they would make. The fact that they were driven by the need for revenge was just the sort of thing they were looking for. It didn't take long for a target to be identified and at last they were now going to see if their pairing was going to work for real.

The man they were waiting for was a notorious Serbian commander. He had been responsible for much of the ethnic cleansing in this local region. It was actually quite amazing how much intelligence there was on these people. Although this man wasn't the one responsible for attacking Arianna's village he was almost certainly the man who either led or authorised the attack on the farm where she had met Goran.

'The troops must've been waiting for him to turn up. I wonder where he's been?' Goran whispered in her left ear.

'Frankly, I don't care. What I want to make sure is that he doesn't go anywhere and cause more death and misery,' Arianna whispered back.

'Well, if you're quick you are about to get your opportunity,' Goran observed as he studied the scene before them through his high-powered binoculars.

Their man walked down the line of parked vehicles and seemed to be in conversation with one of the drivers at the rear of the convoy. Arianna settled into her firing position, looking through the telescopic sight on the top of her rifle. She set the crosshairs of the sight on the back of the man's head. He was starting to go bald and the white patch made a perfect aiming mark. There was a gentle breeze down the valley so she aimed just to the left of the spot to allow for the wind. Her finger gently took up the first pressure then she gently held her breath as she squeezed the trigger just that much harder. The gun kicked hard into her shoulder. At the same time, there was the muffled crack of the weapon firing, heavily muted by the suppressor fitted to the end of the barrel. She watched with fascination as the left hand side of the man's head literally exploded. Blood, bone and brains sprayed over the soldier he had been talking to. His knees buckled and he simply slumped to the ground. For a moment the standing soldier simply froze, as did all the others standing around and then chaos broke loose. Soldiers started running for cover but clearly hadn't worked out where the shot had come from. Some simply started spraying their rifles at the scenery. Arianna knew that it wouldn't take long for someone to take charge and then they would be the hunted not hunters.

'Time to go Goran,' she said as she slid herself backwards and completely out of sight of anyone in the valley.

'Bloody good shot but you're right let's get the hell out of here,' Goran said as he took Arianna's rifle and swiftly broke it down and placed it in its leather case. They had their escape route already mapped out and so it didn't take long before they were jogging down an old game trail and clearing the area. Within minutes, they were pulling the camouflage net off the old American jeep they had been given. It had the advantage of not looking like a modern military vehicle so if necessary could blend in with normal traffic. Although old, it was well serviced and started the first turn of the key.

Within a few more minutes, they were charging down the old farm track that led to the main road, which led back to Croatia. As they bounce their way down the rough road, for the first time in months Arianna felt a weight lift from her shoulders. It was only one act of revenge but in her heart, she knew there would be many more. She laughed out loud in delight.

Chapter 10

The walls of Long Lartin Category A high security prison stretched far into the distance either side of the central entrance lobby. Rupert Thomas parked his car outside the main doors in the visitor's car park which was almost empty. He had driven up from London that morning and was feeling the effects of fighting through the capital's traffic followed by the miles of motorway that followed. He had considered stopping in the nearby town of Evesham for a restorative coffee but in the end kept going. The sooner his business was concluded the better.

As he walked across the car park, he was surprised to see a large white stretched limousine with a uniformed chauffeur sitting patiently at the wheel. *'Not the sort of thing one would usually see outside a high security prison'* he thought. However, speculation about the vehicle was hardly relevant to his visit. He entered the entrance lobby and showed his MI6 pass to the duty officer, who checked it against the day's list of expected visitors. He issued Rupert with a temporary pass and directed him towards an officer holding two wands. The officer waved them all around Rupert's body before conducting a full body search. Once satisfied, he waved him into the inner lobby where yet another but more high-ranking officer was waiting for him.

'Good morning, you must be Mr Thomas. We've been expecting you.' The man held out his hand and gave a firm shake.

Rupert responded in kind. 'Yes, that's me. Hopefully, I won't take too much of your time. Just out of interest, what on earth is that stretched Limo doing in the car park?'

His guide let out a bark of laughter. 'Ah, that's for one of our really bad boys. He has been our guest for several years now. He's out on parole and we're pretty sure that his mother arranged the lift. I'm pretty sure that there are a couple of presents for him waiting inside as well.'

'I assume you mean ladies of negotiable virtue,' Rupert responded with a grin. 'I don't suppose the chap I'm coming to see will ever get that sort of treatment when he gets out.'

'I guess you're right there. We had to put him in his own accommodation for his own safety. It seems that child molesters and

Retribution

traitors fall into the same category in this sort of prison. If you would follow me? I'll take you to your interview room.'

They walked together through a seemingly endless maze of corridors, all painted an institutional dull yellow and separated by countless locked doors. Eventually, his guide opened a small door in a wall and ushered Rupert in. 'Please take a seat Mister Thomas. Your guest will be with you shortly.'

Rupert didn't have to wait long. The door opened and the man he had come here to interview was ushered in with his own guard. Rupert indicated that he should sit once the guard left them alone. He studied his man. He hadn't seen him for five years and barely recognised Lieutenant Horridge Royal Navy as he had been known at that time. Rupert had been responsible for his interrogation after he had been caught by his friend Jon Hunt in his attempt to flee to the Russian Embassy. At that time, Horridge was a middle aged, slightly overweight man who clearly spent most of his time indoors. He had managed to retain the complexion of someone who rarely saw the sun but that was about all. He was now thin to the point of looking gaunt and nearly all his hair had gone. A red scar marred the left hand side of his face. When he saw who it was in the room, the look on his face was a strange mixture fear and maybe a little hope. He took his seat at the desk opposite.

Rupert didn't offer much by way of greeting. 'Good morning, Mr Horridge. I expect you're wondering why I have come to see you again. How are they treating you? You seem to have lost some weight at least.'

Horridge just grunted a curt acknowledgement. 'I might have lost some weight but I almost lost an ear,' he said pointing to the scar. 'I presume they told you I spend my days on my own now. So what is it you want? You pumped me pretty dry when we last met.'

Rupert opened his briefcase and took out a buff file, which he opened and studied for a few seconds. He then looked up. 'Firstly, I would like to go over some of the details of our previous conversations, and then I have some new questions for you.'

'What on earth do you think I can tell you after all these years? You bled me dry last time. Not only that, you promised me that by cooperating, I would get a reduced sentence. I got fourteen years. I hardly call that reduced.'

Rupert was unsympathetic. 'Believe me, it could have been a lot worse. We still actually have the death penalty in this country for traitors. That may not have been likely but a life term was on the cards, so I strongly suggest you consider yourself lucky. Now let's go over your story again.'

They spent the next two hours going over Horridge's previous account of events. He confirmed that he had been approached by someone from the Soviet Embassy and that in the end, he had agreed to spy for them simply for money. At the time, he had been undergoing a painful and expensive divorce and saw it as the only way to get out of his problems. He also confirmed what information he had passed and when.

Rupert couldn't fault the man. His account was as close to his previous as could be expected after years in prison. However, he now had an idea of where to look, where maybe there were deliberate gaps in the man's account.

'All right, Horridge, let's call a break there for a minute,' Rupert said as he stood went to the door and asked the guard outside to arrange some tea for them before sitting again. When a tray with two mugs of tea been delivered. He continued the interrogation.

'I have one key question Mister Horridge. You have said all the time that you were working alone and that no one else in the ministry was involved. Do you still maintain that that is true?'

Horridge looked slightly discomfited by the question but was adamant that he had been working alone. Despite repeated questioning on the subject, Rupert could not get him to admit to any other answer.

He decided a change of tack was required. 'Now, your sentence was fourteen years, when do you think you might get parole?'

The man's head jerked up at the question and a fleeting look of fear shot across his face. 'What are you saying? You must know that I will be eligible next year.'

Rupert smiled back. 'Of course, I know that Mister Horridge but if I thought one minute that you haven't been completely honest with me then I would be honour bound to say so to your parole review board, now wouldn't I?'

The man's face crumpled. 'Look, I've told you everything I know. I was working alone. What more is there to say?'

Rupert had an idea. 'Just remind me again exactly what the Air Marshall's secretary said to you on the telephone that warned you that you were about to be discovered.'

Horridge sighed, 'I've told you that repeatedly. She rang to say that Commander Hunt was coming down for one of his private files but she also said something odd was going on because the office was full of policemen.'

'And why was that enough to make you think that you had been compromised?'

'Look, I had been spying for almost a year and the pressure was enormous, believe me. I simply panicked. I knew I would not be able to get away with it forever but the Russians just wouldn't let up. But they had said they would give me sanctuary if and when things went wrong. I had to assume that this had happened. I had no choice.' The man's voice screeched his last words. He was clearly getting very upset.

'Calm down Mr Horridge. Did she say why the policeman were there?'

'No, only that they had arrived about half an hour before and had gone into the Air Marshall's office. She said she had heard raised voices through the door but that was all.'

Rupert's suspicions went up another notch. He was now certain he was talking to the wrong person but he knew where to go. However, he wasn't quite finished. 'One final question. You say you were working alone and I believe you so don't worry about your parole.'

The look of gratitude on Horridge's face was almost pathetic. 'Thank you, I'll tell you everything I can, you know that'.

'Good, now, you were working alone, fair enough. However, were you aware at any time that there might be others doing similar work within the Ministry of Defence? Did your Russian handler ever hint that he had other sources?'

Horridge frowned, 'no never directly but I did wonder on several occasions when he didn't seem surprised at some of the information I passed on. But believe me, that's as far as it went. As far as I was concerned, I didn't want to know, I just kept my head down.'

Rupert decided he had gone as far as he could and he had more substantive evidence for his new line of enquiry which was about all that he could realistically have hoped for. He also realised that the big mistake that everyone had made was complacency once Horridge had been arrested. They were all so relieved that they had caught their man that they hadn't looked as far as they should have elsewhere. He called for the guard and made his farewells.

When he was in his car heading back down the motorway, he used his secure car phone to call into his office. Natalie, his secretary answered and he gave her the information that he needed to be looked into before settling down to fight the increasing amount of traffic as he neared London.

Just as he was getting near Heathrow his phone rang. 'Her name was Jeanette Morgan and she had worked in the civil service for over ten years. She had been the Air Marshall's secretary for two years. There is nothing on record but I did some digging with her contemporaries and there was a suspicion that she and the Air Marshall had been more than just friends but nothing definite. However, this is where it gets interesting. Shortly after Horridge was arrested, she put in for a transfer. Before anything could happen, she was run down by a hit and run driver outside a London wine bar. She died at the scene. They never found the driver.'

Rupert thanked Natalie and hung up. He now had a lot to think about but at least he now felt he was starting to make some progress.

Chapter 11

The autumn term at the Naval College simply sped by. Jon found that despite his worries about the apparent conspiracy that Rupert was looking into, the day-to-day workload kept him so occupied that he often found himself forgetting all about it. It was only when Ruth called him and they got together in a local pub that is all came flooding back once again.

The Dartmouth Arms was part hotel, part public house. It was a very old building and the bar area was full of dark oak beams and comfortable leather armchairs. Ruth had called him several days previously and they had agreed to meet that evening. Having bought them both drinks, Jon sat back and almost felt himself disappearing in the thickly padded armchair. Ruth looked quite different from the last time he had seen her in her tracksuit. Today she was wearing a pleated grey skirt which showed off her knees to perfection as well as a tightfitting wool jersey which did the same for her breasts. Jon suspected that she had dressed to impress.

'Well Ruth, thanks for coming all this way. I assume you thought it necessary rather than talking over the telephone,' he said as he took a sip of his pint.

She nodded. 'Yes Jon, I don't think the telephone is safe to use.'

'Good God, you're serious?' Jon looked worried.

'I'm afraid so, modern techniques are getting very sophisticated, especially if someone has a watching brief on your communications. And there's a good chance that's exactly what's still happening to you. Rupert made sure that your name was taken off the watch list at GCHQ but that doesn't mean others aren't listening in.'

'Do you actually know that or are you just guessing?' He asked.

'Just being cautious Jon, we still don't know where this is going.' Ruth looked at him hard. 'Jon when you got back to England in your ship, did you have any idea of what your next appointment was going to be?'

'Now that's an interesting question because I've been doing a little casual digging around that question myself. A colleague of mine in the Naval Secretary's division told me that I had an interview arranged, strangely enough, with the First Sea Lord, after I had handed over command. I suppose that was unusual, as normally

I would have gone to see my appointer rather than a Three Star Admiral. I actually knew him quite well from previous operations and I assumed there must've been something extra in what I was going to be asked to do but of course, I never got around to finding out.'

'So, you had absolutely no idea what your next job was going to be?'

'None at all. You know I suppose I could go and talk to the man. He's retired now but I assume he would know what it was all about.' Jon said as the thought struck him.

'That might be worth doing Jon but at this stage, I think we should leave him out of it,' Ruth responded. 'I'll talk to Rupert and see what he thinks is the best way to deal with this. But as you say, the job was probably not run-of-the-mill if the First Sea Lord was going to brief you on it.'

'And of course, we don't know whether he was part of the conspiracy,' Jon replied looking worried. 'Bloody hell, I'm beginning to suspect everybody.'

They left it there with Ruth promising to talk to Rupert and let Jon know what he thought would be the best approach. With the rest of the evening ahead of them Jon invited Ruth to dinner. The hotel restaurant was pretty good as he knew from previous experience. They confined their conversation to small talk during the meal. Even so, Jon got to hear about Ruth's divorce and that she had never had any children and probably a little bit more about her private life than he really wanted to know. She, in her turn, tried to find out more about his past. She was clearly well informed of some of the things he had done with her brother over the years. While they talked, he studied her and realised she was actually quite attractive. He then realised it was the first time he had actually noticed a girl in that way since Helen had gone. What was worse, was that he didn't feel guilty and that, of course, made him feel guilty. But he couldn't deny to himself that Ruth, despite her rather forthright manner was actually a very pretty woman as well as having a delightful figure.

Ruth was having similar thoughts. Rupert had told her so many things about this man that she didn't really believe anyone could be that special. She realised that in fact, if anything, Rupert had been sparse with the truth. By the end of the meal, they were talking almost like old acquaintances. Although neither said it, they both realised they would have to be very careful or things could move further. And neither of them actually knew whether that was what they wanted. They said their goodbyes at the bottom of the stairs leading up to Ruth's room. It was one of those odd moments where neither of them knew quite what to do.

Jon broke the awkwardness. 'Well Ruth, I can only thank you for coming down and telling me what's been going on in London. For goodness sake, tell Rupert to be careful. This whole thing stinks but if he thinks I should approach the last First Sea Lord just let me know.'

She nodded and left for her room, leaving Jon feeling strangely disappointed.

Six weeks later and the College term was coming to an end. Everyone was preparing for the annual Christmas Ball and the inside of the main building was barely recognisable as the midshipmen were turned loose decorating various rooms. Jon had been thinking about inviting Ruth but had never actually got round to it even though they had spoken several times on the phone since their last meeting, taking great care to keep their conversation bland. He was just thinking that maybe tonight he would ring her and see if she was free when he spotted the Captain's secretary, a portly Lieutenant Commander, heading down the corridor towards him.

'Sir, I've just come from the Captain and could you spare him a moment please,' the man said, with an odd smile on his face.

Nodding, Jon let the man lead him back down the corridor and up the stairs to the Captain of the College's office.

The Captain looked up from his desk as Jon knocked on his door. 'Jon come in and close the door please.'

Mystified Jon did as he was instructed and then sat in the chair that the Captain indicated while wondering what on earth this was about. He was rarely called in to see the great man at this time of day.

'I just wanted to be the first to congratulate you before anybody else got the chance,' he said. 'I can't say that I'm glad to be losing a really good Executive Officer but this is well deserved I doubt there is anyone in the service who would disagree.'

Suddenly, Jon knew what the Captain was talking about and it was confirmed when he was handed several sheets of paper stapled together. He looked at the first page and there was his name. Commander Jonathan Hunt, selected for Captain, with affect, first of June the next year. He didn't know what to say.

'First shot to Captain, well done Jon.' And he got up and opened the door to allow his secretary to come in with a tray with an open bottle of champagne and two glasses on it.

As Jon sipped at his first glass, he suddenly realised that that phone call to Ruth might be a really good idea.

Chapter 12

The room was noisy and full of the smell of badly washed bodies and cigarette smoke. The debate has been going on for what seemed like hours. Arianna and Goran were sitting at the back of the army's forward operations room on the Serbian border wondering what on earth they were doing there. They had been called to the meeting after their last successful mission but had not been given any explanation as to why they were needed. So far the conversation in the room had been focused on future plans. However, it seemed that there was also an atmosphere of acceptance of what was going on only a few miles away from them. It was almost as if ethnic cleansing was becoming an accepted policy these days. At least refugees from Serbia were being allowed in and helped to resettle as much as possible. None of this helped Arianna's deep conviction, which had only grown over recent months, that the Serbians must be taught a serious lesson.

Finally, the Colonel who had been leading the debate called it to a halt. Arianna realised that nothing had been agreed amongst the various regimental commanders present. Her frustration boiled over but she knew as a mere non-commissioned officer anything she had to say would not be listened to. As the Colonel strode down between the assembled officers, he caught Arianna's eye and motioned her and Goran to follow him.

They followed the Colonel to his office which was situated across a muddy square which was littered with military vehicles various sorts. It was getting very cold and with a start, Arianna realised it had started to snow. Inside the Colonel's office, it was relatively warm and he indicated to them to sit in the tatty military chairs opposite his desk. He reached inside his desk drawer and pulled out a bottle and three small glasses which he proceeded to fill. He then handed them to Arianna and Goran and tipped the contents of his glass straight down his throat.

The Colonel looked over the rim of his empty glass at them both. 'Well, what did you think of our so called planning meeting. It's alright, an honest opinion would be appreciated please.'

Arianna thought for a minute. She knew this man, he was one of those who had given her the opportunity to fight for her country all those months ago. He was also the man responsible for giving her the tasks she had been undertaking. 'It seems to me Colonel that we are about to give in to what people seem to think is the inevitable.'

'And why do you think that is Arianna?'

'It's a war we can't win. Despite creating the Federation of Bosnia and Herzegovina which has allowed us a much larger military arsenal we seem to be content to draw new borders and let the Serbs literally get away with rape and murder. In military terms, we can only match the Serbs. If we were to go on the offensive the chances of military success are small. And were we able to actually win what would we do then? We cannot reform the Republic, I think most people just want to see a new status quo established.'

'I don't want to know what most people think, I already know that. I want to know what you two think.'

Goran spoke for the first time, 'these thugs murdered the family I worked for including their small children. They shot me in the back when they didn't even know who I was. As far as I'm concerned they should all go to hell.'

Arianna agreed, 'these people murdered my family and tried to rape me. That is just one small part of what they have been doing. We know they have set up camps solely for the purpose of raping Croatian women and continue to murder men and whole families, No Colonel, I'm not prepared to let them get away with it. We don't care what others may think. We will continue this fight for as long as I can.'

The Colonel smiled at them both. 'And what if we could win this war, would that satisfy you?'

It was clear the Colonel had something in mind but Arianna couldn't see what it could be. They just didn't have enough firepower or men to make a decisive strike against their enemy and she said so.

'Of course, you are correct my dear,' but that is only if you look at our forces. What if we were able to get NATO to come in on our side? Don't you think that would bring enough firepower to the table?'

Neither of them answered straight away but they realised that the Colonel would not have brought up the subject unless he had something concrete to offer. 'Do you really think that's possible?

They've done bugger all so far, apart from sending a few people in to look at what's going on.' Goran observed cynically.

'That's not NATO Goran, that's the United Nations and they are a very different organisation. You must be aware of the coverage the war is getting in the international media. What do think it would take to get NATO to support us?'

'Do you really think that the international media could possibly influence a military organisation such as NATO?'

'Maybe but the problem is providing them with hard evidence. Up until now, it has all been second hand or of questionable provenance. What is needed is cold, hard, irrefutable facts.'

Arianna looked at the Colonel with suspicion. 'What has this got to do with us Colonel? I thought we were employed to conduct covert assassination and sabotage?'

He didn't answer immediately. Looking down at his desk he opened a folder and handed a photograph to Arianna. 'Recognise him?' was all he said.

Arianna went white and her hand started trembling. It was a face she would never forget. The last time she had seen it, it was covered in blood and he was screaming but that was only because she had head butted him and then kicked him in the crotch. Before that this was the man who had organised the raid on her village. This was the man responsible for the murder of her parents.

'What is his name?' was all she asked.

'Radivan Kovac. He was the local commander in the area of your village but has proved so good at murder and rape that he has been promoted. He is now the area commander in the Foca district and it seems your attempt to damage his manhood failed.'

Goran looked over her shoulder. 'Who is he Arianna?'

'Someone I really want to meet again, preferably over the sights of my rifle,' she said grimly. 'Although I will not be shooting to kill.' She swiftly told him the story.

'He is our next target Colonel?' Goran asked.

'Maybe but not quite in the way you expect young man.' The Colonel reached into his desk a brought out two expensive looking cameras. 'This is a stills camera and this one takes video. I want you to shoot this man but with these, not a gun. Not only that you will have to let him conduct his activities without interference. Do you understand?'

Arianna looked far from happy. 'You mean gather the evidence you need but by letting things happen?'

'How else can we prove to the world what is actually going on? It was one thing to allow you to wage your own personal war. But the time for that is over. If we ever want to stop the atrocities and the murders we have to have help. Without it, this could drag on for years. Do you understand? Now you two have proved yourselves adept at sneaking into the enemy positions and catching them off guard. What you bring back on these cameras will be far more important than the consequences of any single assassination that you could achieve.' The Colonel sat back and looked at the two of them with a challenging look on his face.

Goran and Arianna looked at each other. He spoke first. 'We understand Colonel and will do what we can but we must also be able to defend ourselves.'

'Yes of course, your first priority must be to be able to return and for that you may have to fight, that is a given. But do you agree to the task and the priorities I have set out?'

They both nodded.

'Good, then this is where you need to go.'

Chapter 13

Just for once, Whitehall looked clean and crisp. Not only that, there was very little traffic for a change. Jon smiled inwardly to himself, *'just about every year it snowed in England and just about every year it came as a total surprise to the population,'* he thought.

He had been lucky even getting to London but just for once, South West Trains had managed to keep their line open, even if most of the rail network had ground to a halt. He was never quite sure what to make of his regular visits to the Old Admiralty building where his appointer worked. In the past, these visits had varied from almost ending his career to giving him some of the best jobs of his life. He was hoping that today would be one of the good meetings.

He kicked the snow and slush from his shoes as he entered the historic building. The hall porter was at his regular position behind his desk. Jon gave him his name and as usual was proffered a seat in the small entrance lobby. As he waited, he wondered whether he would ever visit this building again. The navy along with much of the military were making efforts to move as much real estate as possible out of London. A new shiny building was being built in Portsmouth dockyard to take on many of the MOD departments and if the rumours were true the appointers would be moving into it. He didn't have long to ponder on the situation because his appointer appeared personally.

'Jon, really good to see you but slightly surprised you made it through this appalling blizzard,' Captain Johnson said with a cheery grin as he held out his hand.

Jon smiled back, 'not really a blizzard Sir, not if you've spent any time in the Arctic that is.'

'Ah but the great British public don't have your experience old chap especially those who maintain our roads and railways.'

'Yes, I reckon I was lucky today, although I suspect I was on the last train to get into Waterloo for a while.' Jon said.

'Well, let's go into my office so we can have a chat.' Captain Johnson led the way down the corridor to his well appointed office at the far end. When they entered, he poured Jon a coffee and one for himself and they settled down in two comfortable chairs.

'So Jon, do you have any ideas on what you would like to do now that you are getting your fourth stripe?' The Captain asked. 'As I'm sure you expect, I have a couple of ideas myself but I would like to hear your views first.'

Jon had been thinking of little else all the way up on the train. He knew that his time working in the MOD was limited but he also knew it was one place he really didn't want to be. What he really wanted was a command again although this clashed with his need to be able to react if Rupert came up with any results. Practically, he knew he would probably have very little choice and that being the case he would do his best to get the command he wanted.

He looked Captain Johnson in the eye. 'There is only one thing I really want to do Sir and that is to be on the bridge of my own ship again, preferably one that has plenty of aircraft on it so I can sneak the odd trip in when no one is looking.'

'Sorry Jon but both carriers are spoken for as I'm sure you will be aware. And anyway we don't give command of those ships to Captains until they've had some time in the rank.'

'Yes Sir I understand that but we both know that they are building HMS Indomitable on the Clyde as we speak,' Jon said firmly.

Captain Johnson laughed. 'She's a carrier Jon.'

'Well only sort of, her and HMS Ocean are being built on merchant ship hulls rather than to full military specification. So there'll be no command and control function in the normal sense. She'll be more akin to one of the wartime Woolworth carriers rather than the current ones. Sort of a large flat top ferry.'

Captain Johnson smiled. 'So, you are definitely not looking for a nice cushy desk job in Whitehall then?'

Jon shook his head firmly and then a thought struck him. He knew he would be taking a risk but now might just be the time to find out what had been planned for him several years ago. 'No Sir as I said, all I want is sea command but forgive me for asking, when I returned to the country in Prometheus, apparently I was scheduled to meet with the current First Sea Lord who was going to brief me on my new job. Do you have any knowledge of what that might have been about?'

Captain Johnson looked confused for a second. 'Goodness, no I'm sorry Jon, I know nothing about that.' He picked up a large buff file on his desk which Jon realised must be his personal file and

Retribution

leafed through several of the top pages. 'Yes there is a note here that 1SL wanted to talk to you but nothing more than that I'm afraid.'

'Maybe I will have to ask the Admiral myself then.'

'That will be a little tricky Jon. I am surprised you haven't heard. His obituary was in the papers yesterday. It seems he had a heart attack while in his garden last week and nobody knew until it was too late.' Captain Johnson said, looking sombre.

'Oh dear, that's really sad and he wasn't that old either. I really liked him.'

'I think everybody did Jon. He was one of the good guys. He was my Captain in Intrepid some years ago. But back to business, I actually think I could swing you command of Indomitable. But you must realise she is not going to be ready, even for sea trials, for at least eighteen months. We already have a Commander standing by her and we won't be appointing her Captain for at least a year so in that case we will have to find something for you in the interim.'

Jon thought he knew where this was going. 'Let me guess Sir, there is a desk with my name on it within a few miles of where we are now.'

Captain Johnson chuckled. 'Well that is definitely one possibility Jon but actually there is something else that you could be useful for. Just remind me again how many languages you speak.'

Jon looked mystified but answered the question. 'Well, Russian obviously from my previous appointment in Moscow and French and Spanish although I haven't used either for some time. Where is this going Sir?'

'Well as you know, the Balkans are going to hell in a hand basket at the moment. Everybody is decrying what is going on, particularly the atrocities being carried out by the Serbian army but at the same time nobody is prepared to do anything about it. The only people taking any action at all, surprisingly, are the United Nations in the guise of the UN Protection Force UNPROFOR. Basically, they have a team of observers out there on the ground and a small military presence in certain designated safe areas. We received a request recently to send a senior officer out there as part of the mission. They particularly wanted somebody with language skills.'

Jon frowned. 'Well fine but I don't speak Serbo-Croat. How could I be of any use?'

Retribution

'There are two answers to that Jon. Firstly your knowledge of Russian will be very useful because several of the UN team are Russian. Also with the skills you have in learning languages, we could give you an abbreviated course, not enough to get you fully fluent but sufficiently competent in the time. My plan would be to send you down to HMS Excellent for a month after Christmas and then for you to join the UN team for a year. It will mean you having to put up your fourth stripe early as well which I'm sure you won't find a hardship. Indomitable should be ready for her first Captain when you get back. How does that sound?'

Jon realised that Captain Johnson had had this plan available right from the start. He didn't particularly want to be out of the country for that length of time with all the other things going on in the background. He briefly considered asking what other options might be available but the chance of getting the command of a brand new warship was too much of a carrot for him to ignore. Anyway, Rupert wanted him to keep clear, so maybe it wasn't such a bad idea.

'Sir, what actually is this UN mission doing?'

'Good question Jon, they are there to observe and the military forces they have are only there to protect the observers, there is no mandate to intervene. That said they have set up several protected areas. In some ways it's a classic case of mission creep. Mind you, the current thinking is that it won't take much more before they request intervention from the West, in other words NATO and I suspect that the key element of your job will be to help decide when that request is made.'

Jon sat back in his chair. It actually sounded quite attractive. He, like everybody in the country, had been watching the appalling pictures coming out of Serbia and Croatia. This would be a chance to do something positive and then the prospect of a ship at the end of it. 'Sir, it sounds very interesting I would be delighted to accept.'

'Excellent, I will set the wheels in motion.' Captain Johnson stood up and so did Jon and they shook hands.

Jon looked out of the window. The snow was really heavy now. He realised his chances of getting back to the West Country were just about negligible. He would need somewhere to stay. Christmas was only a few days away. He had been planning to go and see his parents although the prospect was not that enticing as they were both getting quite old and doddery. He suddenly remembered that Ruth had told him, when they were talking at the Dartmouth Christmas ball a few days ago, that she would be in town over the Christmas period. Suddenly the idea of Christmas in St John's Wood seemed very attractive.

Less than half a mile away from Old Admiralty, the elegant dining room of the ultra-exclusive private club overlooked Westminster. Both the Abbey and the seat of government could be seen along with the grey river flanking them. The snow was starting to fall hard and almost obscured the view. The room was quiet with only the murmur of lunch time diners in the background.

The older man looked up as he was joined by his younger colleague. 'Gerald, so glad you could join me. Here, try this Claret they've just got it in. It's rather fine.'

The younger man took his seat and the proffered glass. He savoured the wine for a second and then looked enquiringly at his senior.

'Not now old chap,' the older man said. 'Let's have lunch first. You know how I hate to mix business with pleasure.'

For the next hour, they enjoyed several courses of excellent food and talked inconsequentially about the state of the government, the weather and their respective families. It was idle chatter but by the time the meal ended both men were relaxed and sated. The waiter cleared their plates away, set down some coffee and discreetly left them to their privacy.

'Now Peter, you dragged me away from my select committee, which actually was no great hardship, nothing seems to really come out of them anyway. What is so important?'

The older man looked out of the window contemplating the view. 'Gerald, remember the little contingency plan I had put in place a few years back.'

'The one that backfired rather spectacularly?'

The older man frowned. 'That's debatable, as it actually achieved my aim.'

The young man didn't know how to answer that so remained silent.

'Well anyway, I thought I had covered my tracks perfectly. However, I hear rumours of yet another witch hunt so I've taken some extra measures. Luckily, I was able to get the final evidence removed in time although I had to pull several strings and that in its own right has caused repercussions which I have also had to correct.'

'Sorry Peter you'll have to be a little more precise than that.'

Peter spoke for several minutes and explained exactly what he had achieved.

When he had finished, the younger man spoke. 'Well, it seems to me Peter that there's not a lot else to do. Even if anyone tried to follow it up now there's no evidence to back any accusations. I have to say I'm surprised this wasn't done sooner but I guess we all thought the matter was finished satisfactorily at the time. So, what exactly do you want of me?'

'Firstly to be aware of what has happened and then to keep an eye out for anyone following this up. After all, you are in a much better position than me to keep out a weather eye and take action if needed. Not that I expect it will be, mind you.'

Later, as the younger man crossed Whitehall and made his way back to the Houses of Parliament he reflected on his lunchtime conversation. Had Peter really solved the problem he would never have spoken of it to him in the first place, so clearly he was still worried that more might come of it. He sighed to himself. It was all so unnecessary now. The political concept they had signed up to had been swept away only a few years ago and there was no use contemplating its return. The world had turned and nothing could be gained by looking back. That was unless the past came back to bite them and this definitely could. He would have to put some discreet feelers out and be on his guard.

Chapter 14

Arianna and Goran were dog tired even though the trip to the village had been relatively easy. This time, instead of having to walk or travel back roads in an old car, they had been given the luxury of a ride in an old Alouette 3 helicopter. The night flight had been quite frightening as it was all conducted at low level but their pilot seemed to know what he was doing. They had been dropped off a mere five miles away and could expect a similar ride home once their mission was accomplished.

It had taken them all day to get from the drop off point to the village. Unlike other parts of the country, the area was not heavily forested and they had to take great care when crossing open fields. This was despite the fact that they were dressed as local civilians. Had they been stopped, one look into the packs they were carrying would be enough to incriminate them. The weapons probably wouldn't have been an issue as nearly everyone was armed these days but the two cameras and assorted lenses were a different matter. One was for stills the other was a modern video camera and very definitely not the sort of thing two local farmworkers would be expected to own.

They had studied the photos and maps of the area carefully before they left and had a good idea of the terrain and likely observation points. However, photos could only tell them so much and the place they had hoped to use didn't allow them to get close enough without the risk of being observed themselves. In the end, they had hidden their packs and taken the bold decision to walk straight through the village. No one took the slightest notice of the two dirty, shabby people, walking slowly and avoiding eye contact because that was what everyone else was doing. When they got to the far end of the main street, they had to be more careful. In what had clearly once been some form of farming complex, was a military camp. The whole area had been surrounded by a wire fence and armed Serbian guards were everywhere. They didn't dare approach too closely and it was clear that one of their potential targets was going to be impossible to get near. This was one of the infamous Serbian rape camps. The sort of place Arianna could have ended up in had she not escaped from the man attacking her the previous year. From where they could see it, there was nothing to indicate the hell that existed inside, although as they walked clear, several lorries full of smiling Serbian soldiers approached and were waved inside. They both knew why the soldiers were smiling. Without speaking they trudged down a side road and looked for their primary target. Seeing it from the street, it looked similar to all the other houses along the stretch of road although it was somewhat larger and had a much larger garden. They walked past and kept going until they were well clear of the village.

Arianna was shaking with barely suppressed anger and frustration. 'Why don't we go back there and kill as many of those bastards as we can?'

Goran understood that she was only letting off steam but he shared the sentiment. 'Maybe after we have the evidence then we can come back. At least with photographs we will be able to track down the bastards at any time. They will no longer be anonymous.'

Shaking off her rage and forcing herself to concentrate, she looked at her companion. 'So did you see anywhere we could use?'

'I might be wrong but it seemed to me that the houses either side were empty. All the windows and doors were shut, unlike all the other houses. It's a very hot day after all.'

Arianna thought for a second. 'That's quite likely isn't it? They wouldn't want neighbours with what they get up to.'

Goran snorted mirthlessly. 'Or the neighbours didn't want to be next to such scum in the first place.'

They slowly retraced their steps and retrieved their bags. This time, they went behind the village and approached the houses from the rear. There was a small copse of trees which masked their approach until the last minute.

'I'll go first,' Arianna stated firmly. 'I'm smaller and quieter than you.'

Goran nodded, he knew it would be a waste of time to argue.

Arianna ran doubled over to the rear fence of the neighbouring property to the target. She vaulted it in one go, despite the large pack on her back. She was then able to keep up against the boundary fence and out of sight as she made her way to the house's back door. Unsurprisingly, it was locked. One skill they had both been taught was how to pick simple locks and this one was easy. Within seconds, she had the door opened and carefully stepped inside. The room had clearly been a kitchen once but someone had stripped almost all the fittings out. The place was deathly quiet and after a quick look into the other ground floor rooms, all equally looted, she went back and signalled to Goran who was able to join her in a matter of minutes.

'No one's been here for ages Goran,' she said as he entered. 'We've been lucky.'

He snorted as he looked around taking in the devastation, 'maybe but the owners haven't been. I'll bet they weren't Serbs.'

'I'm sure you're right. Now let's have a look upstairs and see if we can get a good view. They were in luck. A window in one of the bedrooms overlooked the target property. They had a clear view of the large garden at the rear and also the veranda on the side of the house.

'No one at home?' Arianna queried as she carefully studied the building through her glasses.

'Probably all down at that camp,' Goran replied. 'What's the time?'

'Three,' Arianna responded after a quick check of her watch. 'I expect someone will be back soon enough. Let's set up the cameras and have something to eat while we wait.'

It wasn't long before they heard the crunching of tyres on gravel. Carefully looking out, they saw a large Mercedes pull up outside the house. The rear door opened and two men got out.

Arianna hissed in anger. 'That's our man. I will never forget that face.'

'Any idea who the other one is?' Goran asked.

'No never seen him before but it doesn't matter. We have our target. Shit, what I would give for my sniper rifle now.'

'Now Arianna, we have a bigger job to do, you know that.'

She sighed and sat back against the wall. 'I know Goran but it doesn't make things any easier. Still, if the intelligence is correct and he has one of his famous parties tonight then we'll nail the bastard.'

For the next two hours little happened and then two armed men came out and set up what was clearly a barbecue and then a long table and some chairs.

'Those men look like common soldiers,' Arianna observed, as one of them proceeded to light the barbecue and the other reappeared evening, as he made his way to Admiralty Arch where the Admiral had apartments, Jon had mixed feelings about the man but was intrigued as to the reason. Was this something to do with the last time he had been summoned only for events to get in the way? He would soon find out.

When he arrived at the imposing archway, overlooked by Nelson on his column in the middle of Trafalgar Square, he forced himself to stop speculating and entered through the large double oak doors. There was no one to greet him but he knew the way. This was the second time he had been here. The lift was to the left of the small lobby and to the right of it a small speaker. He pressed the button and a disembodied voice asked who he was. When he answered, the lift whirred into action and very soon the doors opened and he stepped in. When the doors re-opened he was in the lobby of the Admiral's apartment. A white coated steward greeted him and took his coat before ushering him through the doors to the large spacious living room that overlooked the Mall down towards Buckingham Palace.

The Admiral rose to greet him. Like Jon, he was dressed casually. Jon noted that the sandy hair was now thinning noticeably and his face was now lined with age but his eyes still held the challenging, alert look he remembered from their last meeting.

'Jon, have a seat, what would you like to drink? We have all the usual suspects,' the Admiral asked.

'A scotch would be good Sir,'

To Jon's surprise, the Admiral poured the drink himself before handing it to Jon, who realised there was no one else in the room. The steward who had met him was nowhere to be seen.

'First of all, congratulations on your promotion Jon, very well deserved and you are off to the Balkans soon I understand?'

Jon knew that the Admiral would be quite aware of where his next appointment was so he presumed the subtext was that this meeting was about something else. The Admiral's next words confirmed it.

'Jon, I'll cut to the chase. Do you recall that when you were returning to the UK in Prometheus you were invited to attend a meeting here with the current First Sea Lord?'

'Yes Sir but events rather got in the way.'

Retribution

The Admiral snorted mirthlessly. 'An understatement old chap. Did you never wonder what it might have all been about?'

Jon had to think furiously. Clearly, the Admiral knew nothing about MI6 and Rupert's current assignment and he had absolutely no intention of telling him. He would have to play this straight down the line, whatever it was. 'Yes Sir, although it's several years ago now and I had almost forgotten about it.'

'Well, I'm going to tell you. It appears that my predecessor wanted to speak to you about a couple of things but the only one I have details on is what it must have been primarily about. However, firstly I need to explain that what I am about to tell you is highly classified but in a way you are not used to.' Seeing the puzzled look on Jon's face, he continued. 'Jon, amongst the military and other senior levels of government and industry there is a group of people who take it upon themselves to provide an oversight function of this country that is not subject to a five year whim cycle based on empty promises made in order to gain power. It's called the Ramon society. Selection is made by the members and takes no account of rank or status, merely of achievement. Because of your bravery and dedication, you were due to be invited but events got in the way. We are now making that invitation.'

Jon looked completely nonplussed. 'Sorry Sir, you've lost me. What do you mean by oversight?'

'Good question Jon and straight to the heart of the matter. What would you say if I said our sole purpose is to ensure that the government does not make a fatal decision in some form or other and in that case we would step in to stop it?' The Admiral looked hard at Jon as he said it.

Jon's thoughts were churning about how to make a response that would sound reasonable. In the end, he decided he couldn't. 'I would say that you've asked totally the wrong man. That what you've just said sounds very like treason and that although I recognise its flaws, I would never do anything to subvert this country's democratic purpose.'

Jon was definitely not expecting the Admiral's response. He roared with laughter. When he finally spluttered to a stop he replied. 'Wonderful Jon, I expected to have to attempt some more convincing than that but you cut straight to it, well done.'

'I'm sorry Sir but you've lost me.'

'No, it's me who should apologise. If you had answered in any other way, this conversation would have been over and I would deny it had ever happened. As it is, we would definitely like you to join us. Let me explain a little more. Several hundred years ago, when the industrial revolution was underway and we still had a functioning monarchy, a group of senior military officers were worried about how the power of Westminster was eroding the power of the monarch. They decided to form the society purely to advise the King and then, of course, the Queen of anything that they felt parliament was getting wrong. It was called the Ramon society because that is the name of the patron Saint of secrecy, believe it or not. It still does advise the current monarch but only through individuals, she has no idea that we exist as an entity. We see our job as acting as the country's conscience. We would never attempt anything overt, although apparently there was a great temptation to do so when the Wilson government was cutting the military to the bone in the sixties.'

'I think I heard about that,' Jon replied. 'So, there was some truth in the matter?'

'Yes but cooler heads prevailed. It was a bit of a wake up call but the reality was that nothing could be done without a consensus and that was definitely not forthcoming, even under what many saw as very strong provocation. What we have achieved is the ability to influence decisions purely because we act as a consensual group. As I said earlier, we have members from government, by which I mean the civil service, we have no sitting MPs and wouldn't want them anyway. There are also members from the academic world and even the clergy.'

'How many Sir? That sounds like a pretty large group.'

'We keep the numbers at forty. That said, it's not an exact requirement and numbers can fluctuate a little. We meet annually, unless a member calls for a special meeting. Our next formal get together will be this winter and as I understand it, you should be back in the country by then.'

Jon had always had a lifelong aversion to secret societies. He had several friends who were Free Masons and hated the way they kept their actions under wraps, even if they were doing no harm. This sounded every bit as bad and the thought must have crossed his face because the Admiral clearly saw that he wasn't happy.

Retribution

'Jon, we only do this for the good of the country, it wouldn't work if who we were and what we do was in the public domain. But before you give me an answer I would like you to look at some documents we have for new potential members. It summarises our purpose, lets you see our membership and outlines some of the actions we have taken over recent years. I'm sorry, I can't let you keep them as I will be burning them after you've had a look. There's a desk over there, take a seat and I'll refresh your glass while you do so.'

Jon did as he was bid and sat at the leather covered desk as the Admiral plonked a full glass next to him. 'Take your time Jon. I have a few things to be getting on with so don't worry about being thorough.'

Jon read the documents carefully. The defined purpose of the group was as the Admiral had said and it was explicit that no direct action could ever be taken. Advice and influence were the only tools allowed. Some of the more recent successes and some failures were included. Jon wasn't surprised to see that the group had fully supported Margaret Thatcher's response to Argentina's invasion of the Falklands but in that case little needed to be done. He was surprised to see that there had been an enormous amount of discussion about the situation in the Gulf both before, during and after the war to liberate Kuwait. The group had made concerted efforts to stop the Americans blundering all the way into Iraq. He noted with interest that the reasons had nothing to do with the military situation. It was primarily based on an almost unanimous assessment that the Americans would have no clue how to manage the country if they did effectively take it over. The destabilising effect that would have on the whole region was in all the member's minds. In that case, the influence was mainly effected through the military although surprisingly, certain Bishops also went straight to Number 10 and were listened to.

Jon sat back and thought hard. He was well aware of the honour being paid him to be invited to such a group and from what he had seen in the documents, they only seemed to have the good of the nation at heart but his innate dislike of secrecy remained. Suddenly, he realised he hadn't looked at the membership list yet. He picked it up and scanned through the names. Many he recognised, some seemed familiar, some were completely new to him and then one stood out from the page.

'Oh shit, him again' he thought. 'Why am I not surprised? And maybe this explains why Rupert found my name on that GCHQ list.'

He put down the paper. He would probably have agreed to join anyway but this made it certain.

'Admiral,' he called over the room. 'I've seen enough, count me in.'

Chapter 16

It was Jon's last night in the country. He would be flying out the next day to Belgrade. He, Ruth and Rupert were having a final dinner in a rather expensive but extremely good St John's Wood restaurant. Jon was slightly surprised that Rupert had made no comment that it was obvious that he and Ruth were now more than just friends. However, they went a long way back and knew each other very well so he was grateful for his tacit acceptance.

They were seated by a rather obsequious waiter in a quiet corner. He left them with menus and an order for drinks. As they were left alone, Rupert turned to Jon. 'What times your flight out tomorrow Jon? Maybe I can give you a lift to the airport.'

'No, that's alright Rupert, Ruth has already offered. It's not till midday and I'm flying from Northolt in a UN chartered private jet. Apparently, getting into the city is quite dangerous for obvious reasons.'

'So, how did the briefing go Jon?' Ruth asked. 'Are you up to speed on the situation?'

Jon laughed cynically. 'I suppose so, as of today that is. It seems the situation changes by the moment. You know, when I was in Beirut I thought the place was a mess with all the factions operating there but this is just as bad. What's worse is that the bloody Serbs seem intent on killing everyone they don't like and we seem to be able to do nothing to stop it. You've seen the media reports. Apparently, it's far worse on the ground. Then you have all the outside parties trying to influence things. The Russians have always supported Serbia. It's how the First World War started after all. They've been giving all sorts of surreptitious aid to Milosevic and yet I apparently have at least one Russian Major who will be working for me and there are loads of Russian soldiers there working for the UN as well. Then, the really good news is that we are not allowed to carry arms. The soldiers protecting us are but if we are operating as observers we must be seen to be impartial. I'm really looking forward to that.'

'But surely now that you're a Captain you won't be actually going into the war zones?' Ruth asked, looking worried.

Retribution

Jon looked surprised. 'Ruth, there is virtually nowhere safe if I'm to do my job. The whole place is a mess. NATO has already intervened in a limited fashion. The UN have declared various safe zones and we have troops guarding them. My job is to oversee several of them but as a UN officer I can only report. We can use force to protect them but only if attacked. I can't stop the bastards killing each other or worse. There's talk of NATO stepping in to fully support us but nothing has been authorised yet and I'm not sure what it would take to get that sort of commitment.'

Ruth started to look concerned. 'Goodness, it sounds quite dangerous. I thought as a UN officer you would be reasonably safe.'

Jon barked out a laugh. 'Ruth we have already lost over a hundred UN soldiers although thankfully only two observers. The problem was that the old Yugoslavia was an armed camp. The Tito regime left weapons dumps all over the place and many of them are still there. Some of them the UN have under control but in many places it's too late. It's given many groups the opportunity to take revenge over grievances that often go back a long time.'

They broke off the discussion as the waiter had returned with their drinks and to take their orders. Then Jon called a halt to discussions on shop while they ate. Once the meal was over, they all walked the short distance back to the house and went upstairs to the living room. Jon poured them all a nightcap but kept his small. He had a very busy day coming up.

Ruth cuddled up to Jon on the sofa while Rupert took an old leather armchair. Since his meeting with the First Sea Lord, Jon had been in a quandary. He had given his solemn promise to keep the conversation secret and was loath to break it but the reason he had given it in the first place was at least partly because it seemed to directly link to Rupert's ongoing investigation. He knew he needed to talk to both of them but it was against his nature to be disloyal, especially to the head of his service.

With a mental gulp, he made his decision. 'Rupert, Ruth, I need to tell you something. I had an interview with the First Sea Lord a few days ago before I went to my initial briefings. It was the interview that I should have had when I got back from the Gulf in nineteen ninety.'

He stopped and saw that he had their undivided attention. 'Go on Jon,' Ruth said as she pulled back a little from him.

'Well, I was sworn to secrecy but I think I need to share this with you. Please, this must go no further than this room. If it ever got out that I had told someone about this my career would be over.'

They both promised readily. As secrecy was second nature to both of them Jon knew he was on safe ground. 'I have been recruited into what, for a better phrase, is a secret organisation. It's a cabal of senior military, industrial and government people. They see their role as overseers of the country and will seek to influence events if they feel things are going wrong. They feel that governments are often too focused on gaining or keeping short term power to always act in the country's long term interest.'

He sat back and looked at his two friends surprised by their lack of response, he ploughed on. 'I was due to be offered membership after my time in the Gulf but as we know that never happened and I was out of the country and then the First Sea Lord changed so the invitation was never renewed, until now that is.'

'Did you accept?' Ruth asked. But to his surprise, there was a slight element of mirth in her tone.

Slightly annoyed, he carried on. 'Yes, I saw something that relates to your work Rupert but probably would have accepted anyway. Hang on a second. Have I just said something funny? Why are you two smirking like that?'

Ruth couldn't hold it in any longer and let out a chuckle. 'Oh I'm sorry Jon, we know this is serious. It's just that you've told us one of the worst kept secrets in the country.'

'What? You know all about it? That's crazy,' Jon exclaimed.

'Ruth's right Jon,' Rupert replied. 'When we say worst kept secret, that only really refers to the intelligence services. We've known about it almost since it came into being. After all, we are in a similar line of business. Our job is to protect national security as well and we're not elected either. Several of our senior guys have been approached in the past. Some have even joined. We call it the Old Farts Club by the way. Sorry, that doesn't mean I think that's what you are. In fact, I'm quite amazed that you've been invited and bearing in mind you were only a Commander when the initial invite was about to be made that's quite unique. You should be flattered.'

Jon was actually relieved as clearly he hadn't actually breached any confidences. 'Well, this old fart is now a paid up member although I won't be getting to meet any of my new best friends until I get back from the Balkans later in the year.'

'Hang on Jon,' Ruth interjected. 'You said you saw something that related to our investigation. What was it?'

'Air Marshal Peter Johnson, he's been a member for ten years.' Jon replied.

'That man's name keeps coming up now doesn't it?' Rupert said. 'I told you that his secretary died in a road accident sometime after we arrested Lieutenant Horridge. I've been trying to dig into his past for some months now but I'm having to be terribly careful. He seems to have some very high up friends. Although we know about the Old Farts we don't have any of our people in there at the moment and they're quite good at keeping their membership list under wraps. That said, I'm not surprised such a senior man is a member. But Jon why did you think his membership was an issue?'

'Not sure but try this. I virtually trap him into being exposed as a Soviet spy, only for one of his minions to be caught instead. Remember, he was the only man who directly knew the detail of the fake information we had planted. There's no doubt that Horridge had passed it on by accessing the file illegally but that doesn't mean the Air Marshall wasn't doing the same. So, I'm in his bad books either way. I get a pier head jump to sea and I'm out of his way and then although he's retired from the RAF, he finds out I'm about to be invited to join his exclusive club. By now he's in the Department of Trade and puts my name on the watch list to keep an eye on me. Then my car crashes and burns out. Suppose it was booby trapped so that I could be removed if he discovered that I was still sniffing around, maybe purely as a contingency plan. It was only bad luck that Helen was driving when that drunk hit her. Even at the inquest, there was surprise that the car had caught fire and burned so fast. I tell you one thing Rupert, if that's true then he's a walking dead man.'

'That's a big leap Jon. Just back off for a moment. All we currently have is conjecture.' Rupert responded. 'As I said, I'm trying to investigate as carefully as I can. Unfortunately, my boss has given me some more mundane work as well so that no one asks what it is I'm really doing and its quite time consuming. But if he is what we think he is, he almost certainly won't be working alone and I want to get all of them whoever they are and however long it takes.

You've got this new job to keep you fully occupied for the rest of the year so just let me and Ruth do our jobs OK?'

'Just out of interest Rupert, who have you spoken to regarding our man? I realise you have to be careful but you must have made enquiries.' Jon asked.

'Well, I've been trying to establish his circle of friends. He seems quite popular in government circles. It's one of the reasons I have to be so careful. As you know, he's very well off and apart from a house here in London, he has a bloody great country estate near Oxford and another shooting estate in Scotland.'

'I'm surprised he keeps working then. You said he was doing consultancy now?'

'You know what some people are like, they just can't stop.' Rupert replied.

'Or he wants to keep near the centre of things to ensure he knows what's going on,' Jon said. 'What about family Rupert?'

'A sister who lives in France, that's all. Both parents are long gone. Oh and his wife of course. You know her.'

'Oh, he did marry her then?'

'Yes your old flame, Inga.'

Chapter 17

Arianna and Goran waited anxiously for the sound of their helicopter. They had spent the day holed up in a spot they had previously prepared at the edge of their pick up field concealed by a small stand of trees. They weren't able to carry a radio with sufficient range to say that the mission had been a success so were praying that the aircraft would stick to the agreed schedule.

There had been little to do during the long hot day while they waited. There was no habitation in sight and no one came near them. The fields were cultivated but there was no livestock about. After taking it in turns to try to sleep while the other kept watch, they abandoned the idea after a few hours.

'I'm going to have nightmares for the rest of my life,' Arianna said quietly as she lay with her head on Goran's lap.

'Me too,' he responded. 'But at least we have the evidence we need to expose these bastards. We just have to get it home now. I've taken out all the video and film from the cameras. What shall we do with them?'

'Split them up, put half in my pack and half in yours. We're not home yet and it's possible we could get separated.' Arianna answered.

'Always the pessimist,' Goran laughed but started to do as she suggested.

'Realist my love. That's why we're still here.' Arianna replied. 'Always plan on the worst. Mind you if our ride doesn't appear tonight we are going to have to walk a very long way.'

'Well, we could always steal a Trabant again. As long as you put some oil in it this time.' Goran suggested.

Arianna laughed for the first time that morning. 'I still don't really understand that but don't bother trying to explain again.'

'No, I realise that would be a complete waste of time. I've never met someone so completely lost when it comes to mechanical things.'

'Oh, I don't know. I can make a rifle work when I have to.'

'Good point.'

By midday, they were both starting to feel the oppressive heat. In order to stay hidden, they were lying inside a large bush which instead of providing shade only seemed to trap the hot air. They really only had enough water for drinking although that didn't stop Arianna from stripping to her underwear and using some to cool herself down.

Goran admired her figure as she sat next to him. 'Well, I didn't expect to come all this way into enemy territory and be treated to a wet T shirt competition.'

She turned to him. 'Not much of a competition with only one contestant. You're enjoying the view then? I always knew you had a dirty mind.'

'Nothing dirty my love,' he responded as he made a grab for her and was rewarded with her sinking into his arms. They made love there, in a bush, in hostile territory as though it was the last thing they would ever do. It was only afterwards the Arianna realised the risk that they had taken with the noise they had inevitably made. She didn't care. After the previous day she needed confirmation that life could still go on. That what they had seen was not all there was or would be. That love still existed. As she lay back sated, she was about to say something to Goran when he started to snore. She realised she should stay awake and keep a watch but fatigue finally overcame her as well.

By midnight, they had all their packs ready and had crept out into the field. When they had arrived the pilot had to risk using his landing light in the last few seconds of his approach in order to see the ground. This time they put out four torches in a 'T' shape which would allow the pilot to judge his landing. They were so dim and directional that it was highly unlikely anyone else would be able to see them. Even so, they would not switch them on until the last moment. They crouched there in the darkness waiting for the sound of the whine of the helicopter's engine and rotors.

After half an hour they were getting anxious. 'Where the hell is he?' Goran whispered through clenched teeth. 'He's late.'

'We were warned that his arrival time was flexible Goran. Midnight was only an approximate time,' Arianna replied trying to keep him calm even though she felt the same concern. She wasn't too worried about being discovered. They hadn't seen a soul all day so it was even less likely anyone would be around at this time. What worried her was what on earth they would do if he didn't come at all. Goran's joke about stealing a car was starting to seem less and less funny.

They waited another twenty minutes that seemed like hours and then Goran heard it first. 'He's coming, I can hear him over there.' He pointed to the west. 'Quick, let's turn on the torches.'

The noise grew and they stood back as a roaring black shape appeared as if from nowhere. Their faces were blasted with the downwash and suddenly a light appeared as the pilot opened a door. They knew what to do and ran in under the spinning rotors. Arianna opened a rear door and they both threw their packs in. Arianna clambered in after them. Goran stepped forward and jumped into the co-pilot's seat. Within seconds, the little Alouette was airborne and accelerating away into the darkness.

Arianna fumbled around in the dark cabin and found the seat strap. She strapped herself in and then reached up to find a headset dangling where she expected it. Goran was ahead of her and already speaking to the pilot.

'Any problems?' he asked. 'You were a little late.'

The pilot chuckled. 'No, none at all. We never fly the same route twice to make sure no one is waiting to take a pot shot at us when we return. That's why we never guarantee a pick up time. Well done with the torches by the way. They were exactly right. Now, let me concentrate. This next bit will be the trickiest. There's not a lot to navigate by around here, especially as we are staying low level.'

Arianna said nothing, just sat back. She was still very tense. She hated flying and this was more like a roller coaster than any aircraft she had flown in before. She would only feel able to finally relax when they were back on the ground. The only things she could see were the dim lights of the pilot's instruments sitting in a simple console between the pilot and Goran. Outside was almost completely pitch black. How on earth the man could fly in these conditions she had no idea.

The sudden, vicious jolt and scraping noise came as a surprise to all of them. The pilot reacted instinctively but there seemed to be little he could do. The helicopter seemed to pitch up and Arianna was sure she could see something scraping up the windscreen before there was an enormous bang and she was flung violently forward. Her lap strap held but it didn't stop her face impacting the back of the seat in front of her. The pain was sharp and her vision blurred. It didn't stop her seeing that the pilot was still valiantly trying to keep them airborne.

'We've hit some wires,' he shouted. 'But they've broken, we can still fly.'

As if to make a mockery of his words the machine started to vibrate violently, so much so that the pilot could hardly keep his hands on the controls. The last thing Arianna heard him say was, 'we'll have to land.' And then everything went black.

Light filtered through Arianna's eyelids. She had no idea where she was. There was a blinding pain across the front of her head and something wet was trickling down her nose. She knew she should try to wake up. There was something she should do but the temptation to slip back away from the pain was almost overwhelming. Suddenly she realised she could smell something sharp and overpowering. The smell was fuel. She was sure of that. All of a sudden, she remembered what had happened. The helicopter had crashed. She forced her eyes open and tried to sit up. Her stomach ached where the lap strap had bitten in but she quickly realised it had saved her life. Slowly focusing her eyes, she tried to make sense of what she was seeing. In front of her, there should have been two seats. There was nothing, just a tangle of shattered glass metal, all painted red. As her eyes started to work properly again she realised what she was seeing. Something must have smashed through the glass roof of the helicopter and cut violently through the two front seats. Goran and the pilot were still there. Actually, that wasn't true, half of them were there. They had been cut in half. The red was blood. She threw up. With shaking hands, she undid her lap strap. Getting out was easy. The door was no longer there. She fell to her knees, shaking in shock and pain. Pain from her head and pain from the loss of Goran. She vomited again. The smell of aviation fuel was all pervasive. She suddenly realised just how much danger she was in and was about to start running away when she remembered the packs with the film in them. Forcing herself back, she looked into the rear of the wreck. At first, there was no sign of them, then she glimpsed one jammed under the pilot's seat. Sobbing with effort, she reached in and pulled it free. One would have to do. She half ran half stumbled away from the wreck, her head still whirling with pain and grief. She realised she had no idea where she was or what she should do next.

Chapter 18

Jon looked out of the car window as it rolled up to the Hotel Metropole in Belgrade. He was surprised at how pristine it looked. In fact, the whole city looked like nothing he had expected. He had seen cities at war and this looked nothing like that. The streets were busy with well fed happy looking people. The buildings were all well kept and the streets were clean. He supposed he shouldn't be surprised, they were well away from any fighting. However, he couldn't help but compare what he was seeing with the shelled out wreck of the city of Sarajevo that he had been shown in his briefings. That and the precautions they had taken when flying into the airport just outside the city. The terminal buildings had been crowded with heavily armed troops. Luckily, his uniform with its UN armband had done the trick. The armed escort that was waiting for him did no harm either. One of them was now sitting next to his driver and four more were following in another white painted Mercedes off roader.

The car swept into the entrance and pulled to a halt by the large glass doors. The soldier jumped out of the front seat and opened the rear door before Jon could get to it. 'This way Sir,' he said in French. 'Your bags will be taken to your room.'

Jon nodded and followed the man into a large entrance lobby. Although the UN had taken over two whole floors of the hotel, it was still in general use and he was surprised how busy it seemed to be. The soldier led him to one side where there was a separate desk manned by another UN soldier who looked up as he approached and quickly made a call on a phone on his desk before standing to greet the new officer.

'Good morning Sir, You are Captain Hunt I expect?' the soldier said. Jon recognised him as a Sergeant but his nationality was not clear. He spoke perfect English but his uniform was not anything Jon had seen before.

'Yes, I am to meet Major Anasov,' Jon replied. 'Excuse me Sergeant but what nationality are you?'

The Sergeant laughed. 'I am from the Ukraine Captain but I was raised in Nottingham which is why I speak English better than Ukrainian. I am afraid you will find almost as many nationalities here as there are personnel. Ah, here is the Major,' and he pointed behind Jon's shoulder.

Jon turned around to see a Russian approaching. This time he had no problem with the uniform. Two years in Moscow had familiarised him with all their military clothing. He took a few seconds to study the man as he approached. He was surprisingly small and slim. Jon was used to Russians being large, especially their military. He had close cropped hair and piercing blue eyes hiding behind an incongruous pair of gold rimmed spectacles.

'Captain Hunt, welcome, we have been expecting you. I am Gregori Anasov. I will be your deputy. How was your journey?' He spoke in strongly accented English and held out his hand in welcome.

Jon was surprised how firm a grip such a slight man could exert and also how surprisingly deep his voice was. Not to be put out, he responded with a similar grip of his own and replied in perfect Russian. 'Major, good to meet you. Yes, my journey was fine although getting through the airport was interesting.'

A look of surprise came over the Major's face at Jon's reply. 'So you speak Russian Captain. I wasn't warned. That will make things easier.'

'I also speak French and Spanish and even a little of the local dialect but I suspect even that won't be enough with all the nationalities here.'

If the Major was surprised he managed to keep it to himself. 'Luckily for you Sir, nearly everyone on our team speaks some amount of English. It's not the same with the locals however and being able to tell when they are not being honest will be of great value. Might I suggest that you don't let them know you can understand them. It could be very useful at times.' He grinned at Jon as he said it.

Jon was immediately starting to like this man. 'Yes, that idea was suggested during my briefings in London. I'm not totally fluent I'm afraid but I can certainly follow a conversation.'

'Good, well may I first escort you to your room? After you have had time to settle in we can start on the local briefs later this afternoon.'

The Major took Jon over to the lifts and up to the fourth floor where he showed him into a palatial suite overlooking the city. His

Retribution

bags were already waiting for him as he surveyed the room. 'My goodness, the UN certainly look after you.'

'Here in Belgrade, yes Sir but don't be fooled. When we go up country it gets a lot rougher,' the Major replied with a wry grin.

'Why am I not surprised?' Jon replied.

'I'll leave you now Sir. Food is available around the clock in the restaurant or you can use room service if you wish. I have arranged a meeting with all your staff and for initial briefings at sixteen hundred. We have exclusive use of the conference facility on the first floor. You can't miss it when you exit the lift it's on your left.'

Jon thanked the Major who left quietly leaving Jon to contemplate his bags and start unpacking.

Sometime the next morning Jon opened his eyes and immediately wished he hadn't. He immediately recognised that a gorilla had been in his room and thrown his clothes all over the place, left the lights on, hit him over the head and done something horrible in his mouth. Either that or he had stayed up drinking with his new team until some dreadful time in the morning. Being with a Russian was bad enough but put into the mix an Israeli, a Frenchman and a Norwegian and it had become a night to remember. Jon looked at his watch and winced. He really had to get up. Mumbling to himself that he really should be old enough to know better, he made it into the shower. Ten minutes later and feeling marginally more alive, he struggled into his working uniform and considered what he was meant to be doing next. Just as his thought processes were kick-starting there was a knock at his door. When he opened it a smiling Gregori stood there.

'Come on in Gregori. How on earth do you manage to look so well?' Jon asked. 'No, don't answer that. You'll only tell me that you're Russian. I've been there and got the T shirt. So, what's on the agenda today, remind me.'

His new deputy just smiled. 'Good mornings Sir, we have a busy day today. First, we go to visit the Serbian Defence Ministry, then lunch with the minister. This afternoon they will give us a tour of the military headquarters and then there is a formal reception here at the hotel this evening.'

Jon groaned. 'So I have to be polite and believe everything they say?'

Gregori chuckled. 'Polite, yes. Believe them, no. I can guarantee that just about everything you hear and see will be a lie. I have never known a race that seems to believe its own propaganda as much as the Serbs. It may seem odd but it makes it hard to believe that they are not telling the truth when they seem to believe it so strongly themselves. My advice would be to try and not get angry when they look sincerely at you and tell you something that they know is a bare faced lie and you know it as well.'

'Don't worry Gregori, I worked in Moscow for several years. You lot gave me plenty of practice.' Jon replied with a grin.

Gregori barked out a laugh. 'Well, as you know Russia and Serbia have been friends for many years.'

'Yes Gregori and that is something we must talk about if you don't mind and now is as good a time as any. During my briefings in England I was made aware that your country is doing much to support the regime here which is very much in contravention of international agreements. Now before you say anything, I realise that this is nothing to do with you personally but you are part of a UN force and are now under my command. I would hate you to find that you have a conflict of interest. Do I make myself clear?' Jon looked hard at his man.

Gregori already knew something about this British Captain. Several of his previous exploits had made the international press. He had also been warned by his own command to take the man extremely seriously. Although he wasn't given any details, it was clear that Jon had impressed his government during his recent time in Moscow.

'Understood Sir. I can guarantee that while I serve as a UN soldier, I answer only to you and the UN.'

'Excellent, I'm glad we both understand each other. Now let's go and be nice to our hosts shall we?'

Chapter 19

Rupert sighed and sat back in his chair fighting a wave of frustration. For the third time that day he picked up the report on his desk and started reading. It was comprehensive and thorough. There was absolutely nothing in the life and career of Air Marshall (Retired) Peter Johnson that indicated anything other than an exemplary life of service to his country. He was born to rich and landed parents, attended the best schools and joined the RAF straight from a first class degree from Cambridge. Already a keen flyer with the University Air Squadron, he had trained on fast jets including the Lightning and later the Tornado. As was common in the Air Force, fast jet pilots seemed to get preferential treatment. Rupert was always amused by this, as if being able to fly an aircraft was somehow a qualification for higher command but it had always been the RAF way. Try as he might, there was absolutely no indication that the man wasn't what he seemed to be. Yet Rupert also knew to trust his instincts. There were just too many coincidences surrounding the man. The one that had really concerned him was the death of the secretary. The police had given up after several months of investigation and confined it to the cold case files. No evidence of any sort had ever been found. No witnesses, no CCTV coverage, nothing. If it had been deliberate, it was very much a professional job. He was just starting to think that he was wasting his time when his phone rang. It was his boss asking to meet. With a frustrated sigh, he walked to the lift and went up to the top floor.

The ensuing conversation wasn't what he was expecting.

'Rupert, you've been on this case for almost a year now.' His boss stated baldly. 'Let's face it, I think we've done our due diligence and I'm inclined to suggest that its time you moved on to a new permanent post and I have one in mind.'

Rupert sighed to himself and sat back in his seat. 'If I had a shred of evidence more than I've managed to dig up so far then I would argue but I haven't. You know my suspicions. I suspect you have yours as well.' He saw his boss nod so continued. 'Frankly, if you hadn't called me here I would be requesting a meeting anyway. It's time to move on.'

'Good,' the Boss responded. 'In that case, I've got some good news for you. I'll be honest Rupert, one of the reasons for giving you the temporary assignment was to align you with an important role that was liable to be coming vacant. You probably know that Jenkins is about to retire. It has been agreed that you should be offered the role.'

For a second, Rupert was nonplussed. 'But that's the whole of Europe.' He blurted without thinking.

His boss smiled. 'Yes a significant promotion and one that many feel is well deserved and overdue for that matter. You are prepared to take it on I presume?'

Rupert was completely taken aback and couldn't find the words for a moment before he, at last, managed a nod. 'I don't know what to say, yes of course, I would be delighted.'

'You realise that this means the end of field work, old chap? From now on you will only be a pen pusher like the rest of us senior wallahs?'

Rupert hadn't thought of that but he was also enough of a pragmatist to know that his time running around operationally had to end at some time. However, he wasn't completely prepared to give up on the last twelve month's work.

'As I said Sir, I would be delighted to accept but I wonder if there is one way I could at least keep one avenue of enquiry open regarding my last project?'

'Go on.'

That evening Rupert sat down with Ruth in the St John's Wood house. When he told his sister about his promotion she looked suitably impressed. 'Well done big brother, you'll be running the whole show in a few year's time.'

Rupert looked startled for a second. 'Bloody hell Ruth, don't think that. This new job is going to be demanding enough as it is.'

Ruth laughed. 'You are just like Jon Hunt. You both do bloody well at your jobs and neither of you seem the slightest interested in climbing the greasy pole. Then when you get promotion, it seems to come as a complete surprise. Anyway, changing the subject. What about our little pet project? I take it we are giving up? It seems such a shame.'

Retribution

'Ah, that's where you're wrong little sister. Yes, officially it's all been put in the 'nothing to be found' folder and sent off to gather dust in the archives. However, I talked the boss into continuing at a low level. That is if you are prepared to take it on. You would ostensibly be doing background work for my new department. In reality, you would continue as before and only report to me. It would be at least a further year's contract. What do you think?'

Ruth looked at her brother. 'You're not just doing this to keep me in work I take it?'

'Hah, absolutely not. I've got a budget to manage now, amongst other things. But I still feel there is some unfinished business despite our lack of progress, as I know you do too. However, doing it this way will officially draw stumps on the project. Who knows, maybe someone will get careless if they think the heat is off.'

'That assumes that we've not been discreet enough and someone knows what we've been doing.'

'Come on Ruth, you know our world. We might have kept under the radar when we first started digging about but as soon as we went out into the wide world someone will have noticed.'

Ruth looked thoughtful. She liked the idea on several levels, not the least that it would keep her busy and also ensure that she kept in touch with Jon. 'Fine by me Rupert, I'm in.'

It was a lovely Spring morning and many of the benches along the south bank of the Thames were in use. One in particular, just down from Westminster Bridge, was occupied by two men. Both were dressed in the standard Westminster uniform of grey suit, brogues and unassuming tie. One was reading a newspaper, the other apparently watching the river traffic under the bridge.

'Thanks for coming Peter. Sorry for the short notice but I was sure you would want to know this as soon as possible.' Gerald said quietly, while not making eye contact. 'I have it on good authority that the investigation you were worried about is over and nothing untoward has been discovered.'

'That's good to know old chap,' Peter replied, careful not to show the rush of relief that had washed over him at the words. 'So, it's all over then?'

'Done dusted and put to bed, so we can get on with our lives now. I hear you have a new job?'

'Goodness, word gets around fast. Yes, I'm consulting for a small company. Nothing special but it keeps me busy.'

Gerald laughed. 'That's not exactly what I heard. You just keep your head down old chap. Things could get very nasty, very quickly over there.'

'Don't I know it but I know the risks and anyway what's life without a little excitement?'

'So true, anyway back to the corridors of power, see you later in the year.' He stood and nonchalantly wandered back towards the steps leading up to the bridge. The other man waited a few minutes and continued his stroll down the south bank.

Chapter 20

Arianna's eyes opened slowly and for the second time in a day, she realised she had been unconscious. This time she was able to recall what had happened immediately and the memory hit her like a blow. She tried to sit up but was overcome with a wave of dizziness and lay back with her head pounding. A strange face floated into view. It was the old woman who had found her and she was smiling. She put her hand under Arianna's head and lifted it slightly and offered a glass of water for her to drink. Suddenly realising how thirsty she was, Arianna tried to gulp it down but the woman stopped her, allowing only sips.

'How long have I been out?' Arianna asked between sips.

'It's about noon now my dear,' the woman answered. 'And I'm sorry but you will have to leave soon. Soldiers came as soon as it was light and they are searching everywhere. My husband has been watching them. They started with the crash site but now some of them seem to be checking all the local farms. Will they know that you escaped?'

Arianna forced her muddled mind to think. There was no reason for the soldiers to know that there had been three people in the aircraft. Then, she had a sudden thought. 'Where's the bag I was carrying when you found me?'

The old woman reached down beside the bed. 'Here my dear, is it important?'

'You've no idea,' Arianna replied as she dug into the contents. The first things she encountered were several rolls of film and two videotapes. For a second, a wave of relief washed over her but she kept digging. With dismay, the next thing she found was one of Goran's T shirts and then some of his underwear. It was definitely his pack. The soldiers would have found hers by now and realised that there was a female in the aircraft. Presumably, that was now why they were searching the local area.

'I have to go,' she said urgently. 'But where am I? I was in the back of the helicopter and have no idea where it came down.'

'This is the village of Hresa my dear. We farm the land out the back.'

'Hang on, that's quite close to Sarajevo isn't it?' Arianna asked as she realised just how difficult her position was becoming.

'Yes, its only ten kilometres from here which is why the army are everywhere. They've been besieging the city for months. What are you going to do?'

'Christ, I don't know. Why are you helping me anyway? You and your husband must be Serbs. You must realise I am Croatian?'

'Not everyone is a murderous maniac my dear,' the old lady stated sadly. 'Many of us don't agree with what is going on. As far as I'm concerned, when we found you last night you were just another human being in need of help. I've put some stitches into that cut on your forehead, I used to be a nurse you know and I can't find anything else wrong apart from a few bruises.'

'And I really thank you for that but I mustn't put you and your husband in peril. Is there any direction I should go? Do you know where the soldiers are based?'

'They seem to be everywhere these days. The only main road is to the north, you can just follow the lane outside the house but that's probably not very safe. If you go cross country to the south and east that should take you clear.'

Arianna realised she had no choice. She had to get out of the area even if it meant going the wrong way, away from the Croatian border. Suddenly, her decision was made for her. The old woman's husband appeared. He had a large bag in his hand. 'Quickly, you must go. The soldiers are almost here. Take this, there is some water and food inside. It's the best I could do but you must go, now.'

Arianna had no desire to get these two good people into trouble and thanking them, she made her way to the back of the little farmhouse. She looked carefully out of the rear of the building. There was a small stand of trees not too far away. With a final heartfelt call of thanks to her two saviours, she ran to the trees.

It wasn't a moment too soon. As she dived into cover she saw a truck draw up in the road in front of the farm and several green clad men clamber out. Praying that her benefactors would not get in trouble, she carefully wormed her way through the trees to the other side. When she was well clear she stopped and took a quick inventory of the bag the old farmer had given her. As soon as she looked in she saw why it had felt so heavy. Two large bottles of water and some bread, cheese and ham were part of the reason. The other was a large revolver that must have dated back to at least the last war and a box of shells. Blessing them for their foresight, she then saw something even more useful. It was only a road map but now she could at least navigate with some confidence. That said, she was under no illusions over the task facing her. She was in the heart of disputed territory with troops everywhere and almost certainly some of them were looking for her. She had to assume the worst and that they had discovered the other half of the films in the wreck of the helicopter. It wouldn't take long for the contents to be understood and then she would be even more in demand. She had to get away and fast but where to go? She studied the map carefully. To the west was Sarajevo, a city under siege. She knew it well but it was the last place she wanted to go to now. Presumably, Serbian troops were all around it. To the south was the main M5 AutoRoute that led into the city. Clearly she needed to avoid that. The obvious way to go was north and skirt around the city before heading east towards Croatia and safety. The map showed one more road, the R447 that she would have to cross and then it was open country for miles. However, she had no intention of walking all the way home. Once clear of the danger area she would look for some isolated property and find a telephone. If there was any resistance, she had the pistol to back her up and once she had made contact she was pretty sure another pick up could be quickly arranged. The thought of another helicopter flight didn't please her but the contents of the films were of paramount importance. She owed it to those poor girls. She had vowed that their sacrifice would be avenged. She knew the telephone lines were still open across the borders. It was just a shame she hadn't had time to think of the idea when in the farmhouse but it was too late now and anyway she would have to get some considerable distance away from the area before anyone would risk flying in.

Realising she was now wasting time, she took the provisions out of the farmer's bag and stowed them in her pack. She loaded the pistol and put it in her waistband, then hoisted he pack on her back and looked at the sun to work out where north was. She started to trudge doggedly on, knowing it was going to be a long day.

Within a few hours, she was beginning to weaken. She realised she was probably still in shock from the crash and the loss of Goran. Sweet, supportive Goran who had been with her for what seemed like forever. The blow to the head probably hadn't helped either. With the last of the adrenalin from her narrow escape leaking away, she realised she couldn't go on. Looking around for cover for the night, she saw a hay rick in the corner of a distant field. That would do nicely. Within fifteen minutes, she was climbing the side of the mound of hay. It was the old fashioned type made by hand, not agricultural machinery and once on top she was able to burrow into the loose material and make herself a nest for the night. Within seconds, she was asleep.

The next morning, she woke with the dawn and a raging headache. Fumbling around in her pack she pulled out a water bottle and drank deeply. After eating some of the food, she started to feel better. Carefully crawling to the edge of the hay, she looked out. Nothing was moving and only a kilometre away she could see the road she needed to cross. Once past that, she would be able to get clear and hopefully find the telephone that she needed.

Brushing the straw from her clothes, she set out north again. There was no sign of the R447, it must be hidden in a cutting she realised. Either that or she had completely underestimated the distances from the road map. In the end, she stumbled on it almost by accident. Rounding the side of a small hill that she decided wasn't worth the effort of climbing, she was suddenly aware of the sound of engines and voices. Throwing herself to the ground, she continued in a crawl. What she saw made her realise all her plans were going to be for nothing. The road was completely full of military vehicles heading towards Sarajevo. It must be another attempt by the Serbian army to take the city. There were trucks full of troops and even a few Soviet designed tanks. There was no way she could make any progress in this direction, not for days at least. She would have to turn around and try and find a telephone somewhere else. She had just started to crawl slowly backwards when she heard voices from behind her. There was a shout and then a coarse laugh. With mounting dread, she turned her head to see the barrels of five AK 47 rifles pointing straight at her and the smirking faces of the soldiers that were holding them.

Chapter 21

The small UNPROFOR convoy wended its way along the road making slow progress. They had left the small, local, UN base a couple of hours ago and should have easily been able to enter Sarajevo within an hour. However, the road was crammed with Serbian troops and there seemed to be road blocks every couple of miles. It was clear they weren't welcome but Jon was not going to let that stop him. Inside, he was seething with frustration.

That morning he had been called for a briefing with the French Brigadier who commanded the small detachment of UN troops that were camped to the east of the city. The man did not seem happy to see Jon, in fact he didn't really seem happy about anything. A small, thin soldier, with tired eyes, he looked surprised when Jon introduced himself and even more annoyed when Jon explained why he was there.

'Yes, I do remember seeing something about your visit,' the Brigadier curtly acknowledged. 'But I don't see why someone who is meant to be on the staff in Belgrade feels the need to tour this benighted country. You won't learn anything except that we are here with no power to do anything to stop these animals.'

Jon was taken aback by the vehemence of the Brigadiers tone. 'Well, two things to answer that Sir. Firstly, I don't feel I can do my job until I understand what is actually happening on the ground. Secondly, I was ordered to do so whether I wanted to or not.'

The Brigadier grimaced again. 'Well, when you find out what is going on please feel free to tell me. Look, I do understand why you're here but the problem is that there as so many factions in operation around the country. Yes, there is meant to be a Serbian army but its command and control is terribly fragmented and most people seem to be out to settle old scores, real or imaginary. Add to that, the Muslims hate the Christians and vice versa. Plus Tito left the country and armed camp and everyone who wants one has a gun or rocket launcher.'

It was Jon's turn to grimace. 'Yes Sir, I've already seen much of that. At least we can carry arms to protect ourselves.'

The Brigadier barked out a laugh. 'Oh, yes, of course. Do you know what the original UN mandate was?'

Jon did know but kept his council.

'We were allowed to use force to protect people and then some moron further up the chain interpreted that to mean we could only use force to protect ourselves. Not only that, we were meant to have over thirty thousand troops and what have we got? Seven thousand, that's what. So, we are too few and without the number to do anything significant even if we wanted to.'

'But we can call in air strikes. We've done it once or twice already.' Jon responded.

'Don't start me there Captain. To get an air strike we have to go up the UN chain and then across to NATO who actually have the assets. When and if approval is granted, it has to come back down the chain. Meanwhile, the reason for the strike has melted away and even if the aircraft are approved there is nothing to strike. Mark my words, there is going to a tragedy here one day soon and I don't mean what they are doing to Sarajevo. And we will be powerless to do anything. My only fear is it will take something terrible to get the world off its ass and involved properly. These Serbs are bullies and until someone stands up to them they will just continue to laugh at us and do what they want.'

Jon was going to remember these words.

In the end, the Brigadier gave them a small escort of a platoon of French troops and let Jon go on his way. He had already been travelling with his Russian deputy and very tough looking South African Sergeant who only seemed to answer to his rank, although Jon actually knew his name was James De Groot. They had been using a white painted UNPROFOR Mercedes off-road car and now had a white truck following. Everyone was armed but only with personal small arms, although the following troops at least had rifles.

The Brigadier's last words were that he expected them back by evening. 'Sarajevo may be a UN protected area Captain Hunt but that doesn't mean they will let you pass. We haven't got anyone in or out for several months. But good luck, maybe you will get lucky.'

Jon was reflecting on the Frenchman's word when yet again they were stopped by a troop of scruffy armed Serbs. Gregori and the Sergeant got out of the vehicle and confronted them while Jon waited with the driver. There was clearly an altercation starting. The Serbs started placing their hands on their weapons. They looked far

Retribution

more belligerent than any other they had so far dealt with. Jon had had enough and got out.

'What's going on Major?' He asked as he locked eyes with what looked like the senior of the Serbian soldiers.

Gregori didn't turn his head. 'This soldier,' he said the word with contempt, 'says we cannot go any further and we must turn back.'

Jon looked around. There was a clearing to the left with a number of trucks parked up and several large tents. The place had an air of permanency about it.

'That is correct, you all must go back. This is not a place for you.' The soldier said in very strongly accented English.

Jon stared him in the eye. 'Where is your Commanding Officer? I wish to speak with him.'

'He will not want to speak to you. Now go away.'

Jon had noted that the man glanced over at the tents as he spoke and without another word strode towards them. The Serb who had been speaking tried to get in the way but Jon just pushed past him. With Gregori and the Sergeant trailing him, Jon entered the first tent. Inside, it was very Spartan with several fold-out tables and chairs. On one, a large radio was in use. An operator was sitting in front of it with earphones on. Standing next to him was a rather overweight soldier with scruffy long hair. Despite his appearance, Jon recognised his rank insignia as being that of a Colonel.

The man glanced around as Jon entered and a look of surprise and then anger went across his pock marked face.

'Who are you and what are you doing here?' he asked in accented English.

Jon took no notice of the man's attitude. 'My name is Captain Jonathon Hunt, Royal Navy and I am an officer in the UN Protection Force. I require access to the city of Sarajevo which is a UN protected area.'

The Colonel barked out a laugh. 'Go away. You are not wanted here and no one goes in or leaves the city. And before you say anything, I know you are not allowed to use force but you had better believe me when I tell you that I am.'

Despite all his diplomatic training and experience, Jon found himself getting more and more angry. It was bad enough that most of the UN people he had met seemed to have just about given up but this blatant disregard for international law and accompanying arrogance was driving him close to the edge.

Gregori stepped close to Jon and said in quiet Russian. 'Sir, we are not going to win this one. It's clear they are up to some new offensive with all the troops and equipment we've seen. We'd be better off returning and reporting what we have discovered.'

Jon knew that the Major was right and that there was little he could do but he hated the idea of backing down in front of this arrogant bully. Suddenly, everyone's attention was distracted by an unearthly scream. It seemed to be coming from someone in extreme agony. Before anyone could react, the Serbian Colonel picked up a field telephone and spoke urgently into it in his own language. Jon had enough fluency to follow the conversation but kept a straight face as if he didn't understand.

The Colonel was almost shouting down the phone. 'Get someone over to the interrogation tent and tell that idiot to stop torturing the girl until I've got rid of these UN idiots.' He slammed the phone down and looked at Jon. 'Go, now, please.'

Jon now had absolutely no intention of going anywhere except to discover what these barbarians were up to.

'What was that scream Colonel? What are you doing here?' he asked angrily.

'None of your business Captain but if you must know we have a medical facility and sometimes our soldiers don't react well to treatment.'

Jon laughed in his face as he swiftly un-holstered his pistol and before the Colonel could react, pointed it straight between his eyes from a few inches away. In Serbo-Croat, Jon spoke through clenched teeth. 'This UN idiot understood everything you said on the telephone you arrogant bastard. We may have a limited mandate here but we are certainly allowed to step in to stop war crimes and it seems to me that is exactly what is going on here.'

The Colonel looked confused as if not believing any UN officer would react in such a way and Jon took the opportunity to tell the Major and Sergeant to get his soldiers to dismount and fall in with weapons ready. He also told them of what was going on although he knew that both men had a smattering of the language as well. The Sergeant disappeared through the tent flap.

Retribution

'You cannot do anything Captain,' the Colonel finally blustered. 'We outnumber your pathetic platoon. You must leave or bear the consequences.'

By now Jon reckoned he had the measure of his man. 'Yes, you are absolutely correct Colonel but wouldn't it be a shame if you personally became a victim of anything that now takes place. For example, if my pistol were to accidentally go off next to your ear, it would remove the ear and deafen you there for life. Or, if my pistol accidentally then went off and the bullet went through your left elbow. I notice you are left handed and that would cripple you for life wouldn't it? Believe me, there are no end of places my pistol could accidentally go off and I have eleven rounds in the magazine. You do believe me don't you?' Jon looked hard at his man as Gregori gave a laugh of admiration behind him.

The Colonel looked into Jon's eyes and suddenly realised that this man wasn't bluffing.

'Oh and just to make things clear. My Major here is Russian and Spetsnaz trained. I'm sure you know what that means.'

From the Colonel's reaction, it was clear he was aware of the quality of the Russian Special Forces.

'And I might just add that the troops which my South African Special Forces Sergeant is now deploying are French. They are all ex Foreign Legion, I expect you also know what that means. So Colonel, if it comes to a fight, how well do you think your pathetic, scruffy soldiers will actually do against mine? My money is on them all running away very fast, not that I saw that many outside anyway and by the time you are able to get reinforcements we will be long gone.' Jon turned to Gregori. 'Major, do me a favour and make sure that radio over there won't work for a while.'

The Major grinned and went over to the radio and unceremoniously yanked the wires out of the back of the set making sure that the connections were ruined in the process. The radio operator simply looked on. He had heard the conversation and had no desire to get involved.

'Now Colonel, do me the favour of taking me to this interrogation tent of yours.'

With the Serbian commander ahead of him and Jon's pistol lodged firmly in his back they left the tent and walked towards a similar tent further down the line. The Colonel seemed to be rigid with fear which was fine by Jon but just to make sure, Jon told the Sergeant to deploy the twelve soldiers around them. When they reached the tent the soldiers took up position outside and Jon, Gregori and the Colonel went in.

The sight and smell that met their eyes was like something out of the dark ages. A sturdy wooden chair and small side table were the only furniture. Strapped into the chair with tape was a semi naked young girl. A large soldier was standing behind her with one hand around her mouth. He had clearly been doing something to her hands. Jon looked more carefully. She was naked from the waist up and there were livid red marks across her breasts. However, it was her right hand that took his attention. Protruding from under a finger nail was a long metal needle. Blood was slowly dripping onto the floor below. Jon could see several more needles on the small table and the soldier was presumably waiting for the go ahead to carry on with his treatment. The girl, although wide eyed in surprise, was sobbing and breathing hard around the soldier's large, calloused hand.

A red mist clouded Jon's vision. He knew he was in a dangerous position and should be careful. He knew he should act diplomatically. He knew he was going to do neither of those two things. Without conscious volition, he marched over the interrogator and smashed his pistol into the sneering man's face. The man was taken completely by surprise and staggered back with blood pouring from his mouth. He recovered quickly, only to be confronted by two cocked pistols held by the Major and Sergeant. Nursing his bleeding jaw, he took one pace back.

Jon hadn't felt this good for a long time. In fact, it was just like the last time when he had punched that grinning, idiotic journalist back at Culdrose.

'Keep them both covered,' he told his two men and he went and carefully knelt in front of the poor girl. It was clear she had been through hell. There were bruises and what looked like whip marks all over the front and back of her torso and her right eye was almost closed with blood encrusting it. 'I'm sorry, this will probably hurt again,' he said in her language and he very carefully pulled the needle out from under the finger nail. She whimpered slightly but that was all. Her bindings were simple gaffer tape but a lot had been used. Luckily, he had a pocket knife which he unfolded and carefully used to cut through the tape.

As he did so, the Colonel got up the courage to speak again. 'You cannot do this, she is a prisoner of war. She was in a helicopter crash a few days ago and had been spying on us.'

Jon spun around and stood nose to nose with man. 'Fuck off, you stinking animal. If she had been in a crash, she should be in hospital not being tortured. I have mandate from the UN to stop this sort of medieval barbarity. As far as I'm concerned, you and your thug here are both guilty of war crimes. So, not only am I taking this poor girl with me but you two are coming as well. You can answer for your behaviour to the international criminal court.'

Jon turned to his men. 'Gregori, get a couple of the men in here to secure these two scum and then help me with the girl.'

Jon was surprised to see that despite her ordeal, the girl was recovering fast. She had managed to stand and go over to a pile of clothing in the corner and put on a shirt. When she saw Jon looking at her, she went over to the small table and picked up some black objects which she handed to him. To his surprise, he saw there were several rolls of camera film and two small video tapes.

The girl spoke for the first time and in English. 'You might want to get these developed.'

Chapter 22

Arianna lay in her hospital bed in Belgrade. She really didn't like where the UN troops had taken her but was reassured by the permanent armed guard outside her room. She was surprised how quickly her bruises and other damage was healing. She wasn't so sure about the damage to her state of mind.

When the Serbian troops had found her, they seemed to think that she was fair game for anything they wanted. It was only the intervention of an officer that stopped her being gang raped on the spot. He had looked in her backpack and immediately seen the films. Luckily, she had already disposed of Goran's video camera and as it used specialised film cartridges they would have no way of playing back the two video tapes. She doubted that they had film developing facilities to hand so she needed to do everything she could to stop them realising what was on them.

Unfortunately, the officer's first words to her didn't bode well. 'You were in that helicopter crash weren't you? We found a backpack with female clothing in it and more of these films. What is on them?'

She vowed to herself to keep quiet for as long as she could. The officer didn't hesitate and back handed her across her face so hard that she fell on her back with blood pouring out of her eye which started closing. She stayed mute. At a gesture from the officer, she was hauled to her feet, taken to a truck and thrown unceremoniously into the back. Two soldiers got in as it drove off and used the short journey to enjoy themselves by groping her despite her struggles. When they arrived at the small base, she was taken to a tent where a more senior officer started asking her the same questions. When she stayed mute, he tore her shirt off her back and ripped off her bra. He then got a thin cane and while a soldier held her, whipped her back. The pain was unimaginable but she focused her thoughts on Goran and what she had lost and managed to remain silent. She was spun roughly around and the cane was used on her breasts and stomach. At some point the pain became so unbearable she passed out. When she came to, she found she was sitting in a hard wooden chair and her wrists and ankles were securely taped in place.

Retribution

Her interrogator was looking down on her. 'You can stay here for the night, maybe in the morning you will feel more inclined to cooperate. There will be more of the same treatment if you don't. That will be interspersed with my men using you as they see fit. I suggest you think on all that until the morning.'

The night had been unbearable. At one point she had to let go of her bladder and strangely that at least felt good. Pissing on her enemies felt right somehow as well as relieving the pressure. She even managed a little fitful sleep despite the pain from her beatings. The next morning a man came in and gave some water. He was actually very nice although he didn't say anything and when he left, the large soldier from the previous day came in. There was no sign of the officer.

Without a word, he started by pawing and slapping her breasts, then twisting her nipples savagely. He didn't ask any questions at all. He then forced his hand down the front of her trousers and savagely twisted her pubic hair. Arianna wanted to scream but was damned if she was going to give him the satisfaction. Panting heavily, she just looked him in the eye.

He finally spoke. 'You know what we want you to tell us. I will continue to give you pain until you do. All you have to do is ask me to stop. Do you understand?' and he underlined his words with another backhanded slap across her face.

She shook her head with the pain and her vision blurred but she said nothing.

'Very well, we'll continue.' He reached into a pocket a brought out several metal needles. He then knelt down by her right hand and took firm hold of her right index finger. He positioned the needle under the finger nail and then looked Arianna in the eye as he slowly forced the needle in under the nail.

Arianna had never felt pain like it and finally let out a gut wrenching scream of sheer agony. The soldier sat back and studied her for several minutes as the pain subsided from pure agony to a deep throbbing ache. 'I have nine more of these for your hands then we can start on your toes, how does that sound?'

She knew she would never be able to stand that. She was close to breaking. The only thing that was holding her back now was the certainty that even if she did tell them what they wanted to know, their treatment of her afterwards would probably be the same. At least by holding out, she was denying them information. Suddenly, the tent flap opened and another soldier came in and said something quietly to her interrogator. She didn't catch what it was but it made him stand back.

'It seems we have to wait a little longer my lovely. Some unwanted visitors have arrived. Don't worry, we will get back to our lovemaking very soon.'

A sharp glimmer of hope flashed across her mind. Whoever these visitors were, they clearly had enough clout to stop her captors. She was about to scream for help when the man must have realised what she was about to do and clamped his hand firmly over her mouth.

Two minutes later it was all over. Three UN officers entered the tent and after the altercation took her away sobbing in their car. She also saw that the officer and her interrogator were being taken. What was surprising was that none of the soldiers she saw offered up the slightest resistance and it was a matter of minutes and they were speeding away to safety.

Her eyes were just starting to close again, the painkillers they had given her made her very sleepy, when the door opened and one of her rescuers came in. It was the naval Captain who had hit the Serbian officer. She would have liked him just for that.

'Hello,' he said in a gentle voice. 'How are you? Are things improving?'

She nodded. He had been very attentive on the road away from Sarajevo. They had stopped once at some small UN camp but she had been kept in the car. After that, they shared the car all the way to the hospital. She knew his name was Jon and that he was a Captain but couldn't really work out where that put him in the rank structure. He was certainly senior to an army Captain but looked far too young to be a Colonel equivalent which is what one of the soldiers had told her. She also thought he had sad eyes. 'Yes, they've given me some painkillers and everything is a bit numb.'

He grimaced. I'm just sorry that we couldn't have got to you earlier.'

'Don't be silly, you didn't even know I was there. Now tell me, have you developed the films?' Arianna had told Jon all about her mission and the subsequent crash on the way to Belgrade.

'I'll be honest with you Arianna, I wasn't sure whether to really believe you or not. You were in a pretty bad way when we rescued you. But yes they have been developed and we've also watched the video tapes. I get more disgusted with these people the more I see of them.'

'And what will you do with the information?' she asked. 'I hope all this wasn't for nothing.'

'No, of course it wasn't. It's dynamite there is no doubt about that. Not quite so sure about my career mind you,' he said with a rueful smile.

'What? You can't be in trouble after all you did.' Arianna looked amazed.

'Well, I did assault that bloody Colonel and had the effrontery to arrest him and his goon. No one knows what to do with them. When we stopped on the way back I went into see a French Brigadier who was in charge of the area and he almost had me arrested on the spot. We had what you might call a firm discussion. I'm afraid by then, I wasn't prepared to back down to anyone and just walked out on the man. So, when we got here I was very quickly hauled over the coals. However, that all changed fast when the photographs were developed and we found a way of playing the tapes.'

'So you know what is going on now? You have the proof. What are you going to do with it?' she asked anxiously.

'Look Arianna, I understand that your people want NATO to become fully involved and this is just the sort of evidence that is needed to convince the world what is going on.'

She looked sharply at Jon. 'That sounds like there is a catch. Is there?'

'Arianna, I'm not going to lie to you. There are some among my superiors who don't think this is the right time to make this public. They think there is still a good chance that the situation can be resolved without resorting to more force.' Jon did not look convinced as he said the words.

'You don't think that, do you?' Arianna said bitterly.

'I'm going to be totally honest with you. When I got back to Belgrade I was immediately hauled in front of the General commanding the whole UN contingent. He's from Belgium and in my view a complete incompetent. A few weeks ago, I had talked him in to letting me go on a front line tour as I felt I needed to understand the situation in the field if I was to be able to do my job here in Belgrade properly. He wasn't keen so when I returned he couldn't accuse me of disobeying orders but I had to repeatedly point out the wording of our UN charter or he would have accused me of being in breach of it. In the end, he had to back down when the photographs were developed. It seems he immediately recognised that government minister. Apparently, they are friends, which really doesn't help. So, at the moment there is a typical UN debate going on about what to do. Has anyone come here yet to take a statement from you?'

She shook her head. 'You have been my only visitor.'

Jon almost said something, then held it back. He didn't want to worry Arianna any more. One of the more outrageous suggestions that had been made by one staff officer back at HQ was that the girl should be handed back to her captors along with releasing the two Serbian soldiers. Jon had blown his top completely at the man but the fact that it could even be considered scared him.

'Right, well if you feel up to it I can write it down for you and then you can sign it. Is that alright?'

She nodded and for the next hour Jon put her story on paper. He was amazed at her experiences as she insisted on going right back to the murder of her parents and her subsequent recruitment into the army. He convinced her to go lightly about her operations with Goran. The last thing he needed was some bloody staff officer to counter accuse her of war crimes.

When they had finished she signed the statement and looked expectantly at Jon. 'What happens now Jon?'

'That's up to you, at least in part,' he responded. 'You may need to stay here to provide evidence or you may be able to go home. I'll find out and let you know as soon as I can but you're going to be in here for a few days more whatever happens.'

'And when I go home how will I be able to do that? Technically, I am in the capital city of my sworn enemy.'

'Again, I'll have to look into that but I give you my word that I'll ensure you have safe passage home one way or another.'

Arianna realised that she trusted this strange man. The efforts of the past hour caught up with her and she drifted off to sleep.

Seeing her eyes close, Jon waited a few minutes before leaving. The girl was a complete mystery to him. Looking at her small frame he couldn't imagine what she had gone through and yet not only had she endured but she had fought back very effectively. Not only that but despite the bruising, and lines of fatigue and sorrow on her face he couldn't help himself but observe just how pretty she was.

Chapter 23

The road side café was like any that could be found in any capital city in the world. Jon was sitting outside at a table drinking beer. He was trying hard to get drunk but it was proving to be an uphill struggle. Inside, his emotions were in torment. When he was a junior officer, seeing someone with fours stripes on his sleeve would generate instant respect and obedience. Now that he had those fours stripes, he was finding things a different matter. As far as the UN command chain went, he seemed to be in limbo. The really senior officers took what few decisions needed to be taken and the more junior ones did all the dirty work out in the field, not that there was even very much of that. For the life of him, he couldn't see what his purpose was apart from sitting at a desk and shuffling reports.

The waiter brought him another beer and he sat back and looked around at the crowds. It was a warm evening and pretty girls were everywhere. Couples were walking hand in hand. Old people were sitting chatting. It was all so normal. Yet only a few miles away, girls were being raped and murdered. Girls were having needles forced under their finger nails and all by the same race of people he was seeing here. And why? Yes, he understood the fundamental issues. He had sat through enough briefings and read all the documents. But none of that excused what was going on. Maybe he should rent a large cinema and show the two tapes of the rape and murder that Arianna had filmed to these people. How would they react?

His thoughts turned to how his superiors had reacted to the tapes and photos and it was this thought that made him realise why he felt so low. Firstly, no one had seemed that surprised and then none of them seemed to want to do anything about it. Clear, unequivocal evidence, of a war crime, which included one of the ministers of the very government that was hosting them and no one wanted to do anything. In the end, it had taken a nose to nose confrontation with the Belgian General and production of Arianna's written statement to get the bloody man to agree to release the evidence to the headquarters in New York. That and Jon's threat to go straight to the papers himself.

Was the world going mad he wondered? Commanding a ship or squadron was child's play to coping with the situation here and this was despite his two years in a diplomatic posting in Moscow to fall back on. The sooner he got away from here the better. There was a large warship, with his name on it being built back in Britain. He would just have to bite his tongue and endure until then.

His thoughts were interrupted by a voice. 'There you are Sir, I see you are taking the Russian approach to coping with the situation,' Gregori boomed out as he took in the number of empty bottles on Jon's table.

Jon looked up at his deputy and smiled. 'It's not bloody working though. Come on, take a seat and join me.'

Gregori took the seat opposite and signalled to the waiter to clear the table. He also said something else which Jon didn't catch but it soon became clear, when a full bottle of vodka and two shot glasses were placed on the now tidy table. Gregori poured two slugs.

Jon grimaced but joined him in a Russian toast and they both emptied the glasses in one gulp before Gregori immediately refilled them. 'And you can stop calling me Sir when we are out of uniform, my name is Jon as I'm sure you know.'

'I will try,' Gregori replied. 'But it will not come naturally. Now, let me guess you're frustrated and sickened by both our people and by these hypocritical Serbs and are wondering what you can do about it, Jon. Is that correct?'

Jon looked surprised at the simple accuracy of Gregori's assessment. 'Got it in one. I'm only here for a short term appointment but if it's all going to be like this, then I'm not sure I will last. I had to threaten a General today to get him to do anything at all with Arianna's evidence. Getting through the next few months without being court martialled is going to be hard.'

Gregori looked sympathetic. 'Sir, sorry Jon, this is something we have all experienced, believe me. The UN has cleverly put itself in an almost impossible position and we are the people who have to live with that. There seem to be two ways to react to it. Some, in fact most, just accept the inevitable and keep their heads down. The General is probably the finest example of that. But some of us are not prepared to sit on our arses and it's pretty plain to me that you are one of those.'

'Thanks Gregori, at least I'm not the only one. And it leaves me with two problems. Firstly, this evidence that Arianna gave us is sitting on that bloody General's desk and despite his promises, I don't see it moving far soon. Secondly, it's the girl herself. The hospital says she will be ready for discharge in a couple of days. She needs to be safely returned to her own people which means we will have to get her there. When I asked if any preparations were being made all I got was blank looks.'

Gregori laughed again. 'Yes, I'm not surprised. Leave it with me. I'll see if a flight can be arranged. If not, we can drive her there or even take her to the coast and get her on a ferry. I can't see it being an issue.'

'Thanks Gregori. At least that is one less thing to worry about.'

'Jon, can I ask you a question?'

'Of course, fire away,' Jon realised the alcohol was really starting to hit now and his speech was slightly slurred.

'What exactly did you hand over to the General and his staff?'

'Eh, what do you mean?'

'Let me put it another way. Did you give them the negatives and the original film cassettes? You know, the little ones that fit into the camera. When you showed them to everyone, they had been transferred to VHS and only the developed photos were shown.'

Jon suddenly felt more sober. This man was no fool. He felt he could trust him but he also knew how the Russian mind worked. He decided on a compromise. 'In exactly the same place as a photo copy of Arianna's statement old chap.'

The next morning, Jon was called to a meeting with his Chief of Staff. He was another French officer but a Naval Commodore this time and Jon actually liked him rather a lot. He seemed to be one of the officers, who to quote Gregori, 'wasn't prepared to sit on his arse.' Jon arrived with his almost normal post Russian hangover. Gregori knew the city well and they had tried several more bars and even a nightclub before Jon firmly called a halt and headed for bed. Even so, it was very late before he made it back to his room. He was now suffering and once again vowing never to go on a bloody run ashore, with a bloody Russian, ever again.

'Good morning Jon, I take it you've been out with your Russian deputy?' the Commodore said cheerfully.

'Bloody hell Sir, is it that obvious?' Jon asked.

'Don't forget I've known him longer than you and have had to suffer in the same way. It always seems such a good idea at the time, doesn't it?'

Jon laughed. 'Yes Sir. Anyway, what can I do for you this fine morning?'

'Firstly, we need to decide what to do with all the material the girl brought in the other day.'

'But the General has it Sir and has promised to get it sent to New York straight away.' Jon sounded puzzled.

'That's not quite what I meant. That material actually belongs to the Croatian military who sent her on her mission. In law, the source material needs to be given back to them.' The Commodore lifted one eye quizzically.

Jon realised that his assessment of the man was absolutely correct. 'Yes Sir, good point. My deputy is arranging transport to get the girl back to her people. We must make sure she has what is rightfully hers. After all, her people must have had a good idea about what to do with it.'

'Exactly and it will stop any bottlenecks in America. Right, I have something else which might just provide support in the same area. I'm giving you someone extra for your staff. What you probably don't know is that from time to time Head Office like to conduct an independent review of our activities out here. God knows why because they never seem to take any notice of the reports they get but it's not up to us to query their God like powers. In this case, they've appointed an outside consultant to review our charter here and how it ties in with our current level of activity, including our rules of engagement. Your recent experiences is exactly the sort of thing he needs to know about.'

Jon suddenly felt a wave of optimism. Could this be a lever to finally get more freedom of action and this stupid restraint on self protection only?

'Who is this chap and does he have any constraints on the scope of his study?' Jon asked, well aware that it would be all too easy to hamstring someone with limited terms of reference.

'He's a very experienced military officer now retired and no, he has been given a blank sheet as far as I can tell. Now Jon, I know that you and I see eye to eye over this issue, unlike our illustrious

General. I want you to make sure that he gets the full picture. Do I make myself clear?'

'Absolutely Sir, when do I get to meet him?'

'Here's here, waiting outside,' The Commodore pressed a buzzer on his desk and the door opened.

A chill ran down Jon's spine. Despite being dressed in a suit and having not seen him for several years, Jon immediately recognised retired, Air Marshall, Sir Peter Johnson.

Chapter 24

They had let Arianna get up out of bed but she was still confined to her room. All her personal possessions had been returned, including to her surprise, her wallet with the considerable amount of dollars in it that she had been provided with as a contingency. It seemed that the Serbs had been so interested in the film and tapes they hadn't had time to search further. A helpful nurse had gone and done some shopping for her so she now had at least one set of reasonable civilian clothes which she was now wearing. That said, she could see the silhouette of the UN guard through the frosted glass of her door but was starting to wonder whether his role was as much to keep her inside as to protect her from any external threat. The nice Captain had been to see her again yesterday and promised that they were arranging for her to go back to Croatia. He was due again soon and she was hoping she would be able to convince him to let her out. He had also explained that the films and tapes would be returned to her before she left. What he hadn't said was how she was going to be taken back. However, for some reason she trusted him. So, hopefully, she would be leaving soon. It couldn't come soon enough. Her injuries had all faded now and with the exception of a plaster over her damaged nail there was no longer any external signs of her ordeal. Apart from a few books that the staff had let her have, there was absolutely nothing to do and she was slowly going stir crazy. She knew she should be grieving for losing Goran but somehow her mind was in a state of limbo, maybe when she got home she could let her emotions loose.

Suddenly, there was an odd, dull thud from behind the door and she realised there was no sign of the guard any more. A wave of panic overcame her and for a second she stood paralysed with indecision. Then she reacted. She was sitting in an arm chair by the bed so grabbed a pillow and stuffed it under the covers so it looked like she was asleep. She then grabbed the bedside lamp, ripping out the wire in her haste and then went to stand behind the door. The lamp was quite sturdy and was all she could think of as a weapon. It should do some damage, at least she hoped it would.

The door handle slowly dropped down and the door started to open. The centre pane was opaque glass so she couldn't see who it was but what she could see quite clearly was the shadow of a hand holding something pointed. Slowly, the hand extended past the door and the outline of a small automatic pistol, with a silencer screwed to it, came into plain sight. Whoever it was, they didn't want to waste time and immediately there was the spitting sound of four rounds being quickly fired. The bed shook and erupted in little fountains of cloth where the rounds struck. If she had been in bed, Arianna would now be very dead.

The assassin must have expected something more because he swiftly stepped towards the bed. She could see his back clearly now. He was a big man in army uniform with short hair and a bull neck. For a second, she wondered whether she could slip out behind him and make a run for it. Before she could decide, he must have sensed something behind him and started to turn. She had no choice. With every pent up element of frustration, grief and rage, she swung the lamp at his head. The jerk as it made contact, almost ripped it from her hand. However, the effect was most satisfactory as the heavy lamp holder hit the man on his right eye and bridge of his nose. His hand flew up to protect himself and he dropped the pistol. Arianna threw herself to the ground, grabbed the weapon and in one fluid motion pointed it at the assassin. Suddenly, she recognised him. It was the soldier who had tortured her. Her decision was made. With an icy calm, she shot him in the crotch twice. He fell, screaming this time to the ground, grabbing at his genitals, or what was left of them. She didn't want him dead. He could live the rest of his life as a eunuch.

She realised the noise would alert someone very soon. But who the hell could she trust now? This man should have been held securely by the UN people. Who had let him go? First things first, get clear and away from the hospital.

She looked out into the corridor. The UN guard was lying on his front but seemed to be still breathing. No one else was in sight but with the noises coming out of the room behind her, it wouldn't be long. She unscrewed the silencer from the pistol and put it in her pocket. Then making sure that the safety was on, put the gun down her belt at her back. It was hidden from sight by the denim jacket she was wearing. Feigning a nonchalance she definitely didn't feel, she forced herself to walk normally down the corridor. To her amazement, no one paid her the slightest attention. Her clothes seemed to make her invisible. She reached some stairs and saw she was on the second floor. Careful to maintain a calm demeanour, she soon found herself in the main lobby with large glass doors leading out onto some steps and then the street.

In only seconds, she was clear of the building but then realised she had absolutely no idea what to do or where to go next. She had never been to Belgrade and had no idea where the UN were. Then she realised that could be the last place to go if they had betrayed her. She needed to get away to the sea, maybe she could bribe a fishing boat to take her up the coast. Maybe she could pay a taxi driver enough to get her there.

She almost jumped out of her skin when a hand fell on her shoulder and she almost managed to reach the pistol before she recognised the voice.

'Hello Arianna, what are you doing out of hospital? Have they discharged you? That seems a bit daft as I was coming to collect you anyway.' Jon said in a friendly tone.

She was completely stunned for a second and then managed to regain her voice. 'Captain, I had to get out. Someone tried to kill me. They knocked out the guard and then shot at the bed but I wasn't in it. The attacker was the same man you rescued me from, the one who was interrogating me.' She realised the adrenalin was kicking in and she was talking too fast. She forced herself to calm down. 'What is going on? Who released that man?'

Jon looked nonplussed. 'Arianna, I've absolutely no idea what you are talking about. Both those men are in custody at the UN building, at least as far as I know they are.'

'Then where did I get this from?' she answered and pulled out the pistol from behind her back.

'Jesus girl, put that away. I didn't say I didn't believe you. Alright, look, we can't stay here, that's obvious. You'd better come with me, let's get you somewhere safe.'

Jon had a taxi waiting for him and hustled Arianna inside. 'The best place for the moment is my hotel apartment at the Metropole. It's in a UN secure zone and you should be safe there, at least for a while. I'll go to headquarters and see if I can find out what the hell is going on. Is that alright?'

'Yes,' she replied. 'As long as I can keep the gun.'

'Fair enough. What happened to your attacker by the way? I assume you incapacitated him somehow?'

She told him.

'Bloody hell girl, remind me not to upset you.' He responded. 'But don't expect me to condemn you. I saw what he was doing don't forget.'

Arianna realised she was liking this strange man more and more. He didn't criticise and he had a very clear way of dealing with things. She also realised she had to trust him. There was no one else.

Chapter 25

Jon walked into the UN HQ building with rage boiling up inside him but he knew he had to tread carefully. The whole bloody place was a minefield of intrigue and inadequacy. Even so, how anyone would have the incompetence to let those two murderous Serbs loose, defied imagination. That's assuming both of them had been released. He stomped into his office and called for Gregori. When the man arrived, he briefed him what had happened and told him to confirm that both men were free and try to find out who had authorised it.

Gregori seemed to be as angry as Jon and left promising to be back as soon as he could. Meanwhile, Jon made himself a coffee and sat back to gather his thoughts. What the hell were they going to do now? This had all the hallmarks of a major diplomatic incident. A Croatian soldier, in UN custody, shooting and maiming a Serbian soldier in the heart of Belgrade. Yes that wasn't the actual story but he was damned sure that was how the Serbs would spin it. He could counter argue that she was simply defending herself, the bullet holes in the bed would be strong evidence. There again, what guarantees were there that the Serbian police would find them? No, he would need to get Arianna away from here and back to Croatia if possible, as quickly as he could. With the girl gone, the UN could simply deny having anything to do with the shooting and the onus would be on the Serbs to explain why the man was there and had assaulted a UN guard. They would be hard pressed to come out of it with any credibility at all. Of course, all this assumed that the hierarchy here agreed to the idea. If some moron was prepared to release the two soldiers, what else where they prepared to do? He realised he needed Gregori back before he could act.

On top of that, it didn't help that that damned ex-Air Marshall was here. Ostensibly working for Jon, from his initial conversations he had made it clear that he considered the arrangement purely an administrative issue and intended to work to his own agenda. Jon held back from responding as it was clear that if the bloody man was steered in the right direction, he could actually end up being a force for good. And of course, there was still the whole issue of Rupert's investigations back at home to take into account. '*Fucking hell, what a bad day this was turning out to be,*' he thought sourly.

Talk of the Devil, there was a knock on the door and before Jon could respond, Peter Johnson walked in. Jon frowned at the man. He was very well dressed, in an immaculate business suit, quite tall with an imposing head of hair now quite grey but with the physique of a much younger man. '*All that money,*' Jon thought cynically, '*its amazing what it can do.*'

'Yes Peter, what can I do for you?' Jon asked without getting up.

If the man noticed Jon's slightly annoyed tone, he chose to ignore it and plonked himself down in a chair the other side of Jon's desk.

'Just thought I'd check in old chap. I've been having briefings all morning and needed a break. Also, I've been informed of your activities over the last couple of weeks. Very brave stuff I might say.'

Jon didn't think for a minute that the man meant a word of it. His patronising manner was starting to get on his nerves already. Jon had just decided that the air needed to be cleared with a one way conversation when there was a knock on the door and Gregori came in. He took in the presence of Peter Johnson but started to speak. 'The duty officer let them go. Apparently, advice from someone on this floor was that we didn't have the authority to keep them.'

'Who provided the advice?' Jon asked through tight lips.

'Can't find out at the moment Sir but I've got feelers out.'

'Hang on a minute, the duty officer doesn't know who told him to let them go? That's bloody ridiculous.' Jon responded angrily.

Before Gregori could reply, Peter Johnson spoke. 'Oh, are you talking about those two Serb soldiers you arrested Jon. I'm afraid that would be me. We had no mandate to hold them and when I was asked, I said so.' He added airily.

Jon was speechless. He looked over at Gregori who looked ready for murder. Suddenly, an icy calm washed over Jon. 'So, with no authority whatsoever in this organisation, you advised to let two men guilty of the most disgusting war crimes go loose. You have absolutely no idea what they had done and more importantly what they would do when released. Bloody hell, you've only been in the country just over a day you fucking, fucking idiot.'

'Hang on, you can't talk to me like that.' Johnson retorted angrily.

Jon didn't let him get any further. 'Oh yes, I bloody well can. You are not in uniform any more. You are a consultant who is meant to be working for me, just in case you had forgotten. And your actions almost led to the brave young girl, who brought in that dreadful evidence of atrocities, being murdered by one of the thugs we're talking about. He must have gone straight from here to the hospital, assaulted the guard on her door and then, without warning, fired four shots into her bed with a silenced pistol. Luckily, the girl has more brains and courage than you have, because she managed to turn the tables, shoot the bastard and get out. However, we now have the possibility of a major diplomatic incident on our hands because I can guarantee the Serbs will not see it the way we do. And all because you thought you knew what you were doing, you arrogant idiot. If I have my way you will be on the next plane out of here.' Jon's last word were almost a shout.

Peter Johnson had turned white and looked stunned. 'But I only gave an opinion when asked. I didn't order anyone to do anything.'

Jon looked disgusted. 'Come on, you've been around this sort of organisation for enough years to know how things work.' He turned to Gregori. 'The three of us are going to see the Chief of Staff now.' He didn't wait for an answer, just got up and headed down the corridor with the two men following.

Half an hour later, the four men had talked the situation through and Jon was far from happy with the result. The Commodore had been totally sympathetic with Arianna's plight and just as critical of Peter Johnson's actions. Unfortunately, this did nothing to help with the realities of the situation they found themselves in.

The Chief of Staff summed it up. 'So, we have the girl safe for the moment but almost certainly about to be accused of attempted murder. Even if we counter the claim, that the soldier assaulted our guard and attempted to kill the girl, it will inevitably end up in a media scrum. Not only will it cause us all sorts of problems, it will give the Serbs ammunition to ameliorate the impact of the photographs the girl brought us.'

'If they're actually released at all.' Jon said cynically.

'True, Jon I'm afraid. I can see people arguing to keep it all under wraps while our whole mission here is in jeopardy.' The Commodore responded.

Retribution

'So, there is only one thing to do,' Gregori interjected.

They all turned to look at him.

'The girl has to disappear and resurface with her own people along with the evidence which they can use effectively. Not only that but we have to appear blameless, somehow.'

The Commodore grunted in agreement. 'That's the solution but how do we achieve it?'

Jon had made up his mind. 'I started this Sir. I'll finish it.' He motioned to a map on the wall behind the Commodore. 'The obvious thing would be to drive north west and cross the Croatian border. As a UN party, we have immunity. Arianna could become a UN soldier for the duration.'

Gregori interrupted. 'Sorry Sir that won't work for two reasons. Firstly, that border doesn't exist. It's just a line on a map which no one is taking the slightest bit of notice of and its where the heaviest fighting is taking place at the moment. Secondly, we have no female troops with the UN detachments and the Serbs will know that.'

'So, any positive suggestions?' Jon asked.

'Why not just go to the airport and fly out? Then she could be returned directly to Croatia.' Peter Johnson suggested.

There was a moment's silence, then the Commodore responded. 'Could we get there before the Serbian police have her details? Even if we fly out in our own aircraft, they still check all of our personnel.'

'Let me see Sir,' Gregori said and he shot out of the door. He was back in a few minutes. 'Not going to work, the word is already out and they have a good description of the girl.'

'How on earth did you find that out Gregori?' Jon asked, intrigued.

'Ah, well once you've been in this cesspit of a city for a while you make the odd contact. In this case, one in the city police headquarters,' Gregori responded.

'Shit, I hope no one saw me take her to the Metropole,' Jon said anxiously.

'She should be alright for the moment. The word has only just gone out. Mind you getting her out of there could be harder.' Gregori replied. 'I think Captain Hunt's original suggestion is the best. We go by road as an official UN party. We have Mister Johnson here as a consultant so have a perfect excuse to be travelling around and it quite believable that a consultancy would send out a senior man with administration support. Arianna becomes his secretary. I'm sure you could provide some convincing proof, couldn't you.'

They all turned to look at Peter Johnson.

'Hang on a moment, are you suggesting I become party to a potentially dangerous and illicit operation to smuggle this girl out of here and into safe territory in Croatia?'

'Well you're the one who caused the problem in the first place,' responded Jon, with a tight smile.

Chapter 26

Ruth had decided to make a coffee. At last, she was making progress and needed the respite from staring at her laptop screen in order to think. She was working from the St John's Wood house which was very convenient for many reasons. Not the least because she could stay in routine touch with her brother and talk without fear of eavesdropping. Unfortunately, Rupert would be abroad for the next week at some international conference but hopefully by the time he returned she would, at last, have some news to report.

She was staring out of the ground floor kitchen window waiting for the kettle to boil but her mind was elsewhere. It was replaying the telephone conversation she had just finished. In retrospect, it was a conversation she should have had months ago. Before she had met Jon, he had mentioned to Rupert that there had been a fire at the garage that had stored the wreck of the old Triumph. It was also the garage that had restored it in the first place. She had known about the car of course and Jon had even mentioned a wild theory about it having been possibly sabotaged but she had read the Coroner's report which was quite clear that it had been an accident and had put the whole thing out of her mind.

However, Rupert had forgotten to tell her about the fire until a few days ago. It had opened up a whole new line of enquiry. She had telephoned the man at the garage but he had been quite cagey when she had introduced herself. However, it was obvious that he was holding something back and didn't want to discuss it over the phone. She had agreed to travel down there the next day. Maybe this was the breakthrough they had been looking for.

The next day, she got thoroughly lost. The trip down the M4 and then the M5 had been relatively easy and the directions she had been given seemed simple enough. That was until she entered the network of narrow Somerset lanes. The place she was looking for was meant to be on an old farm so there wasn't even anything obvious to look for. When she arrived at a small village with an almost unpronounceable name that seemed to consist mainly of the letter Z, she gave up. It was lunchtime and they had a pub. Half an hour later, restored by a cheese sandwich and some very dubious cider, she set off again, this time with some very specific instructions. Sure enough, in the appointed place, there was a long brick building with a small lane leading to it. As she drove in and turned into the courtyard, she realised she was definitely in the right place. A barn to her right was full of old sports cars in various states of repair. To her left was a modern looking workshop with someone bent over the bonnet of a car. As she pulled up, the man must have heard her because he stood up and wiped his hands on an old rag before coming over to her.

'Ruth Thomas?' he queried as she closed her car door behind her.

'Yes, that's me,' she replied, holding out her hand.

The man was in his fifties, with thinning red hair and a prominent paunch which strained against the old overalls he was wearing. He didn't hold out his hand but apologised instead. 'Won't shake your hand my dear if you don't mind. I've been in the bowels of the engine of that car over there and really need to wash up. Come up to the house and we can talk.'

Without waiting for a response, he turned and went into the main house via a back door which led straight into the stone flagged kitchen. 'Take a seat,' he said cheerfully as he scrubbed his hands in the kitchen sink and then stripped off his overalls. 'Luckily my wife's in town so she can't see me using the sink. I'd be a dead man otherwise. Now can I get you a cup of tea or coffee?'

Ruth declined. 'That's fine Mister Radcliffe. I've just eaten at the pub in the next village.'

'Fair enough. Oh and call me Geoff please. Now look, before we go any further do you have any form of identification? I'm a suspicious bugger, especially when that fire is under discussion.'

Intrigued, Ruth opened her bag and showed him her MI6 warrant card. He took it from her and studied it carefully before returning it.

'As I've never seen one of those before I don't suppose it helps that much but you say you know the husband of the girl who bought the car. What were their names?'

Realising he was testing her she quickly responded. 'Helen and Jonathon Hunt, and please call me Ruth.'

He grunted in acknowledgement. 'I guess I'm going to trust you Ruth. Now what can I do for you?'

'You know very well Geoff. On the phone, you intimated that you had something to say but wanted to do it face to face.'

Retribution

He clearly came to a decision. 'I was the expert witnesses at the inquest, did you know that?'

'Yes, I've read the report.'

'Hmm, well so have I and although it is accurate enough, I still maintain that any car built by us would not have caught fire in that way. I said so quite forcefully at the time but got the feeling they thought I was just trying to protect my professional reputation.'

'Alright, what do you base that assessment on?' Ruth asked.

'Let me ask you a question first. What do you know about cars and old British sports cars in particular?'

It was Ruth's turn to laugh. 'Got me there, the answer is absolutely nothing. I try very hard never to look under the bonnet of any car let alone understand how they work.'

'Fair enough. So, I'll keep it simple. That TR5 had a fuel injected engine which means that the fuel system was pressurised. A pump in the boot pushed fuel through pipes to the engine. Alright so far?'

Ruth nodded.

'In modern cars, there is a safety system to ensure that in the event of an accident the pump is stopped immediately. We, as a matter of course, always fit a similar system to any car we restore. You know how your seatbelt locks up when you have any impact?'

'Yes, although I've no idea how that works,' Ruth replied.

'Don't worry about that, just accept the fact that it does and so should the fuel safety cut out fitted to that car. As soon as there was any impact the fuel system should have shut off. But that car went up like a torch and that should just not have been possible.'

Ruth could see where this was going. 'Unless?' she asked simply.

Geoff sighed. 'Unless it was either faulty or had been tampered with and in all my years working on these cars I've never seen one of these safety switches fail.'

Ruth's eyes narrowed. 'So you're saying the car was sabotaged?' *'Maybe Jon had been right all along,'* she thought.

'No, I'm not saying that because I can't. I examined the switch at the time but it was so fire damaged it was impossible to tell what state it was in at the time of the accident.'

'Go on, there's something else isn't there?'

'Two things actually. Firstly the fire in my storage barn was started deliberately. I'm sure of that.'

'But I looked up the Fire Service report and they say it was accidental.' Ruth frowned.

'Look, there was no electricity in the building and no dangerous chemicals. Yes there might have been some fuel in some of the four cars that were in there but that was the sum total of any inflammable materials. All of the cars had their batteries disconnected. The Fire Service could find no evidence of arson so concluded it was accidental. I expect they thought they were doing me a favour in order for me to claim on my insurance. I can see no reason for that fire unless someone wanted the contents destroyed and the only object that had any suspicious circumstances around it was the wreck of that car.'

Ruth wasn't convinced but Geoff had mentioned two reasons. 'And the second thing?'

'Well after that I got to thinking and decided that maybe I should take another look at that bloody safety switch. The inquest was in Cornwall, in Truro so I gave them a ring. All the evidence was stored in a warehouse operated by the Truro police. When I asked to come and look at it they said they would have to get back to me. They rang last week and said that none of the evidence could be found. They blamed an administrative error but it sounded bloody odd to me.'

'So why didn't you report all this to someone?' Ruth asked.

'Hah, who? It's all conjecture and then you rang me. Obviously you have an interest otherwise you wouldn't be here.'

Ruth thought for a moment. 'Alright, you seem to have grounds for suspicion but where on earth do I go from here?'

Geoff looked at her. 'Truro would be my guess.'

That night, she stayed at a dreadful Travelodge near Exeter but it was all she could find at short notice. The next morning she drove down the A38, over the Tamar Bridge and into Cornwall. An hour later, Truro police station was as easy to find as she had hoped. When she arrived, she made her way straight to the reception desk and showed her ID to the duty Sergeant. Within minutes, she had been whisked upstairs into the office of the station's Chief Inspector.

A tall, thin faced man, with iron grey hair, he didn't look too pleased to see her. 'What on earth can I do for MI6 Miss Thomas?'

'I'm sorry to bother you Chief Inspector but I need to look at some evidence. There was a terrible road accident some years ago and a woman lost her life in the fire.'

'Oh, you mean the Hunt case. That's odd, this is the second time it's come up this year but you should know that.'

Ruth looked surprised. 'I'm sorry Chief Inspector, what do you mean?'

'Someone from you lot came down just after Christmas and requisitioned it all. They told us to tell no one, just say it was no longer available. Didn't you know?'

Ruth was getting worried. *'Was there something going on here that she didn't know about? No, Rupert would have known and told her.'* 'Is there a log of who took it?'

'Hang on a second.' He picked up his desk phone and within minutes a policeman deposited a large leather bound book on the desk.

'We still use manual records,' the Chief Inspector explained. 'You can't put a signature on a computer, at least not yet. So, let's see.' He thumbed through the pages stopping at one near the end. 'Right here we are, all legal and accounted for.'

He passed the book over to Ruth. She studied the entry. The entry was for all the material evidence from the inquest and dutifully signed for. She studied the signature and a sudden chill gripped her. At last, this was what she had been looking for. The name was a fake, she knew that immediately. She had studied her quarry for so long now, she would recognise his handwriting anywhere, especially the way he wrote the letter 'j'. It might not stand up in a court of law but it was totally clear to her that the 'S James' who had signed the book was no other than a certain Peter Johnson.

Chapter 27

To Arianna, it seemed she had swapped one holding cell for another, albeit one that was far more comfortable. It had only taken her a few minutes to explore and then once again she was bored. She used the shower and that made her feel much better. She then discovered a small fridge with drinks inside and helped herself to a beer and sat in front of the television and caught up on the news which was depressing. She then found a channel showing the American sitcom 'Friends' and that cheered her up for a while. Eventually, she fell asleep.

She was woken with a start when she heard the door click open. The Captain came in looking worried when he saw her lying on the bed.

'Arianna, are you alright?' he asked anxiously.

'Yes, don't worry I was just having a little nap what's going on?' She asked as she sat up wiping the sleep from her eyes.

'Sorry, we have to move fast but first I have to turn you into a blonde.' He handed her a bottle. 'The instructions are on it which is good as I wouldn't have a clue how to use it.'

'What on earth are you talking about Jon?' she asked as she took the bottle and glanced down at it.

He quickly explained all that had happened and what they were planning to do. 'So you see, we need you to look as different as possible. You will be this man's secretary. I also have a pair of glasses for you, they are very weak. I borrowed them from one of our admin staff but they will also change your appearance. Once you've changed, I have a polaroid camera so we can take a photo and quickly make you a UN Identity Card.'

Arianna laughed. 'Jon, this stuff will take a while to work, hang on a second,' she grabbed one of the hotel writing pads and pens and wrote down a quick list. 'While I'm doing my hair, please can you go and get these. There's a make up list and my measurements there. I will need some plain blouses, simple black skirts and underwear, alright?'

Jon looked slightly discomforted when he realised he was going to have to do a full female shop but what choice did he have? 'Alright Arianna, there's a big department store just down the road they should have all of this. I won't be long. But I had better get changed into civilian clothes first. Why don't you go into the shower while I do?'

'Don't tell me you're shy, my English Captain? Are all of your countrymen like you?' She smiled as she said it.

'Yes, we bloody well are young lady, now git.'

With a chuckle, she went into the shower with the bottle of hair dye. Jon quickly changed into slacks and polo shirt and left to do his shopping. Almost two hours later, he returned with a new suitcase full of the requested items. The make-up had actually been quite easy as Arianna had been quite specific but the underwear had been a nightmare as all she had given him were some sizes. He had been quite conservative in his choices. He hoped that was what she had in mind. As well as two skirts and four blouses, he had picked out a smart jacket, several pairs of shoes and also a more durable overcoat.

When he opened the door, he was confronted by a wet haired, blonde girl, sitting wrapped up in a towel, watching television. He dumped the bag on the end of the bed. 'Here, have a look,' he said, desperately, trying hard not to stare at her legs and more. The towel barely covered her modesty. With a delighted squeak, she started to open the bag.

'Nice clothes Jon but did you have to get such boring underwear?' she asked with a straight face as she looked at his purchases.

'Well it's not something I've shopped much for in the past,' Jon stammered, feeling like an idiot as he did so.

Arianna laughed. 'Don't worry, I'm only teasing. They're fine. Look, I should be able to dry my hair now and put on some make up. Give me ten minutes and we'll see how I look.' She took a selection of clothes and the make up and went back into the bathroom. Soon the sound of the hairdryer pierced the door. Then he heard a voice from calling from inside. 'Jon come here, I've another idea on how to change my appearance.'

Jon opened the door to find Arianna sitting in front of the mirror. Her hair was now blonde, that wasn't the problem. The fact that she was only wearing a bra and pants was. What Jon thought was quite conservative now looked positively skimpy.

She saw the look on his face. 'Don't worry, I'm not going to eat you.'

'That's not the problem. I might want to eat you,' he said before he could help himself.

She laughed delightedly. 'Later. Now look my hair is too long. I found some scissors and with your help should be able to trim it quite easily.'

Jon didn't know what was more discomforting, the idea of staying in the same room as this pretty, semi naked girl or the fact that she would be trusting him to cut her hair. 'I'll do my best but I've never been trusted with a pair of scissors before.'

They managed. She did most of the work and Jon trimmed at the back. It really didn't help that when standing behind her, he just couldn't help seeing down her front and the bra he had bought barely covered her breasts. Also, it was quite thin and her prominent nipples were poking through quite beautifully.

Arianna was quite aware the effect she was having but she really liked him and was thoroughly enjoying the attention. Part of her felt that she was betraying Goran with the thoughts that were going through her head but she pushed them aside, she needed this. They soon finished and as she brushed the last of the hair strands off her shoulders she made a decision. Standing, she turned, grabbed Jon and kissed him hard on the lips. For a second he froze and then suddenly responded.

Everything was telling him that this was not a good idea. He pushed the thought aside, picked her up, took her out of the bathroom and they fell on the bed. Meanwhile, she was desperately trying to undo his belt. She succeeded.

Twenty minutes later Jon lay back and felt a complete idiot. 'That was silly of me Arianna. I'm so sorry, that should never have happened.' He wasn't expecting the really quite hard punch to his shoulder. 'Bloody hell girl, what was that for?'

'Why should it not have happened? I wanted it, you wanted it. It was fun. You bloody English are so stuck up.'

'No, I didn't mean it like that. Look, how old are you?'

'I'm twenty nine, what has that got to do with anything? How old are you for that matter?'

'Well, I'm eleven years older than you.'

'So what? That's not much of a difference. Look Jon, that wasn't a marriage proposal. It was just something that just happened alright? Hey, you aren't married are you?'

Retribution

She saw the shadow pass across his face and realised she had touched some sort of nerve.

'No, not now. She died in a car accident. Please don't ask me anything more.' He looked down at his watch. 'Oh shit, Gregori will be here soon, we'd better get sorted out.'

They quickly dressed and straightened the bed out and only just in time as just as they finished, there was a knock on the door. Jon peeked through the fish eye peephole on the door and then opened it. Gregori came in.

'All ready? Where is the girl?' he asked looking around the room with a glint in his eye. It all looked a little messed up and why was his boss not wearing any socks? He had a pretty good idea but it wasn't his place to say anything.

The bathroom door opened and a stunning, short haired, bespectacled, blonde girl came out. She was wearing subtle make up that emphasised her eyes and black stockings under a simple dark skirt with a white blouse that emphasised her breasts. For a second Gregori was dumbstruck. Was this the same girl they had rescued from torture only a few days ago? No wonder the boss had made a move. Gregori's estimation of Jon went up yet another notch.

'Arianna, you look totally different,' he managed to say without tripping over his tongue. 'And fabulous I might add. No one will recognise you, I'm sure.' He turned to Jon. 'Do you have the camera Sir? We need to make this pass.'

'Oh yes,' Jon replied. 'It's just here, hang on.' He went over to the desk and retrieved the camera. 'Right Arianna, all we need is a head shot against a plain background. Gregori, can you remove that picture on the wall there please?'

He positioned Arianna against the wall and took the photograph. Within seconds, it had developed. Jon and Gregori both agreed it was fine. Jon retrieved the scissors from the bathroom and cut it to size. Gregori then pasted it onto a UN Identity Card and slid it into a plastic envelope.

'The only thing we are missing is a passport, I don't suppose you have one Arianna?' Gregori asked.

She grimaced. 'No, not here and even if I did, the photos wouldn't match, sorry.'

'That's alright,' Gregori replied. 'We are not required to carry them anyway, although many people do. So, we need to pack. The car is coming to pick us up in an hour. Oh and one other thing.' He handed over a small package he had been carrying. 'In here are all the negatives of your photographs and the original small video tapes. I suggest you pack them with your stuff for safety.'

Arianna took the proffered package and put it on the bed. 'Thank you Gregori.'

Later that evening, three people came out of the hotel, two were military but the third was a blonde female. They climbed into one of several white painted, UN, four wheel drive Mercedes, that were in the hotel car park. The men put several cases in the back, one got behind the wheel and they drove off.

The Serbian policeman who had been one of several detailed to keep a close watch on the hotel recognised the two soldiers. He had seen them quite often when on the early morning or evening shift but he had never seen the girl before. He consulted the briefing notes he had been given before he came on shift. There was a general alert out for a missing Croatian girl who had escaped the hospital that morning and hadn't been seen since, even a rather poor photograph but the girl he had seen looked nothing like the one in the picture. Shrugging to himself he decided he would report it when he got back the station later that evening.

Chapter 28

It was one thing to have suspicions about someone, it was totally different to find out that those suspicions were, in fact correct. Ruth's mind was in a whirl as she drove back to London. On more than one occasion, she had to force herself to concentrate on her driving to avoid rear ending the car ahead as her mind wandered off in different directions. One things was absolutely clear to her. Jon had been right. His car had been sabotaged in some way and the fact that Helen had been the victim was almost certainly pure, unfortunate, happenstance. The more she thought about it, the angrier she became. All that said, she still couldn't understand why it had been done. There was clearly something she had missed over the preceding months but she was doubly determined to find it now. Sitting in her brief case was a photo copy of the log from Truro police station. Her first job was to get the handwriting experts at MI6 to study it and see if there was enough evidence there to take some positive action against the man. She had shown a photo of Johnson to the policeman but he had explained that he hadn't actually been present when Mister 'James' had called, merely being appraised of the situation the next day. The duty sergeant, who had attended, didn't recognise the face. Ruth was not surprised, it was several months ago and if Johnson had any sense he would have used some level of disguise. However, she had the dates and maybe she would be able to track his movements on those days.

Almost without realising, she found herself in St John's Wood and just for once found a parking space without difficulty. She had decided that a trip to Vauxhall Cross House could wait until the next day. There were more urgent things to look at. Although it was well after lunch time, she was too wound up to even contemplate food. She let herself in and immediately ensconced herself in front of her laptop. The first thing she did was review the Coroner's report on the original accident. Knowing what she now did, it seemed that it had gone rather smoothly although there was no evidence that the system had been put under any pressure to reach a verdict. That said, she would get her brother to ask around. He was far better placed to enquire. However, what was useful was a list of the supporting material evidence and clearly listed was the offending

Retribution

fuel cut off switch with several photographs. She e-mailed them to Geoff Radcliffe in Somerset for further appraisal.

She then turned her attention to Peter Johnson. She had been over his history many times and still nothing leapt out of the page to indicate whether he had ever been turned as an undergraduate. Mind you the same could probably have been said of Kim Philby until he made his escape to Russia. She also knew that he was a member of the 'Old Farts'. Despite having retired from the RAF several years ago, most members stayed in until they died and she was therefore probably right in assuming that he was still a member. It also seemed likely that Jon was going to have been invited to join them when he returned from sea. The loss of his wife and urgent appointment abroad must have put paid to that. If that was true, then maybe Johnson was worried that Jon's membership could have posed a threat to him. Then Jon returned and he decided to clear up any loose ends. She sat back with a frustrated sigh. This was all conjecture with not a shred of evidence to back it up but somehow she felt she was now on the right track.

The next morning, she went into the office. The massive, green glassed windowed building dominated its part of the Thames. She was always amused when she saw it. The previous MI6 building in Westminster Bridge Road had always been kept anonymous. This monstrosity shouted its presence to everyone. Still hiding in plain sight wasn't a bad tactic.

As soon as she was inside, she went up to Rupert's office which she had permission to use and sent the handwriting samples down to the experts. She then dug out all the information they had on the so called Ramon society but despite searching diligently for hours nothing really critical came to light. She then took a call from the handwriting expert. He confirmed that it was highly likely that the signature in the log and Peter Johnson's handwriting were the same. However, with such a small sample, it would never stand up in a court of law. She thanked him and put the phone down thoughtfully.

Her last task was to look at Johnson's recent movements which wasn't easy. Despite her and Rupert's suspicions, he hadn't been put under any surveillance, partly because the evidence against him was so flimsy and partly because they hadn't wanted to alert him in any way. All she had was what was in the public domain. One interesting thing that came up quite quickly was that he was now working for a small consultancy that specialised in providing military experts around the world. She decided to give them a ring. Pretending to be a potential client, she soon established that Johnson was out of the country on a UN funded project. She had to be careful not to pry too hard but managed to discover that he was in Belgrade.

When she came off the phone she sat back in thought. Hopefully, it was only a coincidence that that was also where Jon was based. Maybe if she contacted Jon, he could keep an eye out for him. She managed to get the switchboard to open a line to Belgrade but no one she managed to speak to knew where Jon was, except that he was away from base on some sort of mission. Never mind, she would wait until Rupert got back in a couple of days and they could take it from there.

Chapter 29

Peter Johnson was sitting in the foyer of the UN HQ, waiting for the car to pick him up and seething with frustration and anger on so many levels. He was having to force himself to stay calm. *'How on earth had he got himself into this situation?'* He wondered.

It had all seemed such a good idea a while ago when he had been approached with the idea of a consultancy job. In truth, things had been pretty boring, apart from the little clearing up exercise he had been forced to do. That in itself had made him realise that he needed more excitement in his life. So, when the prospect of going into a warzone came up but with effective immunity to any real danger, it seemed the perfect solution. His wife didn't seem at all bothered but that was hardly surprising. He saw little enough of her these days, not that he objected to that, as long as she didn't spend too much of his money, something she had a knack of doing when his back was turned. It would give him an opportunity to use his extensive military experience one more time which would be satisfying. Maybe these UN amateurs could be taught a thing or two. Then, he found he would be working for that bloody naval officer who had caused him so much grief in the MOD a few years ago and had forced his hand only a few years later. The man was only a stuck up Commander when they had last worked together and now he was being forced to work for him. It stuck in his throat.

However, that had only been the start of an avalanche of disasters. The real crippler had occurred on the previous evening, his first night in Belgrade. He had arrived in the afternoon and wasn't required at the headquarters until the next day so had decided to take a look around the town. Later in the afternoon, he was sitting, enjoying a beer in the evening sunshine at a pavement café, when a man plonked himself down uninvited at his table. He had looked up and his blood ran cold. The man opposite was built like a tank with dark greying hair and hawk like nose. Rolls of fat clustered around his neck where his shirt collar was clearly too tight as was his dark and rather scruffy suit. None of this really registered because he immediately recognised him. He had been his handler in the old Soviet Union days. He was KGB. He had never known his real name. 'Boris' was the only one he had given.

Retribution

Before he could speak, Boris got in first. 'Peter, my old friend, fancy stumbling across you here, of all places. We can talk about old times, no?' The friendly tones were not matched by the hard look in his eyes.

Peter finally got his tongue. 'Boris, what the hell are you doing here? Your lot don't exist anymore. My involvement with you is over.'

'Hah,' Boris snorted in amusement. 'The old Union may be gone Peter but Russia is still alive and kicking as you say and who said your involvement was over?'

A chill of apprehension ran down his spine. He had a horrible feeling where this might be going. 'Now look Boris, I supported communism and that has died a death in your country. It's more capitalist now than many western countries. I keep informed. You have all sold out as far as I'm concerned.'

'That may be true old friend,' Boris replied. 'Since that idiot Gorbachev tried to make things better and gave the whole lot away in the process. However, life goes on old chap and seeing as you are here, we have need of your services.'

'Not interested,' he said firmly but with a sinking feeling inside him.

'That is not an option I'm afraid, Peter,' Boris responded with a grim smile. 'What do you think your intelligence services would say if certain information found itself into their hands? We could start with some of the secrets my country gained from you or maybe how you killed the wife of the very man you are now working for.'

'Bloody hell, how much did these people know?' Peter thought desperately to himself. Yes, they knew about his spying. *'But how on earth did they know about the girl and the car?'*

As if he was a mind reader, Boris looked him in the eye. 'Yes Peter, we know everything. So you see we have every confidence that it's in your best interest to cooperate. Isn't it?'

With a resigned sigh he sat back. 'What do you want me to do?'

'Firstly Peter, you know about the close ties between my country and Serbia?'

'Oh yes,' Peter laughed grimly. 'Like how your support provided the catalyst to start the First World War.'

'Some might argue that the over reaction of a certain Kaiser was the cause of that. Nevertheless, there has been a long association between our countries and it continues to this day.'

'Yes, you Russians love the 'Great Game' as you call it,' Peter responded. 'Mind you, it seems to me that nowadays it consists of taking the opposite side to the west on any issue, purely as a matter of principle rather than for any logical reasons.'

'Think what you like my friend. In this stupid war we are providing support to our Serb friends as much as we can without being too obvious. The political reasons need not worry you. Now, we know you have just arrived so it is too soon for you to know what freedoms you will have. However, there is one thing you must know about straight away. The UN have a young girl in custody in the main hospital and she has brought in an amount of material that could be very damaging to our cause. We know it has been seen locally but are pretty sure nothing has yet been done. In typical UN fashion they will probably debate what to do with it for weeks before even sending it on to New York. So firstly, we want you to find out what has happened to it. Secondly, they are holding two Serbian soldiers and again we want to know what their intentions are. If there is any way you could influence their release we would be most grateful. Is that all clear?'

Peter looked at Boris with suspicion. 'What is this material you are talking about Boris?'

'Simply some photographs and film of some of our friends being rather stupid in public. If it were to get into the public domain it could be very damaging.'

Peter realised there was much more to this than he was being told but decided to keep things simple for the moment. He knew his man and this was likely to be only the tip of the iceberg. He needed to be fully briefed before he could even begin to see a way out of this mess.

Boris continued before he could speak. 'So, we meet here again tomorrow by which time you will have a much better picture of what goes on inside that building.'

Before Peter had a chance to react, Boris got to his feet and left without a backward glance.

Retribution

The next evening all was much clearer. Peter knew exactly what was on the photographs. He had been shown them. Despite being thoroughly revolted, he could understand why the Serbs and their patrons didn't want them made public. Not that he had a clue about what he could do about it. One success had been to get the two Serbian soldiers released although he was still smarting from the public tongue lashing he had received for his efforts. He hadn't been spoken to like that since he was a junior officer and having to put up with it had almost been unbearable.

They were scheduled to leave on their routine 'trip' in only an hour after he was due to meet Boris so he only had a short window to speak to him. Luckily, Boris was punctual. The conversation was short. Boris already knew about the release of the two soldiers and the subsequent shooting. He seemed suitably grateful when Peter explained how he had engineered their release but not so happy when he heard of the plan to get the girl back to her people.

'We want the girl Peter,' Boris stated baldly. 'And the negatives and master film cassettes. Once we have the girl, we can accuse the UN of deliberately obstructing a criminal investigation. We can also use the whole situation to discredit the photos, if they even have the balls to release them after the fuss we'll cause.'

'Hang on, why do you need me? Can't you just get the Serbian police to stop us and simply grab the girl and photos before we even leave Belgrade?'

'Good point but I think it will be better to do this quietly away from the city. Somewhere isolated will be much better, particularly if you get an armed escort which you almost certainly will. If things go wrong, we don't want witnesses. And I need you because we don't know what route they will be taking. We could just follow them but that will make it hard to set up something ahead of them and could be risky if we're spotted. Do you know which way they are planning to go?'

Peter thought for a moment. 'No, not yet. We're off in an hour but as I understand it, we won't make that decision until we are clear of Belgrade. It's getting late and the plan is to stop at a hotel once clear of the city. Sorry I don't know which one.'

Boris looked thoughtful. 'I don't suppose you have one of these new mobile phones everyone is starting to use?'

'Actually, I do. But will I get much of a signal in this country? I've got one now but what about when we're away from the city?'

'Actually, it should be fine Peter. Coverage is fairly good especially as you say you aren't going far tonight.'

'I hope you're right Boris but don't blame me if I'm out of range. So, do you want me to pass you the route when I know it? And then what will you do?'

'Yes, I must have that route and where you are staying tonight but that's a good question. We will have to stop them somewhere and search them. If we can get the civilian police to the scene they can arrest the girl and there's not exactly much the UN can do about it. It won't be unreasonable to insist on searching them as well. Call me on this number.' Boris quickly wrote it down on a paper napkin and handed it over. 'I'll see what can be arranged and you can do your part.'

'Well, I'll do my best Boris,' Peter replied looking him hard in the eye. 'But I can't offer any guarantees.'

'Oh I think you can do better than that Peter. Try hard please or it may not be worthwhile you going home and as you rightly said, the Soviet Union is no more and so there won't be a grace and favour apartment waiting for you in Moscow either. Do you understand?'

His reverie was broken by the sight of the car pulling up in front of the doors. Grabbing his case he went to get in. The Russian soldier was driving with Hunt in the other front seat. In the rear was a slim, young, blonde girl. She had a leather brief case in her hands.

'Hello, you must be Peter, my name is Arianna. I'm your secretary.'

Chapter 30

The little convoy sped out of Belgrade in the early evening. It wasn't an ideal time to be leaving but they needed to get out of the city as soon as they could. The ever efficient Gregori had telephoned ahead and found them a hotel a few miles outside the city. Had they been able to drive down the main highway, the E70, they could have been in Zagreb in Croatia in under four hours. It was less than four hundred kilometres away. However, despite their UN status it would mean crossing the most fought over and lawless part of the whole region. Also, it would hardly fit in with their so called 'mission'. Consequently, Gregori had worked out a route that would take them around Sarajevo. They could then decide whether to head for the coast which was largely still in Croatian hands or strike north towards Zagreb. Technically, of course, they could go anywhere but they really needed to minimise any risk of confrontation and using a longer route would be preferable if that could be avoided.

Once at the small hotel that was set well back off the road in its own little grounds, they all went to their rooms and changed before meeting on the small veranda bar overlooking the well tended gardens.

Jon didn't take long to change and was slightly surprised to see Gregori already at the bar when he got down.

'Sir, we need a quick talk before the others come down.' Gregori stated with a serious face.

'Go on old chap,' Jon replied.

'I don't trust that consultant at all,' Gregori stated baldly. 'I asked around a bit after he admitted that he had provided what he called advice about the two soldiers. According to the duty officer he had been most insistent, which wasn't exactly what he told us.'

'Hmm, I don't see why he would do that deliberately. He's only been in the country just over a day. Why would he interfere so overtly after so short a time? But I'll be honest with you I've worked with him before and didn't like him much then. I know our intelligence services have an eye on him. Frankly, I wouldn't put anything past him. We had better keep a close eye on him from now on.'

Retribution

Gregori nodded and was about to speak again when Arianna came in. She looked stunning and both men admired her swaying walk as she approached.

'Good evening my friends,' she said as she greeted them with a wide smile. 'I'll have a beer if you're buying.'

Gregori signalled the barman and they took their drinks to a table just as Peter Johnson came in. He also went to the bar and then came over to join them with a beer in his hand. Suddenly, the atmosphere wasn't quite so convivial. If Peter detected the change he affected not to notice.

'So everyone, we've been rather rushed into things. We now need to review the plan and discuss options,' Jon said as he raised his glass.

'Oh, so we're meant to have a plan?' Gregori replied with a straight face. 'That will be a first for the UN.'

'Now, Gregori, none of your cynical Russian ways here,' Jon responded with a grin. 'Come on, I know you spent much of the afternoon poring over maps. What are our best options?'

'Well firstly, I've arranged an escort for the trip. Another Mercedes will join us at eight tomorrow. I've managed to get the good South African Sergeant and some of his friendly Frenchmen assigned to us. It seems they enjoyed the last trip so much, they all volunteered to do it again.'

'Is that the bunch of thugs you had with you when you rescued me Jon?' Arianna asked.

Jon nodded.

'I'm glad they're on our side,' she said simply.

'Well, let's hope this trip will be a little more boring,' Gregori said. 'It would be good to disappoint them.'

'Why do we need an armed escort?' Peter Johnson asked. 'Surely as UNPROFOR we have immunity?'

Everyone turned to stare at him and he looked a little flustered at the attention. 'No seriously, isn't it just provocative to have an armed guard?'

Jon snorted with derision. 'Peter, I've only been here a while myself but I can guarantee they could be needed. We wouldn't have been able to rescue Arianna without them for a start. The rule here seems to be shoot first and ask questions later. Maybe you think that there is a military command chain. Well there isn't. Yes, there is a formal Serbian army but on top of that there are almost the same number of people in local militias and they all have their own agendas and all are heavily armed. Surely they told you all of this at your briefings?'

Peter looked deflated. 'Yes they did but it's one thing to talk about it in a briefing room quite another to experience it for real.'

'Welcome to the real world my friend,' Gregori said with a humourless smile. 'Now, we need to talk about routes. There are several options but I had a long chat with the intelligence people and I think one particular route offers the best compromise between safety and getting across the border quickly.' He reached into his pocket and brought out a road map. 'Sorry, this doesn't look exactly tactical but it's the best way of showing our options. I've marked over it the known areas of fighting and troop movements.' He spread the map open on the table and they all looked over at it. 'Believe it or not, we need to go close to Sarajevo,' he said deadpan.

As expected there was a chorus of disbelief around the table. Jon voiced his concerns first. 'Gregori that's mad. They've got troops all around the place as you well know. Bloody hell, that's where we rescued Arianna.'

'I didn't actually say how close, Sir,' Gregori replied with a grin. 'Seriously, this is the best option for several reasons. Firstly, although there are concentrations of troops close around the city, it means the area behind them is actually pretty open. Secondly, we have our own small contingent of troops nearby who already know about us and they have been warned we will be in the area. There will be a military radio with our escort so we can call for help if we need it. And of course, it ties in with our exploratory mission for our friendly consultant here so we have good reason to be in the area. Anyway, we won't be around long. The roads we will use are all good and we should be in Zagreb by late evening tomorrow.'

There was silence around the table while they all digested Gregori's words. Peter Johnson pointed to the map. 'So what's our exact route Gregori? Can you show us?'

For the next few minutes, they all listened as Gregori showed them his route and alternatives if their way was blocked at various points.

Gregori then looked at them all. 'One final point we need to consider. We don't know how well informed the Serbs really are. We need to consider the worst case situation.'

'Which is?' Arianna asked looking concerned.

'Simply put, if they decide that the risk of taking positive action against an accredited UN group like us is worth taking in order to get hold of you and the material you are carrying Arianna.' Gregori said.

'You don't mean physically detain and search us?' Jon asked.

'Yes, just that.' Gregori replied grimly. 'There is no reason to suspect that they know anything about what we are doing or what route we are taking but their intelligence seems pretty good. They often seem to know things very fast. We need to have some contingency plan just in case.'

Jon looked thoughtful. 'I suppose getting hold of you Arianna will be a major coup and I don't suppose you will want to spend any more time in Serbian custody.'

She grimaced and nodded agreement. 'And, as we've discussed before, if they destroy the originals then they can muddy the waters even further. To the point that your bosses might just decide not to use them at all. But what can we do if they try it on?'

'Apart from starting a small war, I can't see what we could do. The best would be to try to insist that Arianna stays with us and we all return to Belgrade.' Jon said. 'But can you imagine the fuss that will cause? No, I can't see a way around this. Look everyone, there's no reason to suspect that anyone knows what we are doing or where we are going so we will just have to go with plan A and use our UN immunity to the full.'

No one else could come up with a better idea and in the end the conversation slowly drifted to more general issues. Peter Johnson excused himself shortly afterwards and the mood immediately lightened. However, Jon was not about to suffer another of his Russian comrade's induced hangovers and firmly stated his decision to go to bed well before eleven o'clock. He was just about to drift off to sleep when there was a quiet knock at his door. Cursing, he threw a towel around himself and opened it a crack to see Arianna standing there in a similar towel.

'Sorry Jon did I wake you? I see we have the same taste in night clothes. I forgot to put a nightdress on the list I gave you. Anyway, I wondered if you wanted to see whether its true that blondes have more fun?'

Peter Johnson was also having trouble getting to sleep, albeit for different reasons. He had made the call to Boris but it hadn't been easy. Despite the Russian's assurances, his phone had no signal in the hotel. In the end, he had had to go for a walk in the gardens where he found some higher ground and managed to get a weak two bars showing on the phone. He passed on as much of the route that he had been able to memorise. Boris had been suitably grateful and said something would be arranged but not what exactly. Unfortunately, that other bloody Russian, Gregori, had bumped into him as he came back into the hotel. He was pretty sure his explanation of needing a walk to clear his head had been accepted but he didn't trust the man as far as he could spit. One thing he did know, He was not looking forward to the coming day.

Chapter 31

Boris put the phone down feeling far less confident than he had sounded. It had been pure chance that he had recognised his old contact from the Cold War as he came through the airport. He had been there on routine surveillance, a chore all the intelligence staff from the Embassy shared when UN flights were expected. Johnson had been right of course, the KGB had been disbanded soon after the failed Gorbachev coup. However, it had been impossible to start a new intelligence service up from scratch and unsurprisingly the new organisation was mainly staffed by ex KGB members. There had been a general clearing out of some elements and many old scores were settled in the process. Boris had kept his head down and survived the purges and was now slowly making his way up the hierarchy of the new Federal Security Service.

One thing that was definitely different from the old structure was the ease that a man could climb the greasy pole. In the past, there was a rigid and very hidebound structure, nowadays it was every man for himself. Consequently, Boris hadn't actually told anyone in the Embassy intelligence staff what he had achieved. Following Johnson from the airport and putting the frighteners on him had been purely his idea and once the man had reported back the next day, he had realised what a good decision it had been. He would take credit for the release of the two Serb soldiers in his own time but only if the furore over the stupid assassination attempt on the girl didn't end up backfiring on him. But now, he had a real opportunity to make a name for himself again. If he could arrange for the arrest of the girl and recovery of the negatives he could write his own ticket back to Moscow and greater things. The only problem he now had was that there was very little time. The UN party would be leaving first thing the next morning and would be clear of the country by the end of the day. However, he hadn't been quite honest with Johnson. What he really wanted to know was where they were staying that night. With any luck, they would never get going on their route to Croatia. Within hours, the girl would be in custody, the photographs destroyed and the UN thoroughly discredited. And all because of him.

He reached over, picked up the phone and dialled the number of the police headquarters. Unfortunately, things took longer than he expected as they always did in this backwater country. He eventually got through to the senior duty policeman and convinced him of who he was and what he knew. He was adamant that he would only give the details of where the girl was once he was sitting in one of the cars leaving the city. In the end, they agreed and he slipped quietly out of the Embassy and headed the short distance to where they would pick him up.

Surprisingly punctual, a convoy of six cars and a large custody van arrived and he jumped into the first one immediately passing directions to the driver. They shot out of the city only reverting to using blue lights and sirens when some idiot wouldn't get out of their way.

It took less than an hour to get to the hotel. When they arrived at the short lane leading to it they all stopped. Several police were sent on foot to cover the rear and then Boris, the senior policeman and two more constables made their way to the front. The place was dark with no lights and unsurprisingly the front door was locked. There was a large bell button to one side and when a policeman pushed it they could dimly hear a bell ringing inside somewhere. Suddenly, a light came on and a middle aged man in a dressing gown opened the door.

He looked surprised to see the group of men. 'Yes,' he said testily. 'It's the middle of the night. What do you want?'

'We are here to arrest one of your guests. A young blonde woman who came in with the UN party last evening,' the policeman said and flourished some sort of warrant car in the man's face.

Looking even more annoyed, the man let them in. 'Room seven and her friends are in eight, nine and ten. I assume you will be talking to them as well. Up the stairs there, turn right at the top.'

Without further discussion, they went up the indicated stairs. The policeman went to room seven and rapped loudly on the door. There was no response. He tried the handle and the door opened. When he went in it was clear there was no one there. The bed had definitely been slept in but was now empty. A quick check showed that the bathroom too was empty. Calling to his men they quickly checked the other rooms. Again they were all deserted. The birds had flown.

Retribution

An hour earlier, Jon was just drifting back off to sleep after Arianna had slipped back to her room when there was a loud knock at his door. Before he could react, Gregori burst in. 'Boss, we've got to get out of here now,' he said urgently. 'I've just spoken to my contact in the police and he told me that someone has told them of our whereabouts and that we have the girl with us. We have to get out now. They will be here within the hour.'

'Fuck, OK, go and tell the others. I'll be right behind you.' Jon replied with all thoughts of sleep banished from his mind. He swiftly dressed. Luckily, he hadn't really unpacked and within minutes was out in the corridor. Arianna's door opened and she came out with her bags and then Peter Johnson did the same.

'Right you two, down to the car now.' Jon said urgently. 'I assume Gregori has told you what has happened. There's no time to waste.' He led them down the stairs into the lobby. As the two others went past, he took out a large amount of cash and put it under the blotter on the desk and swiftly wrote a note on the hotel notepad that was lying there, explaining to the manager that they had to leave and if the money wasn't enough to contact the UN in Belgrade. He knew the manager wouldn't as he had left far too much for exactly that reason.

He saw the white Mercedes pull up outside the front doors and ran out, putting the latch on the doors behind him and jumped into the passenger seat. As soon as Gregori saw he was in, he drove quickly into the night.

'Where the hell do we go now?' Jon asked to no one in particular as they pulled onto the main road.

'Well, one thing we can't use is the planned route,' Gregori responded. 'If they knew we were at the hotel, we must assume they know where we were intending to go. But I did have an alternative in mind. I suggest we aim south of Sarajevo now and head for the coast. In theory, we would be in Croatia then although I don't suppose anyone following us will care,'

'The real issue is that we are clearly blown if the police know what we are doing. I wonder if it might be better to head back to Belgrade and tough it out from headquarters,' Jon mused.

'No,' both Gregori and Arianna said at the same time. 'Look Sir,' Gregori said. 'They can't actually know that Arianna isn't who we say she is. If we go back, there is a guaranteed diplomatic incident and all we've done will be wasted. And knowing the hierarchy, our careers will be over, even if we don't end up being court martialled.'

'But the Chief of Staff sanctioned the trip.' Jon replied.

'Really Sir? Did he give you an order in writing? If it's his neck or ours what do you think he'll do?' Gregori said bitterly.

Jon said nothing for a moment as he worked through the logic. They were well clear of any pursuit and no one knew where they were going, although he didn't expect it to take long before their presence was noted and reported back. Clearly an alert of some sort would be put out. But the Serbs still had the problem that they were a legitimate UN party and they would be taking an enormous risk to detain them. At the hotel, the police would have been able to argue that Arianna was in her room when they arrested her but once in the vehicle, the issue would be far more difficult for them. Then something else occurred to him.

'Hang on a second Gregori, how on earth did your contact know where you were? You didn't tell him surely?' Jon asked.

Gregori laughed. 'I have one of these Sir,' and he reached into his pocket and brought out a large black plastic case. 'And anyway, I rang him. I couldn't sleep so went for a walk. When I found I had a signal, I thought it would be a good precaution.'

'Oh, one of those new, small mobile phones. I've been thinking about getting one myself but they seem so expensive but bloody well done, that was good thinking. What I really want to know is how the hell the police found out.'

'Ah, I have a theory about that,' Gregori replied, as he pulled the car over to the side of the road. 'Mister Johnson, you have a mobile phone as well don't you?'

'Yes, so what?' Johnson replied as a wave of apprehension washed over him.

'Would you mind me having a look at it please?' Gregori asked politely.

'Certainly not. It's my private phone.'

Jon picked up on the note of panic in Johnson's voice. He turned around in his seat and looked at him in the eye. 'Do as Gregori says or I won't answer for the consequences.'

The situation resolved itself unexpectedly when Arianna, who had been sitting next to Johnson, made the simple move of reaching into his jacket pocket and pulling out the phone. She handed it to Jon before anyone could react.

'Thank you Arianna,' Jon said with a laugh in his voice. He handed the phone to Gregori. 'Now what?'

'Simple Sir, these phones now have a facility to see what previous numbers have been called. Let me see.' And he started pressing a few buttons.

'Now hang on just a second,' Peter Johnson said with a definite note of panic. 'That's private property. You have no right to interfere with it.'

Jon looked grimly at him. 'I don't see the problem Peter. That is, assuming you've nothing to hide of course.'

Gregori looked up from the phone. 'What's this number Peter? You rang it earlier in the night and please don't say it's your home because it has a Belgrade area code.'

'I'll say it again it's none of your damn business. Now give it back to me.'

Gregori ignored him and pressed a button and held the phone to his ear. It was answered almost immediately and his expression became grim. He quickly handed it to Jon whose expression also went hard.

Jon handed the phone back. 'Gregori, have you got a pistol on you?'

Before Gregori could answer, Johnson wrenched his door open and started running back down the way they had come. Arianna was almost as quick and she was certainly a faster runner. The ensuing rugby tackle would have been good enough to get her on her national team.

As they struggled on the ground, Gregori came up and pushed the barrel of his pistol hard into Johnson's ear. 'I would stop that right now Mister Johnson. I would hate to have to report that my pistol accidentally went off, now wouldn't I?'

All the fight left the man. Arianna stood up and looked at Gregori. 'So who was on the other end of that call?'

'The Russian Embassy.'

Chapter 32

Boris was seriously worried. It was all going wrong. The hotel manager hadn't known that his guests had left in the middle of the night. He slept in the back of the building and hadn't heard a thing. So they had no idea when they had left although it could have been no more than two hours ago. They had absolutely no idea which way they had gone although presumably they would be making their way to Croatia via some route but there were a multitude of those. On top of that, the police were pissed off at him and seemed to somehow blame him that the girl had got away. It was pointless to point out that if anyone had warned the UN party it was probably someone from inside police headquarters. No one in the Russian Embassy apart from Boris knew about what had been going on. He could hardly admit that to the Serbs.

After half an hour of argument and recrimination, the police announced that they were returning to Belgrade and unless Boris wanted to stay at the hotel, he would have to come with them. They promised they would put out an alert to all their units to look out for the UN vehicle but that was all they were prepared to do. Arresting the girl in the hotel was one thing, stopping and interfering with UNPROFOR in public was quite another.

All the way back, Boris was considering his position. If he admitted what he had done to his superiors, he would be in deep trouble. Not only that but the time wasted would almost certainly allow the UN party to get clear. He needed to keep his council and work fast. The only people who could help now were the military and he had a few contacts and favours he could call in. There was also the outside chance that Peter Johnson could delay them or at least get in contact and tell him where they were going. He knew he couldn't count on that. The man had been very reluctant right from the start.

He realised he could usefully pass the time as they sped back to the city by studying his map. He had to assume that they would change plans as they had no way of knowing whether their planned route had been compromised as well, which of course it had. So on the assumption that they would try another way he looked at likely routes. *'What would he do in their place?'* he wondered. They had

Retribution

clearly been going for the quiet corridor north of Sarajevo but on the assumption that that route was now out, the next best option would be to head west to the coast. '*At least that is what he would do in their situation.*' Of course, they could be trying a double bluff and keeping to the old route. He was starting to get a headache due to lack of sleep and worry. No, he couldn't second guess every possibility. He would have to work on the most obvious assumption.

The police dropped him off at the Embassy but he didn't go in. People would wonder what he was doing there so early in the morning. Instead he went back to his flat. He would call in sick once the day started. He made himself some strong tea and started to make his calls.

'We don't have time for this,' Jon stated firmly. 'We need to get going. We can sort out Mister Johnson either as we go or after we have arrived at Split.'

They were all back in the Mercedes, with a red faced Peter Johnson sitting in the back with his hands tied behind his back with a cable tie from the car's toolbox. An angry Arianna was sitting next to him with a knife in her hands and a murderous look in her eyes.

'One question we need an answer to straight away,' Gregori, who was back behind the wheel, stated firmly. 'Did you tell them of the route we were using? We discussed it in detail last night, at your instigation I seem to remember.'

Johnson seemed to have recovered some of his bluster. 'How dare you do this to me? I'm saying nothing. Hunt, you can't sanction this. Untie me now.'

Jon looked at the man. 'No. I've had my suspicions about you for some time and long before either of us came to this country.' Jon saw the man's pupils dilate at this remark but kept going. 'We have an awful lot to talk about as I think you very well know. However, that is for the future. As far as I'm concerned our immediate mission takes priority. Now, before you say anything more, let me tell you a little about the girl sitting next to you. She escaped being raped by the Serbs but not before they killed her parents. Since then, she has been working as a sniper and assassin for the Croatian army. That was until she was tasked to get the evidence of their brutality which I know you've seen. In doing so, she herself was brutally tortured. So you can imagine how she feels about the Serbs and anyone supporting them.' Jon left the statement hanging. Arianna just smiled at Johnson. It wasn't a smile with any warmth.

He eventually managed to speak. 'So what? You'll torture me or kill me? Don't be stupid. Remember who I am and who my friends are, back in England.'

'I was wondering when you would use that tack, you shit. Well, I do remember you have friends at home and I wonder what they will think of you when they find out you have been warning the Russians here in Serbia and maybe how much else you have been telling them over the years?' Jon said grimly. He saw his shot hit home. 'Now I'll repeat the question. Do the Serbs know our intended route?'

Johnson pursed his lips but kept silent. Jon knew they didn't have any more time and despite his words, he would not let Arianna do anything they would all regret later. He suspected Johnson knew that as well. He turned to Gregori who was on his mobile phone. 'Anything from back at base Gregori?'

Gregori held up a finger as he spoke into the telephone. 'I can't understand you, no, say that again, my signal is very weak. Sorry, I can't seem to make you out. In case you can hear me, we will carry on as ordered, bye.' And he hung up.

'What was that all about Gregori? Couldn't you get a decent signal on that thing?' Jon asked.

'Oh, I heard them alright. I just didn't want them to know that I had. They're pulling up the drawbridge. Our escort have been stood down and we are ordered back to Belgrade. We are to hand over the girl to the local police. I didn't want them to know we had understood until you decide what we should do.'

'So it's over then. We turn around.' Peter Johnson said.

'You can shut the fuck up, Johnson,' Jon replied angrily. 'Whatever we decide, you're not part of the process. And for your information, I am not handing Arianna over to those animals whatever those cowards back at HQ say. Gregori, be honest what are our chances of getting clear?'

'Well, the route I'm suggesting is not as safe as our original. We have to skirt south of Sarajevo and north of Mostar and as you know both cities are currently under siege. But the alternative is to go north west as originally planned. Either way, it's about four hundred kilometres until we're out of danger.'

Jon thought hard. Despite Gregori's assessment, he was worried that with the two major cities being so close, the gap between them would be heavily patrolled. Yes, they were still a UN party and the police would probably not stop them but the Serb army was a different matter. 'The roads are much better to the north though aren't they Gregori?'

'What, you mean the main E70? Yes, it would be far quicker and technically it's actually in Croatia. Mind you, that's rather in dispute at the moment but we could be in Zagreb in about four hours if we could use it but we discounted that idea from the start.'

'Remind me, why was that? Jon asked.

'Well, it's the main route that the Serb army use.'

'Yes, they use it as a transport route but only for that purpose. As far as we know there are no blocks on it and they must be used to seeing white UN vehicles. If we can save time then so much the better before anyone can organise a search for us. Why don't we just get on it and go flat out, stopping for no one. They won't be able to identify us even if they are looking for us. And in terms of a double bluff, we have to assume they know our original route and will expect us to go south so should be looking in the wrong place.'

The more he thought about it the more Gregori liked it. It was just the sort of mad idea this Captain would come up with and it could work. There was only one thing. 'Yes, I like the idea Sir but we will have to head towards Sarajevo first to keep clear of the fighting to the north but not for long and then we can pick up the E70 and go for it.'

'So what are we waiting for? We've enough fuel to make it. Next stop Zagreb.'

Chapter 33

Ruth peered through the crowd at the arrivals concourse at Gatwick airport, waiting for a glimpse of Rupert. His plane had been slightly delayed but he should appear any minute. That is if the gaggle of people holding up cards and pressing forward against the metal railings allowed her to see. Then she caught sight of him. He was peering at the crowd from the other side of the barrier as he slowly walked out, pulling his large wheeled suitcase behind him. She waved above the heads of the crowd and he caught sight of her and gave an acknowledging wave back. Soon, they were clear of the throng on the way to the short term car park.

'What's so urgent sis? I got your email but you were hardly informative,' he said. 'All you said is that you've made a breakthrough, so what is it?'

'In a minute Rupert, let's wait until we're in the car.'

'Jesus girl and I thought I was paranoid.'

He held back his curiosity until they had manoeuvred clear of the car park and were heading for the M23. 'Right spill it, what's happened?'

Ruth told him the whole story. Her trip to Somerset and then onwards to Cornwall. The likelihood that the fire at the garage was deliberate and the discovery of the signature in the ledger at Truro police station.

Rupert said nothing for several minutes. 'So, you're pretty sure that Johnson was the man that removed the evidence from the police station but there is nothing to link him to the fire at the garage. Also, you haven't found any motive for his actions apart from the possibility that it's something to do with Old Farts crowd. There's nothing that would stand up in court.'

'Oh come on Rupert, you know damn well that it's enough to get a proper investigation going. We've moved heaven and earth in the past on far flimsier evidence,' Ruth said with a note of exasperation in her voice.

'Sorry, just being the Devil's advocate. No, you're right of course. It's just that I don't get it.' Rupert said. 'Why do all this several years after the actual crime and why do it in the first place anyway? There's the old adage of means, motive and opportunity.

I'll give him the means and opportunity although they are somewhat tenuous but what the hell was the motive?'

'Well firstly, the second round of clearing up seems to be an attempt to make damned sure nothing from the original investigation was available for a second look. Maybe he got wind of our interest? Your visit to Long Lartin had to be made in public. Also, Jon was back from Moscow and had just been invited into the Old Farts.'

'Hmm, still don't get it,' Rupert responded. 'But there is every indication to me that Johnson was tipped off somehow which can only mean someone in our orbit was warning him.'

'I agree and that means we are going to have to be very, very careful about what we do now. Oh and I have yet to tell you the icing on the cake.'

'Oh, there's more?'

'Yup. You know we discovered that he had left the ministry and was working as a consultant.' Ruth said.

'Yes, some military advisory lot wasn't it?

'Yes and he recently took on a contract to work abroad in a war zone advising the UN. Any guesses where?'

'Oh shit, not Serbia? That's where Jon is.'

'Oh it's even better than that,' Ruth replied grimly. 'He's doing some sort of routine audit for the UN. I spoke to them yesterday and guess who Johnson is working for?'

'You've got to be kidding.'

'Sorry, I'm not. Although it's meant to be an advisory role and although he's formally under Jon's authority, its more for admin purposes than anything else.'

'Oh God, I just hope Jon keeps his cool. He knows enough about the man to cause all sorts of issues.' Rupert said in a worried tone.

'Agreed. We're going straight back to your office by the way. I've scheduled a phone call to Jon from the office on a secure line. I thought I'd wait until you got back in case there was anything you wanted to add.'

'I'll have to think this through but that was a good idea.'

They drove on through the snarled London traffic which gave them plenty of time to talk more but nothing extra could be gleaned beyond Ruth's current findings. Eventually, they pulled up at Vauxhall Bridge House and were let into the underground car park and made their way to Rupert's office. Rupert was just about to get

Retribution

on the phone and try to ring Belgrade when the inter-office phone rang. It was the head of MI6's secretary and would Rupert go up to his office straight away?

'Ruth, I think you need to come with me,' Rupert said. 'Nothing that happened to me over the last week while I was away merits a call from the great man. I've a feeling this may well be about what we've been talking about.'

He was right. When they entered the office, Rupert said he wanted Ruth with him and there was no objection. As soon as the door was closed, the Head of MI6 indicated chairs to them both and then took his own seat.

'Graham,' Rupert said. 'If I was a betting man I would say this has something to do with the task Ruth has been working on. The one you first gave me when I got back from Moscow.'

'Correct Rupert but as you brought Ruth with you I suspect you have as much news for me as I have you. Why don't you start?'

Rupert indicated for Ruth to tell her story again which was listened to in silence. When she finished, Rupert went on to support Ruth's conclusions and say how he suspected there must be some sort of leak in their organisation.

His boss looked worried at the revelations but not surprised. 'Right you two, that's excellent work. It looks like we are actually making some progress at last. Although, as you quite rightly say Rupert, we would be hard pressed to make anything stick at this stage. However, as you have gathered I have some news of my own. It's about your friend and the man who seems to have borne the brunt of all this recent attention from Mister Johnson, by which I mean Captain Hunt. The Embassy has just passed a message on to us. It seems that there is some sort of diplomatic row brewing between the Serbian government and the UN and the good Captain may well be involved.'

'What sort of row?' Ruth asked.

'I haven't got all the fine detail yet but it seems he rescued some female Croatian soldier from the Serbs and she had some very sensitive intelligence on her which could really embarrass the Serbian government. She was being held in a local hospital. This is where it gets confusing. The UN are saying that she was attacked by a Serbian soldier but escaped and injured the man in the process. They have the UN guard on the room who was also assaulted as a witness. However, the Serbs are claiming it was an unprovoked murder attempt and they want the girl to be surrendered to them for investigation.'

'Any idea what this intelligence material was?' Rupert asked.

'Not exactly. Apparently, she had some photographs of senior Serbs committing some sort of crime but I don't have any detail.

'So, what's the problem,' asked Ruth.

'The problem, my dear, is that she is no longer with the UN in Belgrade. The Serbs are screaming of a cover up and the UN are accusing the Serbs of attempting to murder and then kidnap her. But there's more to it than that. Captain Hunt, his deputy who is a Russian officer, the girl and believe it or not our Mister Johnson, all apparently left Belgrade together. There seem to be conflicting stories as to why. One of my sources says it was to get the girl back to her own people and ensure this sensitive material is released. The UN appear to be sitting on it while all this furore is going on. However, officially, the UN are denying that anything was authorised, which is almost the same as saying that Hunt has done this on his own authority. Mind you that stinks of people watching their own backs. Anyway, they left Belgrade two days ago. They should have arrived somewhere in Croatia by last night at the latest but nothing has been seen or heard of them since they left Belgrade.'

Chapter 34

'Jesus wept Gregori, are you a frustrated rally driver?' Jon asked as they slid sideways around another corner.

Gregori just grinned. 'Spetsnaz trained Sir. We cover a great deal during our training. How's the map reading going?'

Jon had the map on his lap but was having trouble concentrating as the car hurtled along the narrow single track road. *Maybe this was how Brian felt when he was flinging his helicopter around,* he thought with amusement. 'Oh sorry, yes we've only got another few miles along here and we come to a T junction where we turn left. After that, it's not far to the main road. And it seems you were right as there's been no sign of any border posts or even limited road blocks.'

'Well it was one united country until recently and they can't put a border post on every small track.' Gregori said happily as he dropped a gear and floored the throttle again.

Jon took time to quickly look over his shoulder at the rear passengers. Peter Johnson looked white but whether it was because of the mad Russian driver or the mad Croatian woman pointing a gun at him was a moot point. Jon smiled at Arianna and she grinned back but the pistol never wavered. They had decided to free Johnson's hands in case they had to stop for any reason. It would look extremely odd if one of a UN party had his hands tied behind his back. However, to ensure his continued cooperation they had given Arianna the pistol as well as her knife. What would also not be obvious, was the small cable tie securing the buckle of Johnson's seat belt which would stop him making a dash for freedom when they stopped.

Jon was aching to be able to talk properly to the man but they needed to get Arianna to safety first. What he couldn't understand was how Johnson had managed to do so much damage in such a short time. He was either already briefed before he left England or someone was waiting for him when he arrived in Belgrade. Either way, it was quite clear to Jon that the man was some sort of turncoat. Presumably, now that the Soviet Union was no more, he was working for Russia itself. The phone call on his mobile was direct evidence of that. However, that in itself was odd because if he

Retribution

had been doing it out of some sort of idealism as other British Cold War spies had, then why was he now working for a country that had thrown off the shackles of communism? It couldn't be for the money, he had loads of it. Yes, Jon really wanted a one on one conversation. But maybe with Arianna standing off to one side with that rather feral grin on her face.

He was brought back to reality by a jolt as the car caught a wheel in a ditch which Gregori was expertly using to help the car get around a rather tight bend. With relief, he saw the T junction ahead. The roads should get better now which would make his chauffer's attempts to kill them a little less exciting.

It would never be known who has actually placed the landmine in the ground during the Second World War. It was one of several hundred that had been sown to put a barrier across what had once been a strategic route by one side or the other. When the war was over, the government had cleared the area but it was always going to be impossible to get them all. This one had been undisturbed since it had been laid except for when a local farmer had decided to dig out the ditches along the edge of his field to improve the drainage. The digger had just missed the mine but did cause it to tilt over so that it was now at an angle of about forty five degrees in the wall of the ditch. Over the years, the explosives inside it had deteriorated to a marked degree and the impact fuse was just about rusted solid. Given a few more years it would have become completely inert.

However, when the front wheel of the Mercedes hit the mine, there was enough force to break the corrosion on the impact fuse and force the pin into the detonator. A half-hearted explosion of the detonator caused an equally half-hearted explosion of the main charge. As the mine was over at such an angle most of the blast shot safely away over the fields. However, there was enough energy left to smash the suspension and steering of the car and send it flying out of control across the road. Already half in the air as it impacted a small bank on the other side, the Mercedes completed its roll and slid for a few feet on its roof before smashing into the only tree for several hundred yards. Had it not done so it would probably have slid down the opposite bank into a small lake and drowned the occupants.

Retribution

Jon never lost consciousness during the accident although the violence of the whole event completely stunned him. As the car turned upside down, the windscreen smashed and when it hit the opposite bank it acted like a giant scoop flinging grass, mud and stones into the driving compartment. The impact with the tree was so violent he was only saved by the airbag in front of him stopping his head smashing into the dashboard.

Suddenly, it was quiet. He hung upside down in his seat belt wondering what the hell had just happened and coughing from the dust and smoke. For an unmeasurable time, he just hung there trying to gather a coherent thought. Slowly, he regained his faculties. The first thing he noticed was the silence. There was a distant ticking as hot metal cooled but that was all. Then he realised he could smell things. One smell above all others galvanised him into action. Petrol. He knew that cars very seldom blew up because of a petrol leak. That fiction was confined to Hollywood but he also knew the dreaded consequence of fire in a crashed car. Afterwards, he would acknowledge that at that moment he panicked but who wouldn't? He desperately scrabbled for his seat belt release. Being upside down had completely disorientated him but his many training runs in the helicopter dunker over the years came to his aid and he closed his eyes and forced himself to think logically. Unfortunately, having found the release, he failed to think through the consequences and landed with a thump on his head as he fell free of the restraints. Within seconds, he was able to scramble free through the smashed windscreen and crawl under the bonnet which was now above him and get clear.

His thoughts immediately turned to the others. He saw Arianna's door fling open and her dazed face appear. Quickly he grabbed her and pulled her out of harm's way. Johnson was still upside down and seemed to be unconscious but he was clearly breathing. Jon remembered they had tied up his seat belt. He fumbled around in his pockets, found his little penknife, reached in and cut the cable tie before releasing the belt. Johnson's body hit the roof like a sack of potatoes but Jon was able to reach in and with a heave, pull the inert body clear.

Looking around, Arianna had disappeared. Then he heard noises from the other side of the car. He found Arianna desperately trying to wrench open the driver's side door. He went to join her and between the two of them, they were able to get it partially open as the top had dug into the ground before it was fully open. Gregori was surrounded by the deflated air bags. He was breathing but there was a deep gash to his forehead with blood pouring out. With Arianna's help, they were able to release his seat belt and lower him clear without too much trouble.

The smell of petrol was getting stronger and Jon had no desire to be around if the wreck did catch fire. Between the two of them, they dragged Gregori around the front and into the road and managed to get well clear. Jon knew that there was a first aid kit in the boot of the car but just as he was contemplating going back for it a gout of flame appeared at the rear and suddenly the whole of the rear of the car caught light. Ignoring it and with no other recourse, Jon took off his military jacket and then his shirt which he ripped into sections before bundling one of them up and applying it to the cut on Gregori's head. He tied another strip around Gregori's head to hold the pad in place.

Meanwhile, Arianna had disappeared. Jon looked up from Gregori's prone body. Initially, he couldn't see her. He assumed she had gone back to make sure Johnson was clear of the fire.

The car was burning well by now. The whole rear was alight and the flames were spreading forwards. A pall of black smoke was funnelling up from the wreck and blowing their way in the breeze. Suddenly, Jon heard a gunshot. His first instinct was to assume it was ammunition from one of their guns going up in the burning wreck. He was quickly disabused of the idea as out of the smoke came two people. Arianna was stumbling. She was being supported by Johnson but he was also holding a pistol to her head.

Chapter 35

'Oh, for fuck's sake, Johnson, what are you going to do with that?' Jon asked in an exasperated voice.

'Get myself out of this mess you moron. Now get me my telephone out of that bloody Russian's pocket. I know it's there. I saw him put it away.' Johnson said tight lipped, with the barrel of the pistol held tight against Arianna's temple.

'Or what? You fucking idiot.' Jon was having a rather nasty attack of déjà vu. This was so like that time in the Falklands when that Argentinian policeman had done something similar.

'Or I shoot this little tart, that's what. So cut the insults and do as you're told.'

Jon looked at the man. He was still clearly dazed from the accident but seemed to be pretty determined.

He looked at Arianna who was furious. 'Don't do it Jon' she said.

'Why do you want the bloody thing anyway Johnson? For some reason I don't think it's going to be to ring the emergency services.' Jon asked, stalling for time. He knew how resourceful Arianna could be. Maybe she could disarm him. After all, she had far more experience of this sort of situation than any of the rest of them.

Johnson's eyes narrowed. Before any of them could react, he took the pistol away from the girl's head and simply shot her in the side of her left foot. The crash of the gun was deafening but Arianna's scream was almost as loud. Jon leapt to his feet but Johnson had forced the gun back to Arianna's head despite her writhing in agony. 'Get back Hunt. Now for the last time get me the fucking telephone.'

Jon knew he would have to comply. The man was clearly on or even over the edge. He fumbled through Gregori's pockets and found the telephone. As he pulled it out he strongly considered throwing it into the wrecked car that was still burning well. Johnson clearly anticipated Jon's thoughts. 'Hand it over Hunt or I shoot her in the other foot.'

Reluctantly, Jon passed it over to Johnson's outstretched hand. 'And just how are you going to use it one handed?' He asked.

Retribution

'Because I can guarantee that the moment you move that pistol away from Arianna both she and I are going to beat the shit out of you.'

Any hope that Jon had that he would unsettle the man was dashed as he simply pressed one button and held the phone to his ear. 'Last number redial Jon. You really need to get one of these and learn how they work.' He then pulled Arianna back several feet, pushed her to the ground and squatted behind her as he waited for the phone to be answered which clearly it had been. At that distance, Jon couldn't hear what was being said but he had a fairly good idea what Johnson was up to.

He spoke for several minutes and then hung up. 'Right, now we wait. It won't be long.'

'At least let me bind up Arianna's foot you bastard,' Jon said. He could see the blood welling up from her shoe.

'Hah and let you close. No but you can pass me the remains of your shirt and she can do it herself. I don't want her dying. I think my Serbian friends will have some questions for her. Oh and on that note where are the photos and film?'

'I've no idea, why don't you ask the defenceless young girl you just shot? I'm sure she'll be delighted to tell you,' Jon replied bitterly.

Arianna was grimacing in pain as she tied part of Jon's shirt around her injured foot. She didn't attempt to remove her shoe. All she wanted was to apply enough pressure to stop the bleeding. Surprisingly she offered the information. 'They were in my brief case you dick head. Please feel free to go and get them.'

Johnson looked over at the wreck which was almost burned out now and realised it was a complete waste of time. 'Never mind, destroying them was always a second option. Now everyone, sit still it won't be long.'

The two Serb soldiers were sitting comfortably around the high frequency radio in the command tent near Sarajevo. One of them had his feet resting on the table the other was stirring his coffee.

'Hey Ivo', one of them said. 'Did you hear what happened in Belgrade the other day?'

'Only a rumour,' the other soldier, called Danijel, replied. 'Something about the Colonel and that bloody Sergeant that the UN people arrested last week. But I didn't get any detail.'

Retribution

'Hah, well I got it from one the guys who has a girlfriend back in Belgrade. She's a nurse in the main hospital and saw the aftermath. There's a real panic going on there. It seems that little hellcat we had in custody was in the hospital and under guard. However, it appears the UN decided to let our two guys go and the Sergeant then decided to pay the girl a visit. Our government are saying that the girl then shot him but where the hell she would have got a gun from, unless it was from the big ape himself, is not exactly clear.'

'Hang on Ivo, are you saying that little slip of a girl took out Sergeant Babic? The man's a fucking gorilla. He was the regimental wrestling champion for years. I don't believe you.'

'Well, the press would hardly make something like that up.' Ivo said.

'Oh really, they seem to make just about everything else up these days.' Danijel replied.

'Ah but the bit they haven't reported is how the girl took him out. She must have got his gun off him somehow. He had a nasty wound to the head apparently and then she shot him.'

'I can't say I'm that sympathetic he was a complete shit.' Danijel said with feeling.

'Ah but I haven't got to the good bit. You see she didn't kill him. She shot him in the balls, several times. He won't be shagging any Croatian tarts any more and if he comes back he'll be shouting at us all in a high pitched voice.'

Danijel looked nonplussed for a second and then roared with laughter. 'Oh that's fucking great. I'd like to see him try and give us a hard time while shrieking like a woman. I shouldn't say it but that girl deserves a bloody medal.'

'Private Cardic, what the hell are you doing in here?' a voice from the tent entrance roared. 'You are not on watch so get the hell out of my command tent and stop spreading malicious stories about Sergeant Babic, understand?'

Ivo looked startled to see the Colonel. He was not normally seen before ten o'clock. He knew better than to argue and made himself scarce.

The Colonel turned to the remaining soldier. 'Get a message out to patrol number four to head to this grid reference.' He handed him a piece of paper with six numbers on it. 'They are to detain the people they find there in a wrecked car until I arrive is that clear?'

Retribution

'Yes Sir, right away.'

Despite Johnson saying that it wouldn't be long before someone arrived, it was over half an hour before the sound of an engine was heard. Gregori had regained consciousness but was clearly badly concussed. Even so, Jon had to order him to lie still. He was praying that the engine they were hearing was a farmer or some other non-military vehicle but his hopes were dashed when it was clear that it was a large army truck. It pulled up with a skid and armed Serbian troops bundled out of the back.

They surrounded the four of them with pointed guns. One was clearly in charge and Jon spoke to him in Serbian. 'Thank you for coming to help. I am Captain Hunt of the UN Protection Force. As you can see we need medical help. Can you take us to the nearest town?'

The soldier looked confused. His orders were simple. To detain the people here. No one had told him they were UN soldiers who had been in a car crash and were injured. The indecision on his face was clear.

Jon was about to follow up, being the only Serbian speaker when Johnson interrupted him. 'Hunt, shut the fuck up. I know what you are trying to do. Remember, I still have a gun.'

'And I speak English,' the soldier replied, now looking very suspicious. 'Where is this gun? Give it to me.'

Johnson looked as if he was about to argue so the soldier pointed his rifle at him and cocked the slide. Faced with the barrel of a loaded AK 47, Johnson reached behind his back and passed over the small pistol he had been concealing.

Jon was about to try again but the soldier spoke first. 'No one talks. My Colonel will be here very soon he can decide what to do.'

A tense silence descended. Two of the soldiers got fire extinguishers from their lorry and put out the last of the fire and then they all waited. In only a matter of minutes a green painted four wheel drive car screeched to a halt. With a sinking feeling, Jon recognised the man who got out. It was the same Colonel he had arrested only days before. The same man he had humiliated in front of his own men. This was not going to end well.

Chapter 36

The Serb army camp they were taken to was very different from the one that Jon had confronted the Colonel in several days ago. What had clearly been a large agricultural complex was now the headquarters of a large regular army encampment. As they were driven into the area in the back of a lorry, Jon saw several tanks, artillery pieces and even a Russian helicopter in the outlying fields. Once inside the farm compound, there were orderly ranks of vehicles and all the soldiers looked smart and alert.

When the Colonel had arrived, he had said nothing to the survivors, despite Jon's repeated attempts to get him to acknowledge them. He did give Jon a piercing look and then simply turned his back on him and started a conversation with the soldiers. Shortly afterwards, they were prodded into the back of the lorry at the points of several rifles. Gregori seemed to have lapsed into unconsciousness again but Jon wasn't convinced, mainly because of the wink he had given Jon when no one seemed to be looking. In the end, they had put the somnolent Russian in a stretcher and put him in the lorry with the rest of them which, to Jon's surprise, included Johnson. He would have said something to the man but as soon as he started to speak one of the guards menaced him with his rifle. Johnson also seemed put out but there was nothing any of them could do.

Once they arrived, they were taken from the lorry and marched into the main building. Arianna was forced to hold onto Jon's shoulder and half hop with him as she couldn't put any weight on her foot. Waiting in the hall was a rather fat, florid man in an ill-fitting business suit. As soon as Johnson saw him, the man said something and the Colonel ordered him to be separated from Jon and Arianna. They disappeared into the building. Jon looked at Arianna and shrugged but before they could react any further they were prodded further on to a set of stairs leading down to what was clearly a basement. Here they were left and again nothing was said to them.

As soon as they were on their own, Jon immediately scouted the room. It was lit by a single bare bulb and there was no furniture at all. The walls seemed to be bare concrete and the wooden steps that led up to the door on the ground floor above them were the only fittings.

He squatted next to Arianna. 'Do you want me to look at that foot?' He had noticed that fresh blood was appearing around the crude bandage that she had tied.

She was sitting on the floor with her back against one of the walls. 'Yes please Jon but be careful.'

He gave her a reassuring smile. 'Don't worry, I've done loads of first aid courses over the years. Now, let's have a look.' He squatted down in front of her and carefully untied her crude bandage. As soon as he did, more blood started to drip from the shoe. 'I'm going to have to remove this shoe alright? It may hurt but I can't do anything with it in the way.'

Arianna just nodded, tight lipped, her face pale.

Luckily, the shoe was laced and Jon was able to untie it, remove the laces and then open it out before carefully pulling it away. Arianna had been wearing short socks with it and he was also able to peel the sock off. All the time she stoically stared ahead and said nothing although from her white face, Jon knew she was suffering. Once the foot was bare, he realised she had been lucky. The bullet had gone through the side of the foot and seemed to have missed any bones. However, it had torn a large wound which was why there was so much blood. With little else to hand, he had to reuse what he had but this time was able to bind it tightly and the bleeding stopped. Once Arianna was settled, he also sat back to consider their position.

'One thing we must remember Arianna is that the longer we wait before we try to escape, the harder it will be. So, any ideas? Now would be a good time.'

She gave a little laugh. 'You sound like you've been in this position before Jon.'

'Actually, I have, although that time it was me that was wounded and it was a lot warmer. I'll tell you about it some time. You know, I wonder what they've done with Gregori.'

'I thought I saw him being taken off towards another building. I just hope it was a medical facility.' She said in a worried tone.

'Actually, I'm not too sure that he's as bad as they might think,' Jon replied and told her about the wink.

Retribution

'Good, he's one tough character maybe he can get away and alert the authorities.'

Before Jon could reply, the Colonel and a soldier appeared at the top of the steps. With the soldier covering them with an AK47 the Colonel approached and looked down.

'My name is Anto Borko, we were never properly introduced last time we met. Of course, this time you don't have your French Foreign legion squad to back you up,' he said with a mirthless smile.

'What are you going to do to us?' Jon asked. 'We are UN personnel and your government will not be happy to find out you have kidnapped us.'

The Colonel just laughed. 'Don't be too sure about that Captain and we did not kidnap you, we rescued you. You were the ones in a car crash. Now, I'm not really interested in anything you have to say. I simply require one thing. I need all your clothes.'

'What? Well, you can fuck right off.' Jon replied angrily.

'Such language from a senior officer.' The Colonel responded and signalled to his soldier who cocked his weapon and pointed it directly at Jon. 'I won't repeat myself. As far as I'm concerned your lives are forfeit but if you want to live a little longer you will do as you're told. Now strip.'

They had no choice. With the soldier covering them, the Colonel picked up the pile of clothes but not before casting an appreciative eye over Arianna's naked form. 'I'm glad you did as I told you. We will have some fun, you and I later.' And with that they left. Jon shouted that they needed some replacement clothes and medical supplies for Arianna but they were completely ignored.

When they were alone again, they huddled together for warmth. It was cold in the basement.

'What are they going to do Jon?' Arianna asked. 'Why did they want our clothes?'

Despite fighting it, a black mood was slowly creeping over Jon. 'Well, if some corpses were found in the burned out car, wearing the remains of our clothes and a certain Mister Johnson attested that they were ours and that he was the only lucky escapee. Who wouldn't believe him?'

Arianna didn't answer straight away. Eventually, she spoke in a small voice. 'So either way we're dead? That's what the Colonel meant when he said our lives were forfeit isn't it?'

'I'm afraid so. They probably want to interrogate you. I don't suppose I have much to tell them though.'

'Oh Jon,' she cried and they hugged each other even harder. They were interrupted by the door opening again. The same soldier came down but this time he was followed by Peter Johnson who was carrying some sort of bundle.

He threw it at their feet. 'Some clothes and there's some antiseptic and clean bandages. They asked me to deliver them. Sorry it's all I could get.'

He turned to leave but Jon called out. 'So, I suppose you're off back to Belgrade to testify to our deaths, you utter bastard. You had better just pray that we don't meet again because if we do, you are a dead man.'

Johnson didn't answer and turned to leave. Jon tried again. 'Before you run away you traitor, I have one simple question. Why did you murder my wife and my unborn child?'

Johnson stopped dead in his tracks and turned back to face Jon. 'I did no such thing.'

'Oh really, well MI6 have been looking at you for some time. Ever since you put my name on a GCHQ watch list.'

'And I'm sure they found absolutely nothing,' Johnson replied confidently.

Jon ignored the reply. 'Why, you fucker? Was it because I was about to be invited into the Ramon society?'

Johnson looked flustered for a second. 'What? No. Don't be stupid. That bunch of old morons had nothing to do with it.'

'Thank you. So you admit it then?' Jon was smiling mirthlessly.

Johnson's expression changed. He had clearly come to a decision. 'Alright, I arranged for your car to be sabotaged. You might as well know, you won't be leaving here alive. But it was meant to be a contingency plan to be able to get rid of you in a hurry if I needed it. Believe it or not, I'm sorry about your wife but it was a drunk Cornish farmer who killed her not me.'

'Why, you bastard why?' Jon had got to his feet completely forgetting about his lack of clothes. The soldier pointed his gun at him but Jon ignored him. 'WHY?' he shouted into Johnson's face.

Johnson took a step backwards, suddenly terrified at the look of naked hatred on Jon's face. 'God, you really don't know do you?'

The soldier stepped in between them. But a red rage was settling over Jon. He was about to do something he would almost certainly regret but the need to get his hands around this man's throat was almost overwhelming. It was Arianna who saved him. She came up behind Jon and pulled him back. 'Don't Jon, he's not worth it. You'll just get yourself shot.'

Jon was suddenly calm. 'Why?' he repeated. 'What was so important that you would do such a thing?'

Johnson wanted nothing else but to get out of the room but in some odd way, he felt he owed it to this man to tell him, even if the Serbs were going to shoot him in a few hours. 'Very well. Did you know what job you were going to get when you came back from sea?'

'No but I had a meeting planned with the First Sea Lord which never happened. It was to invite me to your bloody secret society.'

'Maybe but that wasn't the only reason for the meeting. You were coming to work for me. There was going to be a top secret investigation into how the Soviets had discovered how noisy their submarines were. It was so classified that even the intelligence services were not aware of it. The navy was concerned that the leak might have actually come from there. I only had a short time left in the RAF and giving it to a senior Air Force officer was deemed the safest approach.'

'And you were worried I might find out who the real person was who had passed on the information?' and then the penny dropped. 'And it was you, wasn't it? You were a soviet spy all along. My God, they gave the investigation to the very man who had been the perpetrator. I got damned close to you the last time, too close. No wonder you were worried.'

Johnson turned and climbed the stairs. 'Goodbye Captain, goodbye young lady. Believe me, I never wanted this to happen but it's out of my control now.'

'Just remember to watch your back for the rest of your fucking life,' Jon shouted as the door closed.

Chapter 37

It had all gone quiet in the small sick bay that Gregori had been taken to. The effort of feigning being unconscious had been surprisingly difficult, especially when someone had stitched up the wound in his head. He had managed it though and finally he was pretty sure he had been left alone. He very carefully opened his eyes slightly. At first, he thought he had gone blind but then realised his eyelids were partly gummed up with the residue of the watering they had done during the stitching operation. Also, it was dark in the room he was in. He quickly realised he was alone in a bed with medical screens all around. There was also a drip next to him feeding something into a needle taped to his left wrist. He immediately pulled it free and sat up. A brief wash of dizziness caused him to pause but it soon passed. He realised he was still fully dressed except for his boots. Looking around, he saw them on the floor. With deliberate care, he slowly slid off the bed and put them on.

'What the hell do I do now?' he wondered. His thoughts were interrupted by the sound of footsteps approaching. Quickly, he stood to one side and sure enough, the curtains pulled apart and a middle aged man looked in. Before the man could react to the sight of the empty bed, Gregori had his arm around his neck.

'Make one sound and I will snap your neck,' he hissed into the man's ear.

To his surprise, the man didn't even struggle but he did speak in a whisper before Gregori could react. 'It's alright, I was pretty sure you weren't actually unconscious. I'm not going to do anything.'

Gregori let his grip relax slightly in acknowledgement. 'Alright then, who are you?'

'I'm the doctor who treated your wound. Look, I may work for these pigs but I'm not one of them.'

'Then why do you work for them,' Gregori hissed back.

'Because I'm a doctor and I treat anyone who needs me and they give me little choice. Now please, let me go. I won't betray you. I've told them that you will probably be out for the rest of the night. They want to interrogate you but they've all gone to their quarters now except for one guard at the entrance.'

Gregori realised that he had little choice and if there was any chance of getting away or of rescuing the others, he was going to have to trust this man. 'Alright but don't think that I won't hesitate if you are trying to deceive me.'

The doctor nodded and sat on the edge of the bed. Gregori got a better look at him. He was very thin, with greying hair and wearing the obligatory white coat. 'So you won't betray me but will you help me? You know that me and my colleagues are UN personnel and are therefore being illegally detained?'

'Yes, I know all that but I have also heard what Colonel Borko said. Apparently, you arrested him some days ago but he was then released and that the girl had some evidence that he wanted suppressed. It seems the evidence was destroyed in your accident but the Colonel is a vindictive man. We have a morgue here and they took several bodies away earlier on. My guess is that they are going to use them in the wreck and claim they were you. There was a bad fire I understand?'

'Yes there was,' Gregori responded in a worried tone. 'If that's the case, then they won't want us turning up any time.'

'Which is why I am prepared to help you. You know, although I am a Serb and would like to see my country properly restored that's not at the cost these men are prepared to impose. Think of this as my small attempt to redress some of the wrongs that are being perpetrated in the name of fighting for freedom.'

Gregori could see that the man was sincere. 'Alright, where are they keeping the others?'

I'm not certain but there is only one likely place, which is the basement of the main farmhouse. They use the farmhouse as their headquarters and most of the officers live there. It will be impossible to get in and out I'm afraid. You would be better off getting away and alerting your people to what is really going on.'

'And my friends would be long dead before I could do that.' Gregori responded grimly. 'I have a better idea. You said there was a guard. Where exactly is he?'

The medical bay was situated in what had been an office building for the large farm, set off to one side of the main yard. The soldier who had been detailed to guard it was bored and with no one to tell him not to, had slipped outside for a cigarette. When he finished and with another two hours before he would be relieved, he nonchalantly went back in through the main door to see if he could find some coffee. The last thing he was expecting was the arm around his throat as he turned to shut the door behind him. He certainly wasn't expecting the world to go black quite so quickly.

Gregori lowered the man to the ground and signalled to the doctor. He always used to laugh at the films where the good guy quickly exchanged clothes with an unconscious enemy. In reality, it was no easy task stripping a supine dead weight and then there was the highly unlikely chance that the damned clothes would actually fit. And that was exactly the problem here. At least he had some luck as the man was overweight and so all the clothes were too big. Tightening up loose clothing was easier than trying to fit into stuff that was too small. After several minutes, he was dressed as a rather scruffy Serbian soldier. His disguise would probably not pass muster in daylight but would have to do for what he had in mind. Between him and the doctor, they bundled the soldier into a cupboard and tied his hands and legs with surgical bandages that the doctor supplied as well as making sure he wouldn't make any noise.

Gregori was preparing to leave when he looked at the man who had helped him. 'You know what I have to do now? That is if you don't want your part in this to be discovered?'

A sudden realisation appeared on the doctor's face followed by a nod of acceptance, just before Gregori's fist hit him in the side of his face. He dropped to the floor like a deadweight. Gregori quickly knelt down and made sure he was breathing and then slipped through the door.

At least Jon and Arianna were warmer now, even though they still huddled together. This time it was more for mutual support than warmth. The clothes they had been given were clearly some old castoffs, a couple of scruffy jerseys and jeans. There was no underwear and no shoes. However, Jon had been able to clean Arianna's wound properly and bind it with clean bandages. To pass the time, Jon had told Arianna all about Helen. He had meant to keep it simple but in the end the whole story had come out including how she had been instrumental in getting him out of captivity in Beirut and helping him during the hijack of the Uganda.

'She must have been a very tough lady,' Arianna said with admiration in her voice.

'Oh yes but she was also very beautiful. It was a deadly combination,' Jon responded wistfully. 'And I really meant it, if by some means we get out of here I have only one priority and that's getting hold of Peter Johnson.'

Arianna laughed. 'You must be part Croat Jon, we understand the meaning of retribution. It what's driven me all this time.'

'Yes, people say that revenge is not worth the effort. Well excuse me but I want to find out for myself.'

He was about to say more when there was the sound of a distant explosion, followed by several more and then the sound of running feet over their heads. Jon shot to his feet and ran up the stairs but the door was firmly locked.

'Do you think we are under attack Jon? Arianna asked, a note of hope creeping into her voice. 'Could it be my people?'

'I don't think so Arianna.' Jon replied. 'This is a big camp. I saw that as we drove in and it looked well prepared. Also, we are a long way from any of the main fighting. If you ask me this is a centre of operations for the siege of Sarajevo. No, it's got to be something else.'

They both looked at each other and said the same thing together. 'Gregori.'

'Well, if it is, we need to be prepared. Can you walk?' Jon asked as he helped Arianna to her feet.

She winced as she put her weight on the injured foot. 'If I have to I'll run on the damn thing.'

Jon was about to say something more when there was a dull thud from upstairs and the door flung itself open. The barrel of an AK47 poked around as a Serbian soldier looked in. It took Jon only a second to recognise the face.

Before he could speak Gregori beckoned with the rifle. 'Quick, we only have minutes. Can Arianna walk and where the hell is Johnson?'

Jon helped Arianna up the stairs. 'Johnson has gone. I'll tell you later. Now, what's the plan and what the hell are those explosions?' as Jon said it, the building was rocked by yet another loud crash.

'Silly sods put their fuel dump next to an ammunition store. These people really are amateurs. Mind you, it's lucky the soldier I borrowed this uniform from was a smoker as the matches really came in handy. And as for the plan, we run like hell.'

Chapter 38

Rupert was tearing his hair out in frustration. No one seemed to know anything. MI6 normally had a good relationship with the UN but that was through the main headquarters in New York and in this case they seemed to know as little as he did. There was no direct way to talk to Belgrade although Rupert was pulling all the strings he had with the Foreign Office. Again he had hit a brick wall. After Belgrade had issued the first release of information it was almost as if they were regretting it and were clamming up.

He was sitting in his office when Ruth ran in. She looked terrible. 'Rupert turn on your television, get CNN now.'

Rupert did as he was asked. He kept a small TV on a side table and very quickly the familiar screen of the American news channel was displayed. The grim voice of a newsreader was talking over the picture of an upside down burned out car. UN markings could just be distinguished in the blackened paint. A feeling of dread ran down his spine.

The newsreader was just concluding. 'And it has been confirmed that three UNPROFOR observers were killed in the accident which no one so far is claiming to be their action. Over now to Belgrade where the sole survivor has been allowed to talk to us.'

Suddenly, the face of Peter Johnson appeared. He looked haggard and a large plaster was over his nose. He was sitting on what appeared to be a hospital bed. A question was asked off camera. 'Mister Johnson, you were travelling in the car can you tell us what happened?'

He looked into the camera. 'I can't tell you much, to tell the truth. One moment we were travelling down a small side road and then the car was upside down. I must have been thrown clear somehow. I tried to help the others but there was nothing I could do. Then some Serbian soldiers came and took me to their base.'

'And you can confirm that the other occupants were all dead?'

'Oh God,' Johnson put his head in his hands. 'Have you ever seen a person burned to death? Sorry, the sight will haunt me for the rest of my life but yes there's no way they could have got out.'

'I'm sorry, I realise this must be hard for you. Was there any indication over who attacked you?'

Retribution

'Oh, didn't they tell you? It was almost certainly an old Second World War landmine. The area should have been cleared years ago but it seems that they didn't do too thorough a job. The Serbs found the remains of the thing in the ditch. Our wheel must have just clipped it and it flipped us over.'

Rupert reached over and turned off the television, he felt sick. 'Can this be true Ruth? I don't trust that shit Johnson as far as I could throw him but I don't see why he should be lying over this do you?'

Ruth didn't answer, she was completely overwhelmed. 'We need to see the bodies. What did they do with them?'

'Come on Ruth, what are the chances? It happened in the middle of a war zone and what would it prove?'

'I don't know but I don't believe anything that oily bastard says on principle.'

'Come on, what would he have to hide? But look, I promise I'll continue to dig around. There are still a great deal of unanswered questions. You were getting quite fond of Jon weren't you?'

She didn't answer just sat there sobbing.

In the kitchen of his married quarter in Dartmouth, Brian Pearce and Kathy had just finished watching the same news item.

Brian spoke first. 'I don't believe it. He's indestructible.'

Kathy got up and put her arms around her husband. 'What else is there to believe Brian? There was always some risk to that job.'

'But a fucking World War Two landmine? And what the hell was he doing there in the first place? It's hardly near Belgrade where he was meant to be based. Right, I'm going to open that bloody parcel.'

He went over to a cabinet and took down an A4 sized brown parcel. It had arrived a few days earlier and was addressed in Jon's handwriting. It also had a letter attached which had said Brian was only to open the parcel if anything untoward happened to Jon. Well now was the time. He opened it and another sheet of paper fell out. Again it was in Jon's writing.

Brian,

Sorry about the melodrama but something has happened out here which needs to go into the public domain and I don't trust some of the hierarchy here an inch. My aim is to ensure that it goes through the right channels but you're my long stop. In the parcel are a large number of photographs and some VHS tapes. There is also a copy of a statement written by a very brave young lady called Arianna Kasun. She is a Croat and the statement will explain what this is all about. I strongly suggest you do not let any of your family see the contents. Once you have seen what it's all about you will understand why. My reason for doing this is that I am about to try and return the original material to the people who commissioned it as well as save the life of the young lady who was so brave to obtain it in the first place. As I said, you are my back up plan.

Once you understand what this is all about. Please, please do not let anyone know about it until you have given the whole lot to one of our newspapers. I don't care which one, use your judgement. Again you will understand why when you've studied it. I strongly suggest that you get hold of Rupert afterwards. I won't say any more but good luck and hopefully I'll see you, Kathy and the kids again soon.

Your mate,

Jon.

Mystified, Brian found the written statement and started to read. He quickly realised that Kathy had been looking over at him. 'Sorry love, I need to look at some of this and then I promise I'll tell you what it's all about.'

Recognising the tone of her husband's voice, Kathy made some coffee and handed him a mug. He handed over Jon's letter and then the written statement. When she had finished she looked up at him. He had been leafing through the photographs. 'I don't want to see those do I?'

'Absolutely not and frankly I have no intention of watching the videos either. But what the hell are we going to do?'

'Isn't that clear? Jon was your friend and he asked you to make sure the press get that information. He must have had his reasons and who are we to argue? Its only Saturday morning, you could be in Fleet Street by this evening. I'm sure all the papers keep weekend staff.'

'Right, you can run me to the station.'

Monday morning, Brian's chosen paper, the Times, ran the whole story, with some heavily edited pictures and Arianna's statement in full. Brian had been quite firm that the reasons he had the material were not to be made public and thankfully the paper had honoured their promise. That didn't stop the paper's editorial being scathing about UNPROFOR. Some quick witted journalist had looked at the dates and realised that they had clearly been sitting on it for far too long. Within hours, the story had gone global. Yet another confirmed story about the behaviour of the Serbian nation was making headlines and this time the evidence was unequivocal and even included evidence of the involvement of government ministers. A public outcry was soon underway and a motion was tabled in the UN for urgent discussion. Even Russia seemed disinclined to use its veto this time.

For Brian and Kathy things stayed quiet but he knew it wouldn't be long before someone linked the so called attempted murder in Belgrade with the deaths in the car accident and the mysterious release of the photographs. He decided to take action. Firstly, he called on the Captain of the College and without being too specific managed to get permission to take an urgent week's leave.

The next thing he did was go home and pick up the telephone. 'Rupert? This is Brian Pearce, we need to talk.'

Chapter 39

The ditch was half full of stagnant water and was bloody cold. They had managed only a mile or so from the main camp with Gregori and Jon supporting Arianna on their shoulders before they were forced to rest. The noises from the camp behind them could still be heard and the horizon was a ruddy glow where fires were burning. Clearly, the diversion had worked as no one seemed to be in pursuit. The ditch seemed a good idea until they had slid into it, only to find it was half full. At least it provided good cover for a moment.

'We need decent clothes and more importantly something to go on our feet.' Jon said as he caught his breath.

'Well, unless we can find some habitation we're going to have to make do.' Gregori stated flatly. Look, I have this jacket. We'll cut it up and we can at least bind your feet up with cloth.'

It took them several minutes to make cloth coverings for their feet but at least they could now move in a little more comfort. The terrain was mainly cultivated fields gone to seed but not conducive to running over in bare feet.

They carried on now at a more measured pace. 'Any idea what direction we are going Gregori?' Jon asked as he looked up at the cloud covered sky. There was no moon or stars visible.

'Not really, I just went for the shortest route away from the encampment. Whatever direction we're going, we need to keep straight. The last thing we need is to go round in a bloody great circle. At least we can see where the camp is for the moment until all those flames die down.'

'Or we could find somewhere safe for the night until we can see where the sun is rising,' Jon replied. Just then, he spotted something ahead that had a regular shape. 'Hold on everyone that looks like a house or a barn.'

They stopped and Gregori went ahead to scout it out. He was soon back. 'It's some sort of workers cottage. No lights or anything. I would expect its abandoned, being this close to the Serbian army. Let's take a look.'

They crept carefully forward. Soon they could just make out what looked like a small house. It was eerily quiet. Gregori crept up

Retribution

to the front door and very carefully tried the handle. It opened with a loud creak. They all froze waiting for any response. Gregori unslung the AK47 he had kept but it stayed deathly quiet. He pushed the door partially open to minimise the noise and slipped inside. Seconds later, he beckoned the other two in. They seemed to be in some sort of hallway, although it was so dark they could barely see. Gregori risked lighting a match and they could now work out the layout. It was indeed a hall with only two doors and some stairs leading upwards. They went to the end and found what was clearly a kitchen although it was devoid of any furniture. However, there was a sink and when Jon tried it, the tap offered up a stream of cold water. They all took time to drink.

Gregori had managed to keep his watch. 'It's about two in the morning. I suggest we find somewhere more comfortable than a kitchen if there is one and get some rest. But I will check around and see if I can find any more clothing or something better to make shoes out of.'

Jon agreed but insisted on helping. They went into the other ground floor room and were rewarded with an old sofa. Jon insisted that Arianna lay down and the two men went searching. Upstairs, there were two bedrooms, both empty and a bathroom. They went back downstairs and had a look outside. The cloud was starting to break and a half moon was providing a little light. Enough to see that there was a barn off to one side. Once again it was almost empty but then Jon found an old car tyre leaning against one wall.

'Gregori look around and see if you can find anything sharp and any old rope or twine.' Jon said.

At the back of the barn were several old wooden boxes. Jon looked carefully in them. One was empty but the other contained several old hacksaw blades. Just what he was looking for. Then Gregori returned with a large amorphous lump of tangled bailing string. 'Will this do Jon?'

'Yup, now we can make some decent footwear.'

They went back to the living room and with the ragged old curtains pulled clear, there was just enough light for Jon to see what he was doing. Arianna was asleep so they let her carry on. He used the hacksaw blades to cut out lengths of car tyre and then trimmed away the sidewalls so that there was enough to almost wrap up a foot. 'We need something to drill holes in the rubber, can you see if there's anything in the kitchen please Gregori?' Jon asked as he sawed away at another piece of tyre.

Within minutes, Gregori was back with an old corkscrew.

'I don't suppose you found a bottle to go with that? I could murder a drink.' Jon said.

'Sorry Boss, no food or anything. They really cleaned the place out.'

'Wouldn't you with that bunch of murderous bastards camping nearby? Anyway, let's try one of my elegant shoes on. You know, I saw this done on a Caribbean island some years back, they actually looked quite comfortable.'

Jon had laced one of the rubber shoes with twine. When he put his foot in and tied the laces it wrapped snugly around his foot. He stood to give it a try.

'Hmm, no heel but that's a million times better than what we had before. Come on Gregori, let's finish the others, then we can take turns at watch and get some rest.'

The rest of the short night passed quietly but by half past five it was starting to get light. Jon was on watch with Arianna who had woken earlier. Both were wearing their new fashion shoes and waiting for the dawn. They were both disappointed to see where the sun was rising. The horizon was brightening over the camp they had escaped from which meant that was east. The problem was, that meant that they had fled westwards in the night and that meant directly towards Sarajevo. They now must have the whole Serbian army between them and escape. Gregori came and joined him. Jon indicated the rising sun. 'Guess we could have chosen a better direction last night Gregori.'

'Actually Sir, what we need is communications and the city still has those in abundance. There should also be shelter, medical attention and food. In my opinion it's not a bad place to make for especially as the Serbs should be all behind us.'

'Good point. Let's find anything to put water into and get out of here. It can't be too far to the city and we need to get as far away as we can. They'll be out looking for us already, I'm sure.' Jon was about to say more when he was interrupted by a sound in the sky like tearing calico which turned into a savage roar as two jet aircraft shot overhead. In the blink of an eye they were past and they saw something black tumble from both of them. Seconds later, there were several massive blasts from the direction of the Serbian camp followed by a gout of flame and thick, black, oily smoke.

'Fuck me, those are French Super Etendards,' Jon exclaimed. 'Last time I encountered them they were trying to kill us during the Falklands. Mind you, I suspect that these are French rather than Argentinian.'

They watched as the aircraft pulled up in a steep climb and turned over their heads clearly intent on another bombing run.

'That's not a good idea,' Gregori said. 'Even I know you should never attack a target from the same direction twice. When I was looking around the camp last night I saw that they had some good mobile SAM sites around the perimeter. Still, at least I doubt the Serbs will come looking for us now, what with the little diversion last night and now this. Something seems to have woken NATO up at last. I wonder what?'

Jon was wondering whether his little parcel to Brian had anything to do with it when he was distracted by the scream of the approaching jets. This time they opened up with cannon. It sounded like paper tearing and they could clearly see the stream of gas coming out of the gun muzzles. Once again, they pulled up and inverted over their heads, clearly intending to come back for a third run.

However, this time there were two white streaks of smoke and flame coming up at them from the ground. Both machines rolled upright and the smoke and small glowing spheres of infra-red decoy flares shot out of the rear of each. The second missile was clearly seduced and veered off and well clear. The first one was close enough to the rear aircraft that it carried on regardless. Suddenly, there was a gout of flame from the jet pipe of the second Etendard and bits started to fly off. The whole tail plane then separated and just before the whole machine broke up there was yet another gout of flame from the cockpit. This time, it was from the pilot's ejection seat. A parachute quickly deployed and drifted out of sight behind some trees to the west.

Then, all the noise had gone except for the sound of the sole retreating jet. Jon got to his feet. 'Oh bugger, maybe the Serbs won't be coming for us now but I bet they will be for that poor bloody pilot. We're much closer and we saw where he came down.

I know we have our own priorities but I would like to suggest we see what can do for him, any objections?'

'You've forgotten something else Jon,' Gregori said.

'Oh, what?'

'If we find him he should have an emergency radio of some sort. We could call for help.'

'That's a very good point Gregori. Arianna are you up for it?'

'Well, it's almost directly in the direction we were going anyway Jon,' she said as she peered towards the trees blocking their direct view. 'Let's go.'

They took a few minutes to fill some old plastic bottles they had found with water and set off towards the trees.

Chapter 40

The committee room in MI6 was large enough to seat at least thirty people. Today, there were only four. Rupert, Ruth, Graham Peters, the Head of MI6 and Brian Pearce were sitting at one end looking at a video tape being displayed on a TV monitor.

'Commander Pearce, the evidence you managed to get published was only part of the story. These images were provided separately and show things that happened in the area of Srebrenica in the east of Croatia. They've been in the hands of the UN for a little while as well. I'm afraid the whole incident does not reflect well on the Dutch soldiers who were there or the hierarchy of UNPROFOR for that matter. These are unedited and I hope you have a strong stomach.' Graham Peters turned on the tape.

The four of them watched for almost fifteen minutes and then the tape was turned off. Brian did indeed feel sick. They had just watched Serbian women raped and murdered. One was pregnant. Then there was the mass murder of men in various locations. All the film was taken with some sort of amateur camera. The quality was poor but that didn't detract from the effect.

'So, are you suggesting that my release of the 'rape party' tapes has prompted the UN into action at last?' he asked.

'Impossible to say Brian,' Rupert answered. 'But this morning at the request of the UN 'Operation Deliberate Force' had been authorised. This is going to use air strikes to target Serbian positions threatening all the UN safe areas. Not only that but UNPROFOR artillery has been let off the leash to retaliate. I think the Serbs are in for a nasty surprise as of this morning.'

'Jon's sacrifice wasn't in vain,' Ruth said with a catch in her voice.

'So, no further word about what happened to him?' Brian asked. 'When is Peter Johnson coming home? I assume you are going to be talking to him.'

'Actually Brian, that's going to be difficult for us.' Rupert stated.

'What? The man was in the accident with them and has gone on television stating what happened. And from what I can gather you lot have grave suspicions about him. Where the hell is he now?' Brian asked angrily.

'Still in Belgrade but we are expecting him back any day now,' Rupert replied. 'He will report to a Coroner when he gets back and make a statement and that's it. As you know, he has friends in very high places. We do have some very limited evidence that he may have been involved in subverting the results of the inquest into Helen's car accident but it certainly won't be admissible in court so we are stuck, unless we can get any more evidence that is. Ruth will give you a detailed briefing on that after this meeting.'

'Shit, so you can't get him in the basement and kick the crap out of him then?' Brian asked grimly.

'I know how you feel Brian,' Ruth interjected. 'But we need to tread very carefully here. And by the way, your ideas on how we conduct interrogation haven't been used by us since the dark ages.'

'Who said anything about interrogation? I just want to beat the hell out of him. Sorry that's a bit silly but if he had anything to do with Helen's death he deserves more than that.'

'Commander Pearce, we understand your frustration,' Graham Peters interjected. 'Your release of those photos could have been very unfortunate for you. I hope you realise that?'

'Now hang on, I was merely carrying out the wishes of a dead friend and would do the same again.' Brian said grimly.

'Yes, we understand that but it would probably have been more sensible if you had come to us first.'

'Bollocks, sorry Sir but that evidence needed to be shown as soon as possible and we all know it. I'm not saying the British government would have sat on it but can you guarantee that it wouldn't have? All it would have taken was a request from the UN and there would have been endless discussions wouldn't there?' Brian asked with a note of asperity.

'Yes, you're probably right,' Graham sighed. 'But Commander, you took a real risk to your career. I hope you realise that?'

Brian just looked stubborn. 'I would do it again, at the drop of a hat and bugger my career.'

'Hmm, well, we might just want to ask you to help us a little more.' Rupert said. 'Now that you're involved in this, you could be of great help to us.'

Brian looked interested. 'Of course, you know I'll help. What can I do?'

Retribution

'Before we go into that Brian, this is effectively seconding you to work for us. We will have to ask the navy for your cooperation and we won't be able to tell them why. Even if we are successful nothing will ever appear on your record.'

Brian just laughed. 'Like our time in the Arctic then? We didn't exactly get any recognition for that either. Even if we did help stop World War bloody Three.'

'Point made Brian,' Rupert replied with a wry grin. 'I was involved in that too, remember? Anyway, for the moment, we can't really approach Johnson but you certainly can. You were Jon's closest friend and would clearly like to know more. He can hardly refuse you. You go back to the day job and when he's back in the country we'll let you know and give you contact details.'

'Fine,' Brian replied. 'But what exactly do you want me to do? It's not as if I'm a spook and let's face it, subtlety and tact were never my strongpoints.'

'No, we recognise that but if you were able to get to him in a social situation, he might loosen up enough for us to get some sort of lead.'

'You mean get him pissed and then pump him?'

'Something like that. Err, we might just be able to give you a kick start with that idea. We have a very clever drug that you could slip into a drink. It's just about untraceable but is remarkably effective at loosening tongues. But we would only suggest that as a last resort. The first thing would be purely to get to talk to him and see if he lets anything slip.'

'Fine by me.'

'Right, well, you get back to work now. We will have a quiet word with the Admiralty so that you can slip away at short notice when we have the green light.'

After Brian had left with Ruth, Graham turned to Rupert. 'Are we doing the right thing Rupert? He said it himself, he's hardly the subtle type.'

'I've known Brian Pearce since nineteen eighty two. He's an exceptionally competent man, more so than he thinks and like us he's taken the death of Jon Hunt very hard. They were friends and colleagues since they both joined the navy. You know some of the things they've achieved together. I trust him implicitly.'

'As long as he doesn't end up kicking the hell out of Johnson,' Graham replied. 'He's a large man.'

'You know, I wonder if that would be such a bad thing.'

Chapter 41

Gregori scouted ahead while Jon helped Arianna. The 'shoes' they were now wearing were proving remarkably comfortable and Arianna's wound was hurting her far less. Even so, she found that leaning on Jon's shoulder was comforting in more ways than one. The undergrowth between the trees wasn't too dense but as soon as they entered them, it was proving almost impossible to see beyond a few yards and without a compass, it was going to be very hard to keep in a straight line. Luckily for them, there was a noise in the distance that they could track. It was the sound of burning with the occasional crack of exploding ammunition from the wreck of the Super Etendard. Jon just hoped that the pilot had escaped the fireball as he came down. His ejection had been very much at the last minute.

They soon found out. With little warning, they caught sight of something white in the trees above them and it was quickly apparent that it was a parachute. The pilot was harder to spot as he was dressed in a green flight suit. Gregori was the first to see him, well above the ground, dangling in his harness from a large branch. He wasn't moving.

'Oh shit, how the hell are we going to get him down?' Jon asked, looking at the slightly swinging body. 'Dammit, is he even alive?' The pilot's eyes were shut, his head lolling at an angle and it was impossible to see if his chest was moving.

Gregori solved the problem by efficiently climbing the tree and shinning out along the branch that was holding the parachute cords. 'Yes, he's breathing' he called down. 'I'm going to cut these cords one at a time. Hopefully, that will control his descent. You two get ready to grab him or catch him if I get this wrong.'

Jon looked up as he and Arianna positioned themselves under the body. Gregori's idea almost worked and the pilot dropped in a series of jerks until he was just above their heads. Then suddenly, he fell the last six feet. Jon did his best to cushion his fall but was knocked to the ground himself as the pilot's limp body fell on top of him. He quickly scrambled clear and with Arianna's help got the pilot into a prone position. Meanwhile, Gregori seemed to be doing something further up the tree. Just as they had managed to release the pilot

Retribution

from his parachute harness, something white floated down and covered them. They quickly realised it was the parachute itself.

Gregori joined them, he was breathing hard. 'Had to get that down, it was a beacon for anyone looking for him from the air and they did have at least one helicopter. At least that was before this guy bombed the shit out of them. How is he?'

'Good thinking Gregori.' Jon replied. 'He seems intact and he's breathing but he's definitely out for the count. We're going to have to remove his helmet.'

Jon and Arianna carefully removed his oxygen mask which was still clipped up and then undid the chin strap. Jon looked for the little clamping levers that he was used to on a British helmet but there didn't seem to be any so with Arianna helping support the man's head, he carefully levered it off. There was a large scuff mark on one side although it appeared intact. Jon wondered if this was what had knocked him out but also worried whether he was doing the right thing. If there was a head injury, it might have been better to leave the helmet on. But they were a long way from help and it couldn't stay fitted for any length of time. As the helmet came clear, Jon was relieved that there didn't seem to be any physical signs of damage.

They lowered the pilot's head carefully back and Arianna noticed the pilot's eyes flicker. She leaned closer and he opened them fully. For a second they were unfocused and then they looked straight at her. He said something in French which she didn't understand and smiled.

'What did he say Jon?' she asked. 'You speak his language don't you?'

'Oh yes,' Jon laughed.' And he said, and I quote, 'Am I in heaven because you must be an angel.'

Gregori laughed as well. 'Only a Frenchman would be chatting up girls before he even became fully conscious.'

Arianna realised she was blushing. 'Jon, you'd better talk to him.' But as she said it she couldn't help notice how good looking this French pilot was and he was still smiling at her.

Jon knelt down again. 'Hello, my name is Jon how do you feel?'

The pilot looked at him and gave a double take. 'Who are you? You speak perfect French but you look like a refugee.'

'Sorry about that. Actually, my name is Jonathon Hunt. I am a Royal Navy Captain, working for the United Nations. We were captured by the Serbs and were making our escape when we saw you get shot down.'

Jon saw the man's eyes narrow in suspicion as he looked around and took in Arianna who was similarly dressed and then Gregori who was in Serbian uniform. 'Then who is he?'

'That my friend, is Gregori and he is Russian Special Forces and works for me. The reason he is in that uniform is that he used it to help us make our escape. Look, you can believe us or not but the real Serbs will be here soon. Do you want to risk that? Now, what is your name and are you hurt anywhere else? You seem to have taken a knock on the head, looking at the damage to your helmet.'

The pilot's face hardened. 'My name is Henri le Clerc, Lieutenant de Vaisseau, my date of birth is twenty two April, nineteen eighty two and my number is six, five, seven, three, bravo. I will say no more.'

Jon sighed. He could understand why the pilot was so reluctant to trust them. He was probably in severe shock amongst other things. 'Look, can you stand? We can't stay here.'

Henri grimaced and tried to sit up. He gave a small cry of anguish and lay back, his face white. Jon realised the problem straight away and reached down and pinched the skin of his leg through his flight suit. 'Henri, can you feel this?'

'Yes. Please stop. That hurts. Oh, you are checking if my back is broken?'

'Yes, you've just ejected from an aircraft. It's a common injury. However, I'm not sure it's actually broken. You've probably just damaged some vertebrae.' Jon looked at his colleagues. 'We've got a real problem here. We're going to have to carry him to Sarajevo if we don't want the Serbs to get him.'

'Why do you want to go to Sarajevo? It's under siege.' Henri interjected.

'Hang on, we were talking English then. Do you speak it Henri?' Jon asked.

'Yes, I spent several years on exchange flying British Sea Harriers.'

Retribution

'Good, then you will know my old friends Pete Cummings, Charlie Cannon and Mike Southgate?' Jon asked. 'I am a helicopter pilot myself but I occasionally talk to the stovies.'

Henri's face cleared. 'Yes and I think I know you. You were the pilot who shot down the Pucara in the Falklands War, no? And you helped with that hijacked ship. Yes, oh thank goodness.' He looked around at the other two. 'Sorry but it's been a rather bad day for me so far,' he looked at Arianna and grinned. 'Mind you, a pretty face is always good to see.'

Arianna didn't know what to say for a few seconds and then smiled back. There was something very attractive about this man. He was small and wiry, with a shock of dark black hair and twinkling blue eyes. She would have to keep an eye on him she decided.

'Henri, we need to get you and ourselves to safety and the only direction we can go is towards the city. Do you have an emergency radio or any other survival aids? Jon asked.

'Yes, I have a survival pack. It should have been attached to me. Is it caught up in a tree?'

The three of them looked around. Jon spotted a yellow canister dangling from another of the branches and pointed it out to Gregori. 'Off you go Tarzan. You seem to be the expert tree climber.'

Gregori nodded and was back in a matter of minutes with a fibre glass box. Henri lifted his head and told them how to open it. Inside was a red one man dinghy for use over the sea and also a large pack of survival gear, including flares, some water, a small compass and other minor equipment. Best of all was a small package which Jon immediately recognised as the same that was used by British aircrew. It was a SARBE or Search and Rescue Beacon. There was also a large knife which he knew they would be needing very soon.

'Listen everyone, we could activate this beacon now.' Jon said. 'It makes a distress tone on the aircraft emergency frequency but it will also act as a beacon for the Serbs. I strongly suggest we don't use it until we get well clear of here and even then, it could be the wrong thing to do.'

'I agree,' Henri said. 'Our instructions were to use it very carefully and only when a NATO aircraft was visible and then only for a short time.'

Retribution

Gregori looked thoughtful. 'Let's get to Sarajevo first then. If Henri isn't able to walk, we need to make a stretcher. If that helicopter had survived then the Serbs would already be here but they aren't but it won't take them long even on foot.'

'Oh, don't worry about that,' Henri interjected. I shot it to pieces on our second pass, even though I told our leader that going back a second time was a stupid thing to do. It exploded rather well I thought.'

Jon turned to his two companions. 'We need to make a stretcher. When I did my survival training we had to carry one of our team only five miles with six people and it nearly killed us but we have no choice if we want to get Henri to safety. So, Arianna, you and I will start folding up that parachute and Gregori, you go and cut down two good branches with that knife.'

They set to work and within a remarkably short time had a serviceable stretcher. Getting Henri onto it was a different matter. Luckily, he wasn't a large man and by careful manipulation they managed to get him comfortable. They tried an experimental lift and Jon realised just how hard this was going to be.

Before they set off, Jon turned to the pilot. 'Henri, you've seen the area from the air. Are there any roads nearby?' He asked. 'I'm thinking maybe we could steal a car or even a tractor from a farm. It's a good few miles to the main city.'

'Actually, there are extensive suburbs only a few miles to the west,' Henri replied. 'Our intelligence is that they have been deserted but if we could get there we might find a car. We will certainly find some shelter if we need it as well as water and maybe food. You two could even find some decent clothes.'

'Good point. Right due west it is.'

Chapter 42

The day had proved to be very hot. By mid morning, Jon was only wearing his jeans but still felt light headed with heat and exhaustion. As he had predicted, two people carrying a stretcher was just about bloody impossible. Henri probably only weighed about seventy kilograms but that meant he and Gregori were carrying thirty five each or in English, almost eighty pounds. Arianna had managed to make up some straps so that they could put some of the load around their necks and on their shoulders but even so, if they made half a mile before they had to stop to rest they were doing well. Also, they had run out of water despite being as careful as possible.

'I thought you Spetsnaz people were ultra fit?' Jon asked wearily, as they sat for another stop, in the shade of several trees. 'You seem as knackered as me.'

Gregori barked out a tired laugh. 'Maybe ten years ago Jon, things have changed and I haven't got any younger. Mind you, you're not doing badly for an old man.'

'Look, let me try to walk,' Henri interjected.

'Alright then my French friend, let's see you sit up first.' Gregori replied.

Henri struggled to lift his torso but even with using his hands, he could hardly move a few inches before the pain was too much. He lay back on the stretcher with a muttered oath.

'So, no walking then Henri,' Jon said. 'You'll just have to put up with being chauffeured around by us for a little longer. By the way, where were you flying from? Italy I suppose.'

'No,' Henri replied. 'Our carrier the Clemenceau is just offshore. She is not working that well as the catapults are not the most reliable but it cuts our sortie time down by well over half.'

'Does she have any helicopters?' Jon asked.

'Yes for plane guard but not really suited for extraction. But you have your carrier Illustrious as well and she has several Sea Kings I believe.'

'Good, once we can make contact we should be able to get out one way or another. Right, I think we should get going again it can't be much further. Arianna, how do you feel about scouting ahead? You seem to be able to limp faster than we can stagger.' Jon asked.

Arianna nodded and went on ahead while Jon and Gregori forced themselves to their feet once again. They had only managed a few hundred yards when Arianna came, half running, half limping back to them. 'I think the reason we have not encountered any pursuit is that they have moved ahead of us by road and are combing the ground back towards us. There is a line of soldiers in the open ground ahead. Even if we stay in these trees, they will soon be on us.'

'Shit, Gregori, you are the expert what do we do?' Jon asked.

Gregori looked around carefully. 'We can't run or hide in the trees so we have to dig. We need to scoop out shallow pits and use some of these dead leaves to cover ourselves. The three of us need to do Henri first and then we can do each other. I will be last to make sure you have done it properly.'

They didn't have much time but luckily there was a tangle of some sort of bush just off to one side of the route they had been following and they were able to use that for cover as well. With only minutes to spare, they were hidden. At least Jon hoped they were, there was little else they could have done in the time. Funnily, despite the danger, he was actually enjoying the rest as he lay prone and tried to calm his breathing. For a while, he couldn't hear a thing and then he caught the sound of someone calling in Serbian. For a second, he felt panic rise as he thought that they had been discovered. Then he was able to make out the words and realised it was only one soldier asking his friend for a cigarette. If that was what was worrying them, he suspected that they weren't looking that hard. He seemed to be right because the voices slowly faded into the distance. He was just wondering whether it was safe to break cover when Gregori called softly to them all to do just that.

Brushing dirt and leaves off himself Jon had a thought. 'Anyone reckon on how far away you think their vehicles might be?'

Gregori answered first. 'They sounded pretty fresh. I guess it can't be far what are you thinking?'

'Why walk when you can ride?'

In fact, another agonising hour of walking proved that the road the soldiers must have used was further away than they had first thought but maybe that was because the two men were on the verge of total exhaustion. Jon realised that they would have to stop soon, no matter what. If necessary they would have to hole up for the night somewhere. There was no way they could continue much further, especially with no water.

Arianna had continued with her scouting duties and suddenly reappeared from up ahead. They had been skirting the edge of yet another wood so that they could quickly disappear into the trees if they had to.

Breathlessly, she told them what was ahead. 'I've found a small military vehicle. It has a radio aerial and a couple of soldiers but nothing else. There's no sign of lorries or anything.'

'Actually, that makes sense,' Jon replied. 'If they are combing the ground between here and the crash site then they would send their transport on ahead to pick them up from the other end. The vehicle must be for a radio link. Anyone fancy borrowing it?'

There was no dissent, only talk about tactics. Gregori had an AK47, Henri produced his personal nine millimetre pistol that was in a pocket of his flying suit and they had the large knife.

'Do we ambush them or just shoot them from a distance?' Arianna asked although it was clear from the way she said it that shooting was her preferred option.

'Ambush Arianna,' Jon said. 'Weapons fire can be heard from a long distance. We don't want any friends they have in the area coming to see what's going on.'

She looked disappointed but accepted Jon's logic.

'Well, I am sort of dressed as a Serbian soldier why don't I divert them and you two can sneak up from behind,' Gregori offered. 'Are you sure there are only two Arianna?'

'Yes, I watched for a while. One was in the driving seat, the other in the rear. When he got out I could see that there was no one else.'

'Good, then this is what I suggest we do,' Gregori explained.

The two Serb soldiers were bored stiff. They had been ordered to stay and maintain a radio watch until dusk and absolutely nothing was happening. Occasional calls on the radio made it clear that nothing had been found. They were not surprised. It was a big country and one enemy pilot could easily make himself scarce. As for the escaped prisoners, they could be anywhere by now.

Retribution

Suddenly, they saw one of their soldiers limping towards them. He was dishevelled, had a bandage around his head and had clearly been hurt. He waved, then he dropped to his knees, clearly in pain. The two soldier immediately ran towards him as he slowly toppled, face first, onto the ground. As the two men arrived at his prone body, he suddenly rolled over and they found themselves staring straight into the barrel of a small pistol. At the same time they heard the distinctive sound of an AK47 being cocked behind them. One soldier turned and blinked in surprise when he saw a pretty young girl holding the weapon. Pretty she might have been but the look on her face was pure murder. Suddenly, another man appeared dressed like the girl in jeans. Both had strange looking shoes on their feet.

The man spoke. 'Now that was silly. Your weapons are still by your vehicle. Don't they teach you anything in the Serbian military?'

Ten minutes later, Jon and Arianna were luxuriating in the comfortable boots that they had liberated. Both pairs had proved too big for Arianna but with some of the parachute now wrapped around her feet they fitted adequately and were far better than an old car tyre. They were finishing off tying up the two soldiers with strips torn from their uniforms. Meanwhile, Gregori had unceremoniously ripped out the radio equipment from the back of the old Land Rover that the soldiers had been using and made enough room for Henri to be loaded up. As soon as they were ready, Jon and Gregori jumped in the front. This time, Jon insisted on driving saying that as it was a British vehicle, it was his privilege and not saying out loud that his mad Russian deputy's style of driving was too bloody scary. As he climbed in, he spotted a road map on the dashboard which he passed to Gregori. 'Right, get us to Sarajevo as fast as you can.'

The track they were on soon led out of the forested area. They started to occasionally glimpse houses set back off the road but despite the almost overwhelming temptation to stop and at least try to get some water, Jon insisted that they continue. It was only a few kilometres to go and they would be safe. Suddenly, a metalled road was visible. Jon turned left as directed by his navigator and floored the throttle. It was clear that they were entering the suburbs of a large town although it was eerily quiet. There was no traffic and no sign of people at all.

Suddenly, Jon pulled up. 'There's something we've forgotten.'

'What?' Gregori asked perplexed.

'We're driving flat out, into a besieged town, in a vehicle clearly belonging to the besiegers. What do you think they are liable to do when they see us? Open fire or simply wave us through?'

'Shit, I hadn't thought of that,' Gregori said. 'What do we do?'

Jon called into the back. 'Arianna we need squares of that white parachute material. Tie one to that radio aerial and give one to Gregori. Gregori, tie one to the barrel of your AK and hold it out of the window. I am going to drive quite slowly from now on and we all pray that the inhabitants aren't completely trigger happy.'

Chapter 43

The Cotswold villages Brian was driving through looked absolutely delightful in the mid morning summer sun. He realised it was one thing to look but on a naval officer's salary there was no way he would ever be able to afford to live here. He was also having a little trouble navigating. One would have thought that an estate of the size he was looking for would be easy to find, after all it had over fifty acres of land to go with it. Eventually, he was forced to stop and ask for directions. The drive, when he finally found it, was almost hidden and the large iron gates across it were firmly shut. He parked the car before them and went up to the little intercom post on the side.

Instructions were written on the side so he pressed the button down and talked into the grill. 'Commander Pearce here to see Mister Johnson. I am expected.' He waited expectantly but there was no reply. Suddenly, the gates started to silently swing open. Taking that as his cue, he jumped back in the car and drove into the estate. The road was a single track tarmac strip in excellent repair which wound through a large stand of trees and then into open country side. Sheep were grazing on open fields to both sides but there was no sign of the house he was looking for. After over a mile, the road swung hard to the left and suddenly he could see a roof over yet more trees. Within minutes, he was parking in front of an imposing red brick Tudor house which had a more modern wing built on one side. His wasn't the only car on the drive, a large Range Rover, a new Audi and an old Triumph sports car were also parked up outside of a large outbuilding which looked like a garage and workshop.

He went up to the imposing oak front doors but before he could knock they swung inwards and a very attractive blonde woman came up and gave him an unexpected and quite delightful hug.

'Brian, it's so good to see you, you're looking so well, it's been ages since I last saw you,' Inga Johnson declared as she pulled back to look at him. A shadow then crossed her face. 'I'm so sorry about Jon. I know we didn't part on the most amicable of terms but I always had a soft spot for him. It's so unfair what happened to him.'

Retribution

Brian looked at Jon's old girlfriend from Norway. She hadn't aged very much at all but she had matured. She had been a very pretty young girl and now was a beautiful woman. He wondered just how much was the product of expensive couture, after all her husband was not short of cash.

'Inga, it's good to see you too. You look ravishing as always but as you know I'm here to see your husband. Is he in?'

'Of course, he's expecting you. I just wanted to come and say hello and pass on my condolences. Let me take you to his study.'

As she led him through the house chatting away, Brian was extremely impressed. Not only was it clearly very old but it was impeccably decorated. He mentally reckoned he could retire on the value of the furniture he could see even before they got to their destination.

Inga opened another oak panelled door and ushered him into a snug room with a large bay window overlooking extensive manicured lawns. There were several tennis courts in the distance.

'Brian Pearce I assume,' Peter Johnson said, smiling and extending his hand as he stood from behind a large antique desk.

'Yes, good morning Sir. I'm glad you could give me some time,' Brian replied, giving an even firmer handshake back than the one he had been given.

'None of that 'Sir' stuff please. I retired ages ago. I'm just a civilian now as I repeatedly told your friend. I assume you're here to find out some more about what happened to him in Croatia and you will stay for lunch?'

Brian wasn't expecting such a friendly welcome, indeed he hardly knew what he was expecting and could hardly refuse. 'I'd be delighted thank you.' he replied.

'Good, come and sit with me and I'll tell you all I know, although I expect you probably know most of it anyway. Inga my love, could you get us some coffee?'

Inga left without a word.

Brian studied his host. It was clear he had been in some sort of accident recently. There were the remains of a bruise above his left eye and the way he held himself indicated he was quite stiff.

Johnson started to speak. He told Brian about the contract he had taken on and how he had reported to the UN in Belgrade and met Jon. He inferred that they were working together although Brian had already been appraised that, in fact, he was working for Jon. He wondered how that had gone down with both of them. He very briefly mentioned the release of the two Serbs but didn't mention who had been instrumental in getting them released. He then dwelt on Jon's ideas to get Arianna and her photographs out of Belgrade.

'It was all Jon's idea then?' Brian asked. 'Why did you go with them?'

'Well, I needed to tour the area anyway and it seemed a good idea. It was all seen as very low risk and if we were stopped, I could provide the ideal cover for the girl. She was pretending to be my secretary.'

'So you stopped for the night in the outskirts and then headed off towards Croatia the next day. Why didn't you have an escort? I thought that was standard procedure?' Brian asked.

'Good question. As I understand it they were delayed and Jon decided to push on without them.' Johnson answered without hesitation.

'Hmm, that's surprising. Jon was never one to take unnecessary risks and as I understand it the soldiers had been quite useful in the past.'

'Yes but I think he saw that the greatest need was to get moving fast and just didn't want to wait.' Johnson replied blithely.

Something wasn't adding up for Brian but he couldn't quite put his finger on it. 'So, you were heading around Sarajevo and the car had the accident?'

'Yes but don't ask me what happened,' Johnson replied. 'One moment we were belting down this side road with Jon's mad Russian deputy doing the driving, the next thing I remember is lying in the road with the car upside down and on fire several yards away. Believe me, there was nothing I could do by then.'

'And you're absolutely sure that all three were in the car and didn't get out?'

'Not at first, no. When the fire died down, I went to look but frankly it was all dreadful mess. The first thing I did was to look around in case anyone else had been thrown clear but they hadn't. When I looked closely inside, I could see bodies. Have you ever seen someone who has been burned alive? It's absolutely dreadful. Then the Serbs turned up and took me back to their camp. They were really helpful and confirmed that they had found three bodies.'

'What did they do with them?' Brian asked. 'Presumably, you know where they buried them so we can exhume then at a later date when all this is over?'

A strange look fleeted across Johnson's face for a second. 'That would be a good idea but actually, I'm not sure where they buried them. I think they took them and the wreck back to the camp that I was in and buried them there somewhere. However, I gather from the news that that was one of the targets for these recent air strikes by NATO so whether there is even anyone left to know, is a moot point.'

'You're bloody well lying,' Brian immediately thought, *'that answer was just too bloody glib.'* but he didn't say anything and kept his face straight.

They talked over the issue for another half an hour but Brian learned nothing more. Lunch was a simple affair and with Inga there they only made small talk and then it was time for Brian to leave. He made his farewells and was back on the road to London by mid afternoon.

That evening, he met with Rupert and Ruth in their St Johns Wood House. He recounted everything he had been told.

When he had finished, Rupert spoke. 'Fine Brian, that's what was said. Now, what is your opinion of the man and his story?'

'Where do I start? If you ask me, he's hiding several things. Firstly, he was very vague about why they were on the road in the first place. I know Belgrade have been very cagey about that but I know, sorry, I knew Jon and he would never take silly risks, like not waiting for an escort for a start. And then when I asked him about the location of the bodies, he gave me some bollocks about the Serbs not actually telling him. Sorry but any reasonable person would have checked that. There are a couple of other things as well. During lunch, Inga barely said a word but when I arrived she would hardly shut up and also when I left as she took me back to my car. If you ask me, that is a marriage that is cracking up and maybe we should have a go at Inga without her husband around. There was one other thing as well. When I arrived there was an old Triumph sports car on the drive. It was exactly the same model as the one Helen had bought. It wasn't there when I left. I asked about it at lunch and Johnson said that he had always liked them and changed the subject pretty fast.'

'So what's your conclusion Brian,' Ruth asked.

'Frankly, I'm confused. He's clearly hiding something. My overriding feeling is that he really doesn't want the bodies found but for what reason I just can't guess. I also think he had a great deal more to do with why they were on the road in the first place but again, I can't work out what it could have been.'

'The way you explain it Brian, it's almost as if he was working for or with the Serbs,' Rupert observed. 'But why the hell would he be doing that?'

'Let's assume for the moment that he is or was a Russian spy. He could still be working for them and they are heavily involved in supporting Serbia behind the scenes,' Ruth said frowning. 'So maybe he was following instructions to help get rid of those photos.'

'That doesn't make sense Ruth,' Rupert said. 'He'd only been in the country a few days. How the hell would he manage to get involved so fast?'

They were interrupted by the telephone. Ruth reached over and picked it up from a side table. She listened for a few seconds and replied. 'It's a very bad line can you say that again?'

She listened for a few more seconds, her face screwed up in concentration, then she turned white and her hand started shaking. She looked over at Rupert and Brian with shock on her face. 'Say that again, Oh God, say it again.'

'For goodness sake, who is it Ruth?' Rupert queried.

She kept the phone clamped to her ear but managed to speak as she continued to listen. 'It's Jon. It's really him. Oh my God, it's Jon.'

Chapter 44

Jon was proved right. Literally just around the next bend was a road block. At first, it didn't seem much. Just a few oil barrels set up to block the road but then he spotted the heads of men looking up from behind concrete blocks on either side of the road. He could also see the barrels of rifles several of which seemed to have the distinctive lemon shaped heads of rocked propelled grenades attached. As soon as it was clear what they were facing, he stopped the Land Rover and took the rifle from Gregori. Very carefully, he opened his driver's door and got out. He took the fact that he hadn't immediately become the target for concentrated rifle fire as a good sign. Apart from the boots, he was still dressed as a civilian which was probably a good thing.

Very carefully, holding his white flag aloft, he approached the line of drums. 'Hello,' he shouted. 'I am a UN officer who was abducted by Serbian troops but managed to escape. In the vehicle behind me is a French pilot who flew one of the first raids against the Serbian army. Unfortunately, he was shot down and needs medical attention.'

Stony silence met his declaration.

He tried again. 'We are seeking refuge and help.' Then a thought occurred to him. 'The pilot's name is Henri le Clerc. I'm betting that you have seen something about this on one of the news channels like CNN or the BBC. My name is Captain Jonathon Hunt. There may have been something about me as well.'

The silence continued for a few more heartbeats and then there was a scuffling sound behind one of the concrete blocks. Several men appeared carrying rifles. One of them shouted to Jon while they were still a hundred yards away. 'Why are you driving a Serbian army vehicle?'

'We stole it. The original owners weren't too pleased.'

The men continued to approach cautiously. Jon decided on another gambit. 'I also have a Croatian soldier with me, a girl. She was responsible for taking photographs and film of a Serbian atrocity. Maybe that has also been on the news?'

The men came closer. One covered Jon with his rifle but said nothing. Two others went to the Land Rover. Suddenly, a conversation broke out at the rear of the vehicle. Jon could clearly hear Arianna's voice and she didn't sound pleased. In fact, she seemed to be giving the men a piece of her mind. Jon grinned inwardly. Small and petite she might be but she had the temper and courage of a lion.

The two men came back and nodded to the man covering Jon. They said something quietly in his ear and suddenly the weapons were dropped and Jon was enveloped in a bear hug. 'Welcome to Sarajevo my friend. Yes, we know all about you, although how you all came to be together is going to be a wonderful story. Please, come with us.'

An hour later, Jon, Gregori and Arianna were sitting in the Mayor of Sarajevo's office. With him were several aides and an army Colonel. Jon had just finished their story when someone came in with several bottles of spirits and shot glasses. They were quickly filled and the Mayor offered them all a toast.

'To you, my good friends. You have told us your story now we will tell you what has been happening over the last few days.' He tossed down the drink. 'You were correct about the news. We can still receive television even if the telephone lines and mobile phone masts have been destroyed by our enemy.'

Jon had made the mistake of following the Mayor's lead and tossed down his drink. He immediately wished he hadn't and started coughing. The Mayor stopped and smiled indulgently until Jon was able to breathe normally again. He then went on to confirm what Jon had surmised about news coverage. Clearly, Brian had wasted no time in releasing the photos but he was saddened to hear the news about Srebrenica although not that surprised. Maybe the UN would, at last, get off its collective arse. They had certainly got NATO on the case now. He suddenly realised he hadn't heard what the Mayor had just said.

'Sorry Sir, can you repeat that?' he asked.

'I asked what do you intend to do now? We can still communicate out. There are many high frequency radios in the city. We have some in this building. But getting you out is another matter. We are surrounded as you know.'

Jon had been putting off any decisions about just that until they reached safety. There was a lot to think about and he hadn't wanted to compromise their escape attempt but now he realised he had some serious decisions to make. Underlying it all was a core deep desire to ensure that Peter Johnson faced justice. Coming back from the dead might be exactly the wrong thing to do he realised but they needed to get Henri out whatever happened.

'I think we can organise a helicopter recovery if that is alright with you,' Jon replied to the Mayor. 'We can use the HF radio and we have an emergency beacon they can use to home in on when they are close. I strongly suggest that getting the French pilot back to his ship is a high priority. It will be another blow to Serbian propaganda. But I need to think about what to do about the rest of us. Arianna is a Croatian soldier and should probably return to her unit although I would suggest that that is up to her. Gregori and I need to think about how to handle our return. I told you about the Englishman who said we had died and I know you saw him on the television. I would hate to alert him that we are still on the planet. He could use that as a warning to escape justice.'

'But how long do you think you can keep your presence secret?' The Mayor asked.

'I've no idea so the quicker we can get home the better.' Jon replied grimly.

An hour later, the three of them were sitting together in Jon's hotel room which, given the state of the city they had seen so far, wasn't bad. They even had a working room service although the choice was extremely limited. They were so hungry, it hardly mattered and the burgers they had all ordered tasted like heaven although no one wanted to ask what they were actually made of. They had been promised some new clothes the next morning but for the moment, the fed and showered trio were luxuriating in the soft dressing gowns provided by the hotel.

Jon had just finished his second beer and was starting to at last feel some of the pressure slip away. 'So, tomorrow we go to the hospital and see how Henri is getting on. Arianna, what do you want to do?'

'I don't really know. But Henri has asked me to stay with him for a while,' she said with a challenging look on her face.

'I thought you two were getting on rather well,' Jon replied with a slight smile. 'But you do what you want to do. You've earned the right ten times over. OK, let's assume that Henri can be moved by tomorrow evening, probably still in a stretcher of course but we got him here in one so I don't see why he can't be moved, especially in a proper stretcher rather than that lash up we made. I'm pretty sure I can arrange for a Sea King to come in tomorrow night and pick us up. If I talk to the right people we can then travel onwards. Personally, I want to get back to the UK as fast as possible but I can probably arrange for you two to go just about anywhere you want.'

Gregori looked thoughtful. 'Jon, half of me wants to come with you to help you nail that bastard but although I work for the UN at the moment, I will have to go home sometime. I know it's not like the old Soviet days but I do have a career in the military and I should probably not be seen to help you overtly.'

'Understood Gregori. Both of you, just give me a couple of days before you surface. Right, I need to get dressed again. There's a radio in city hall they said I can use. I'll go and make a call. I should be able to get a phone patch into the UK network quite easily. I have some friends there who will be able to help.'

Chapter 45

Peter Johnson was, at last, starting to relax his guard. After the visit by the naval Commander friend of Hunt's he was half expecting something more. But twenty four hours on and nothing had happened. It looked like he had got away with it.

Then the phone rang.

The voice at the other end asked for a Mathew Smith. Peter explained that it was a wrong number and hung up but his hand was trembling and he had turned white. Luckily, Inga wasn't in the room to see it. He realised he had no choice. The two words were a code alert from his old days and there was only one person in the world who knew them.

He went out into the hall and called for Inga. 'Sorry darling, I have to go out. I shouldn't be long.'

A voice answered from the kitchen where Inga was indulging in her latest hobby of cooking, courtesy of several popular television programmes. 'That's alright but supper will be in about half an hour. Don't be late.'

Peter grimaced. A keen cook did not necessarily mean a good one. He had been hoping that her fad would soon run its course and the cook he paid good money to could take back her evening role. However, he had a terrible feeling that things were about to change for the worse.

He grabbed the keys to the Range Rover and set off for the nearest village where he knew there was still one of the rapidly disappearing payphones. Unsurprisingly, when he got there, no one was using it. The new mobile phones were making them a thing of the past.

He pushed open the door and was grateful to see it hadn't been vandalised and put in his credit card. He dialled a number he had hoped he would never have to use.

The voice at the other end was the same as the one earlier and he knew exactly who it was. 'Peter bad news. The three have escaped. No one knows where they are now.'

Peter didn't answer. He just stared blankly at the dirty glass of the booth. His whole world was crashing around his ears.

'Peter, did you hear me?'

Retribution

'Yes Boris. How the fuck did that happen?'

'I've no idea but it's irrelevant. They sent out search parties but the camp was bombed by NATO that morning so it wasn't exactly thorough. We've no real idea where they went but it was probably towards Sarajevo. You should assume that they will surface some time soon and take appropriate precautions.'

Peter's head was buzzing but one thing was clear to him, he needed help. 'Alright, what can you do for me?'

This time there was silence at the other end of the line for some seconds. 'Peter, I have to be honest, I spotted you in Belgrade and kept your presence to myself. I was hoping to make name for myself. I had no official support.'

'What? So what are you saying?'

'Listen, I've done all I can to give you warning, sorry but that's all I can do. Good luck.' The line went dead.

Peter froze. *What the hell was he to do?* In the old days, he could have expected some form of asylum but that was clearly out of the question. If, or more likely when, Hunt got back, his position would be untenable. His only chance was to call in every favour he had with his friends. Maybe they could get MI6 off his back long enough that he could get away somewhere. Then he had another thought. Hunt had said that the intelligence people had been looking into him so it was highly likely all his phones were being monitored. Thank God Boris had had the sense to invoke the old Soviet safety protocols but it meant he couldn't use the phone in the house. Then it came to him. There was one place that he was pretty sure no one knew he had a phone and it was well placed for a quick subsequent get away.

With his pulse racing, he jumped back into the Range Rover and drove home as fast as he dared. When he got back, he shot back into the house calling for Inga.

'Supper's almost ready,' she said smiling at him. Then she saw the look on his face. 'What's wrong?'

'Forget supper. Pack a bag. We're going to Scotland right now,' he snapped back before she could say anything more. 'Don't bloody argue woman this is an emergency, just do it. We're leaving in ten minutes.'

He was true to his word and soon they were flying out of the gates and onto the road heading for the M5. Inga was looking scared. She had never seen her husband like this. Something very serious had happened but despite all her efforts, she couldn't get anything sensible out of him. He refused to say what had happened, only that once they were there, he would explain it all.

For his part, Peter's mind was whirling with ideas none of which seemed to be practical. His initial thoughts about calling in favours might buy him some time. He was tempted to use his mobile phone from the car but again the risk that GCHQ was listening in was just too much to take. One thing he would definitely do as soon as he could was to contact the company that provided him with a private jet whenever he needed one and get it up to Prestwick as soon as they could. He thanked his stars that a large part of his fortune was carefully hidden away from the British taxman's eyes in the Cayman Islands. So the only question was where to go. There were several countries that had no extradition arrangements with the UK. It would have to be one of those. Brazil would have been a good destination but he knew a treaty had been signed some years ago, even if they hadn't released that train robber who was still there. Most of the rest were the old communist countries or China, none of which had any appeal. Then he remembered a Caribbean island that would suit. The Dominican Republic was poor but that was to the good. Being there with money would allow him to make a good life in the sun. He smiled to himself, maybe he could still have a decent retirement.

The traffic was light this late in the evening, even around the normal log jam of Birmingham and it only took six hours and they were speeding through the gates of his shooting estate in Scotland. The place was locked and all the lights were out but he had the keys and they let themselves in. He would announce himself to the staff the next day. There was no need to wake them in the middle of the night. Inga had finally stopped asking bloody questions. He was seriously beginning to wonder whether bringing her with him had been the right idea. It was too late now. He would have to tell her something.

As they got ready to climb into a cold bed, he made his decision. 'Inga, I'm sorry about all the rush but as you must realise something very serious has come up. It's to do with what happened in Croatia but I can't tell you any detail just yet. Please just trust me alright?'

Retribution

Inga was dog tired. All she wanted was bed but still didn't know what to think. 'Alright darling. Let's just get some sleep and I'm sure things will look more simple in the morning.'

The next morning, Inga was wakened by the light coming through the curtains. Bleary eyed, she looked at her watch. With a start, she realised it was almost eight o'clock. 'Peter, time to get up,' she called as she turned towards him only to find his side of the bed empty and cold.

Chapter 46

The football field hadn't seen a boot on it for several years. It was just bare earth with two sets of sagging goal posts but it was a perfect place for a helicopter covert landing. Jon, Gregori, Arianna and Henri were waiting in tense silence. To everyone's surprise, Henri had been released from hospital that morning. His back was still very sore but X-rays had revealed no broken vertebrae. He had convinced the doctors that he could walk although he was on very strong pain killers. Arianna was staying close to him and offering support.

The previous evening, Jon had managed to get in contact with Portishead radio and he had been able to put a call into Rupert's home number. Ruth had answered and it had been an emotional few minutes especially when Jon discovered that Brian was also with them. However, it wasn't that good a line and he had tried to keep things brief. The first priority was to arrange for them to be picked up. Brian said he was pretty sure he could manage that with MI6 help. Jon called again the next morning and Brian confirmed that it was arranged. Jon gave him the location. He had spotted the sports pitch the previous evening as he had been driven back from the city hall.

He had been in a quandary about what to tell them about Johnson. Part of him wanted to keep quiet until he could get back to the UK so that he could be there when the man was arrested. However, he had to be realistic. There was a good chance that their escape had already been reported back to whoever it was in the Russian Embassy that Johnson had been taking orders from. In which case he could have already been warned. He didn't dare take the risk and so gave them the bare bones of the story. Rupert said he would act on it and make sure Johnson was taken into custody which was the best Jon could hope for.

Suddenly, the distant growl of an approaching aircraft could be heard. Jon looked at Henri who nodded and switched on his SARBE radio. It would be heard in the approaching Sea King which could also home in on the radio signal. Jon expected the aircrew would almost certainly be on Night Vision Goggles as well but the signal would also confirm that they were waiting.

They didn't have to wait long. It was a dark night but there was plenty of ambient light from the city and Jon soon saw the all too familiar shape of the aircraft approaching from down-wind. It briefly hovered over the centre of the football pitch in a cloud of dust and then plonked down, tail wheel first. As soon as it was on the ground, Jon ran in followed more slowly by the others as they helped Henri. An Aircrewman was waiting for them and immediately handed Jon a flying helmet and pointed forward to the cockpit. Jon briefly turned to make sure the others were climbing in and then went forward. The pilot turned and indicated for Jon to plug into a dangling Mic/Tel lead.

'Captain Hunt Sir?' he asked.

'That's me and all my passengers are here as well. What's our first stop?' Jon asked.

'Jump into the other seat Sir and I'll brief you,' the pilot said. 'I understand that you've got a few hours on these machines?'

'Just a few although I haven't flown one for a few years now.'

'Right Sir, well my brief is to take you to the French carrier, Clemenceau first. Then we take a suck of gas and I deliver you to Italy. There's a routine Hercules flight out later tonight and I should be able to get there in time for you to get on it. What about the others? I've no brief about them.'

'They will probably all get off on the carrier. I'll sort it out while we refuel.'

'Right you are Sir. Do you think you could run through the pre-take off checks for me?' the pilot asked and he handed Jon a set of flip cards. 'Normally my crewie does it but I'm sure you remember them.'

An hour later, they were over the sea. In the distance, the shape of a large carrier could be seen and after making contact by radio, the Sea King was cleared to land on the stern. Once safely on deck, Jon climbed out of his seat and turned to see his comrades clustered around the forward passenger door which the crewman was opening and then lowering the steps outward.

Henri turned and shook Jon's hand and then Arianna gave him a massive hug and kiss on the cheek. It was too noisy to speak but it was clear what she meant. Then Gregori made a hand gesture indicating that he too was disembarking and he also gave Jon an enormous hug. And then they were all gone. For a moment, Jon felt

Retribution

a real sense of loss. He had shared some pretty amazing time with those people and it wasn't the way he would have wanted to part. He vowed to himself that when this was all over, he would get back in contact somehow. For now, he had more pressing things on his mind.

The aircraft launched and within another hour they were landing at Abruzzo airport. It was being used as a resupply base for the ships off the Adriatic coast and a C130 Hercules with all four engines already running was waiting. With only a brief thank you and goodbye to his rescuers, Jon was running across the tarmac and into the giant machine. A crewman greeted him and escorted him up the forward stairs to the cockpit. The two pilots turned and looked oddly at him. Jon realised what a sight he must look, still dressed in civilian clothes. He doubted that he looked like what they had been expecting to see.

Another officer, who Jon assumed was the navigator, turned in a swivel chair and faced him. 'Captain Hunt,' he shouted over the roar of the engines.

Jon nodded. 'Sorry I'm not exactly in uniform but the last few days have been interesting to say the least. Where are we headed?'

'Our brief was to carry on with our normal itinerary. Which means our first stop will the air station at Yeovilton. We have a load of stores to drop off there. I was told to tell you that a Commander Pearce will meet you there.'

Jon felt a wash of relief. 'Yes, that's great. He's one of the people I really need to see.'

'Why don't you go down aft Sir and grab some kip. We can also provide you with a delicious RAF bag rat meal if you're that way inclined.'

'Thanks, I'll have to think about that. Are the seats as ferociously uncomfortable as I remember?'

'Oh I'm sure they're worse but if you ask the Loadmaster I'm sure he can rustle up a hammock for you after we take off.'

As soon as they were in the air, the Loadmaster came up trumps and slung a hammock for Jon from the ceiling eye hooks. Jon politely declined the white cardboard box that was offered. He knew exactly what was on offer inside and the thought of curled up RAF sandwiches and a packet of crisps definitely did not appeal. It would be a few hours to England and he was exhausted. He had hardly slept the previous night. The adrenalin from the past and worry over the future keeping him awake. He soon found out that it was the same now. Despite an almost overwhelming need for sleep it wouldn't come. His mind was in a whirl. He kept thinking of Helen. He kept thinking of Peter Johnson. Despite all he knew, he still couldn't reconcile the facts. When they had been escaping from the Serbs, he had pushed it all from his mind. Now it wouldn't go away. Suddenly, she was sitting in the hammock with him. Part of his mind knew that was impossible, part didn't care.

'Hello my darling,' he said with wonder in his voice.

She smiled that glorious smile of hers. Her hair was a halo around her head, silhouetted by the cabin lights of the aircraft. She looked down at him with love in her eyes. 'Do what you feel you must Jon. But put me in your past, please?'

'Never, that's just not possible and you know it.'

She smiled again but sadly this time. 'Then I will just have to wait for you, goodbye.'

He was just about to say something when he felt a hand on his shoulder giving him a gentle tug. 'Sorry Sir, we are about to land, you need to get out of the hammock and take a seat. We'll be on the ground in about ten minutes.'

Groggily, Jon slipped out of the hammock and strapped himself in. He was desperately trying to hold on to the echo of the dream. He knew it had been one but just for a moment it seemed so real. Then his thoughts turned to the future and he felt an almost painful stab of resolve. This was going to end and very soon.

Chapter 47

Brian left the warm confines of the Air Traffic Control tower at Yeovilton and braved the cold predawn air of the airfield. The Hercules was taxying and about to stop on the concrete hardstanding in front of him. The noise and smell of half burned kerosene was intense. He didn't notice it. The aircraft came to a stop and the noise slowly wound down with the engines. A door near the front of the aircraft opened and some steps were lowered. A figure emerged. At first, Brian had difficulty recognising him. For some reason, he expected Jon to be in his normal uniform. This figure was wearing jeans and an old, tatty overcoat. But it was clearly his old friend

They met half way. Jon looked terrible. There were bags under his eyes and his face seemed lined with worry. Even worse, it seemed like the normal irrepressible twinkle in his eyes had faded. Brian gripped his hand. 'Welcome home Jon. Sorry about the transport, it was all I could manage at short notice and even that took some serious string pulling believe me. Come on into the tower. They've got a small galley there and one of the girls is making us a heart attack special. I bet you haven't had one of those in a while.'

Jon smiled wanly at Brian and they went back into the building. The bright light made them both blink and Brian led them down a corridor to a small room at the rear. True to his word, two large plates of fried eggs, bacon and other cholesterol filled items were waiting, along with two enormous cups of coffee. Suddenly, Jon's mouth was watering and he sat down and started wolfing it down.

Brian was pleased to see his old friend eating well. He reckoned it was a good sign. The fact that he was about to impart some bad news was not quite so heartening.

Jon spoke through his mouthful before Brian could start. 'Brian, I'll tell you all about what went on when I have time. As far as I'm concerned there is only one issue I want to discuss. Have they arrested that shit Johnson?'

Brian looked uncomfortable. Jon immediately saw the look on his face. 'What is it? What's happened?'

'They raided his house just after midnight. He wasn't there and nor was his wife. An old couple live in a cottage and normally the wife cooks for them but she had already been told she wasn't needed that evening.'

'Hang on, so they had been there that day?'

'Yup, a car was heard leaving about mid evening but they didn't know where it went. It's not unusual. But when the police and one of Rupert's team got there the bird had flown.'

'Fuck, so where have they gone?' Jon looked worried.

'The police are starting to use this new traffic camera system they're installing on some motorways. Their Range Rover was spotted heading north around spaghetti junction at Birmingham but after that they've not been seen.'

'So, we've lost them then?' Bugger.'

'Possibly not. Johnson has a shooting estate in Scotland near Largs on the west coast. He has probably gone there. However, Rupert immediately got GCHQ to listen to the phone lines from there and there have been no calls at all. You would think that he would be screaming for help to someone or arranging some form of escape but it's been totally silent.'

'Hang on, what if he's using a mobile phone? They seem all the rage these days.'

'We thought of that but the spooks can monitor the cell masts in the area and again nothing has been picked up.'

'So, he's not there. Does he have a boat? Is he already at sea somewhere?' Jon asked thoughtfully.

'Not that we know of but I haven't come to the worst bit. Just before you landed, MI6 were instructed to back off. It's an internal operation and MI6 are meant to be focused abroad as you know. Someone from very high up has said that the police must take over. Also, that they shouldn't do anything until you have been properly interviewed. A specialist police team is on the way here as we speak. They are expected in about an hour.'

'You've got to be fucking kidding. He'll get away before that's all sorted out.' Jon said in exasperation. 'Hang on a second, if he's managed to get in contact with one of his friends in high places then he's using a bloody telephone.'

'Yes but he could have stopped and used a public one from anywhere.'

Jon was about to say something, when a young sailor put his head around the door. 'Commander Pearce? There's someone on the phone for you in the Ops Planning room.'

The two of them shot out and followed the sailor.

Brian was handed the telephone. It was Rupert on the other end. 'Brian, I've made myself really unpopular but I managed to find out who it was who told us to back off. It was a senior civil servant from the Home Office which is how he managed to get the order authorised. He's a man called Gerald Butler. Guess who he is known to be associated with? Anyway, GCHQ owe me a few favours and they managed to track all the incoming calls the man had at his house early this morning. They could only find out what exchange was used not the content of the call. But at about five thirty this morning one was received from Scotland and guess what exchange it was?'

Brian didn't need to think. 'Largs.'

'Got it in one. And half an hour later, we received the order to desist.'

'Well, get the local coppers up there,' Brian said in exasperation.

'None of them will do a bloody thing until Jon has given a sworn statement.' Rupert replied.

'What is it, what's he saying?' Jon asked urgently.

Brian told him. Jon went over to a map of the UK that was pinned to a wall. He looked for Largs and then ran his thumb up the map. 'It's just under five hundred miles there Brian.'

'Sorry Jon so what?' Brian asked puzzled.

'Let me talk to Rupert,' was all Jon said. Brian handed him the receiver.

'Rupert, its Jon, we're going up there. We can be there in about four and a half hours. You can tell the police to stuff their statement. They can have it when I've got the bastard.'

'Jon, what are planning to do? For God's sake don't do anything silly,' Rupert sounded really worried. 'You've only just escaped from a bad situation, for goodness sake don't make it any worse.'

'That's alright Rupert, just tell the bloody police they can have their statement in Scotland. Now for goodness sake, tell me exactly where this place is.' He listened for a few minutes and then put the phone down.

Brian looked puzzled. 'Jon, what the fucking hell are you playing at?'

Jon smiled mirthlessly. 'When I last looked, I owned a helicopter which, if I'm not mistaken, is parked up in that hangar over there. Are you with me?'

Brian barked out a laugh. 'You mad bastard. Right, you go and start getting her ready. I'll get a couple of the lads to help you push her out. She's full of fuel. I only used her the other day. I'll check with the duty Met person. We're going to need fuel somewhere so I'll sort that out as well. See you in a few minutes.'

In fact, it was less than twenty minutes later and the two of them were strapped into Wanda. Jon insisted on flying and was in the right hand seat. Brian was sitting next to him with a quickly prepared map. The airfield was shut but Brian pulled rank on the duty tower staff and told them in no uncertain terms what was going to happen. While he sorted out the final details of their route, Jon fired up the engine and rotors and within minutes they were airborne and heading north.

'We've got a tail wind for the trip so a ground speed of about one hundred and twenty. We should be there in four hours, give or take. The Met man says it should be a clear day so we can cruise at about two thousand feet. The big question is whether you are actually going to stay awake all the way, you silly sod,' Brian said as they settled into the cruise. He could see the strain on Jon's face.

'I tell you what Brian,' Jon replied. 'You take over when we stop for gas alright?' Jon had to admit that he was feeling bloody tired. Hopefully, the effort of flying a steady course in this very simple machine but that need constant pilot input, would keep him awake.

Two hours later, they were approaching RAF Valley, the airfield at Anglesey, for fuel.

Brian used the radio and called ahead. He was astounded to hear that not only where they refused fuel but were required to land and report to the local police who were already there waiting for them.

'Fuck,' said Jon. 'The word must have gone out. I expect all the airfields on our route will have been told the same. I'm not surprised but I have a cunning plan. I think it's time we dropped off the radar.'

Jon lowered the collective and the little machine fell out of the sky. He levelled off at about fifty feet and they shot up a valley in

Retribution

the Snowdonia National Park, quickly ensuring that the radars from Anglesey or anywhere else for that matter couldn't see them. 'I need a course for the closest motorway Brian. Oh and have you got your credit cards on you? Mine seem to have gone missing.'

The service station on the M56 near Liverpool was quiet, as it usually was this early in the morning. Most cars had yet to start out on their daily commute. Most truckers were snug in their cabs taking their mandatory time off. The lad in the kiosk was half asleep. He hadn't had a customer for over fifteen minutes. He was suddenly alerted by a strange growling noise. Then suddenly, out of the blue, a small helicopter appeared. The sight was strange enough to excite his curiosity. It got even stronger when the machine landed next to the HGV diesel pumps. The rotors quickly stopped and a man got out and strolled over towards him. He then saw another man climb out of the other side and take a fuel hose over to the machine. His pump register beeped at him and without thinking he pressed the button to start the pump.

'Good morning,' the man said politely at his kiosk window. 'You do take Barclaycard I hope?'

The lad nodded, still not sure whether he was actually awake. The fuel counter on the pump ran up an impressively large amount before stopping and then the man handed over his credit card which he authorised.

Within minutes, there was the whine of a turbine engine starting up, followed quickly by the departure of the helicopter. *No one is going to believe this when I tell them,* the lad thought as he looked at the amount of diesel that had just been dispensed.

Chapter 48

Peter Johnson looked around at the small lodge that he had built on the side of the Grouse moor he owned. It was there to provide sustenance for his guests during a day's shoot. However, the most important thing was that it had its own telephone line, one that had been ex-directory ever since it had been installed. Unsurprisingly, many of his friends didn't want people trying to contact them when they were here. Consequently, he was as sure as he could be that no one, not even GCHQ knew about it. It was a gamble he knew but one that he was pretty sure was a good one. He had put it to good use. Firstly he had contacted his friend Gerald. At first, he had been angry at being woken so early in the morning and then even angrier when Peter had explained the situation. It was only when Peter made it clear that if he didn't get away, he would take Gerald down with him, that the man had agreed to see what he could do. Forty five minutes later, Gerald rang back and told him what he had achieved. It wasn't much but Peter was grateful. It was about all he could expect.

He then managed to get hold of the aircraft company and they had promised that a trans-Atlantic capable jet would be at Prestwick airport by midday. His one final call was to his broker telling him to transfer as much of his cash and other assets as possible to his offshore accounts. The man had been suspicious at first but the percentage he was offered soon shut him up.

He looked out of the window. It had been light for some time now and the weather was looking good. The view from the lodge was beautiful. It was one of the reasons he had placed it on the side of a gentle slope overlooking the moor. It was with a real pang of regret that he realised he wouldn't ever see it again. That turned his thoughts to his wife. She was beautiful too but he wasn't so sure he actually wanted to see her again. In fact, he was starting to regret his decision to take her with him last night. Inga had a taste for the good life. She had spent a great deal of his money pursuing it. He hadn't minded at first as she was so beautiful and so completely uninhibited in bed. However, lately things had cooled between them and he was definitely not sure how she would take to the idea of being in exile and away from all her London friends. He came to a decision. The

Retribution

Range Rover was parked nearby. He would head to Prestwick without going back to the main house.

His eye was distracted by something moving in the distance. He quickly realised it was a small helicopter. He reached behind him and picked up a pair of binoculars. Once he had the machine in focus, he realised that his first guess had been right. It was either an army Scout or a navy Wasp as it wasn't easy to tell which at this distance. What did intrigue him was that he knew quite well that both types had gone out of service some years ago. Some rich person must have bought it as a toy. He tracked it for a few seconds and then berated himself. He needed to get going. Just as he was about to look away, he realised where it was heading. His main house was just over the rise to his left and it was quite clear that the aircraft was heading that way, maybe even going to land. He looked more carefully and saw that the machine had four wheels not skids, so it was the navy version of the aircraft. What the hell was it doing? The only track off the moor went almost up to the house before joining the main road out of the estate. If it did land, he would be able to see it as he drove past. With no choice, he was about to jump into his car when he had a thought. He turned and unlocked a cabinet on the wall and took out a hunting rifle complete with telescopic sight. It was one of several, single shot weapons, they used in the deer stalking season. He then reached into a drawer and pulled out a handful of rounds. He loaded one into the rifle and pocketed the rest. It was always best to be prepared.

Brian was flying now and Jon navigating. In normal times they would probably have been exchanging friendly insults over each other's ability to do the other's job. Not this time, the atmosphere in the aircraft was deadly serious.

'That's the road we follow Brian,' Jon said, pointing out of the cockpit window slightly to his left. 'The house should be in about five miles, off a track to the left.'

They flew on for a few minutes and then the house came into sight. It was definitely the right place as there was no other habitation around for miles. It also looked deserted.

'So, what the hell do we do now?' Brian asked tight lipped. We can't just go and land on the front lawn. Supposing the bastard has a shotgun or worse.'

Retribution

'I've been thinking about this. We'll approach the front lawn but just before we get there, go low and I'll jump out. You then take your time going in to land. If Johnson comes out I'll try to sneak up on him while you keep him occupied. If its Inga or one of the staff, we can simply talk to them.'

'Sounds, sort of, like a plan. OK, let's fly over first.' Brian responded. They levelled off at five hundred feet and flew over the house. There were several outbuildings and a large lawn to the rear but still no sign of life and no cars on the front drive which Jon thought was odd. Rupert had said they had a Range Rover, so where was it?

Brian flew well past then turned back southwards into wind, looking for somewhere to drop off Jon. They both saw it at the same time. There was a plume of smoke or dust coming down a small track that led off the moor to the west.

'If I didn't know better, I would say that that's a Range Rover,' Jon said, tight lipped. 'And we know who owns one of them, don't we?'

'So, what do we do? We can't follow him far we've only got about thirty minutes of fuel left Jon.'

'We have to stop him somehow. Look, he's got quite a distance to go before he can get off that road. Plan B, go and land over there on the road and block it. There's a ditch on both sides so he won't be able to shoot off cross country.' Jon pointed to their left. 'There, just before the house, it's over a rise. He won't be able to see us. I can jump out and hide. You land on and block the road. Just buy me some time.'

Brian threw the little machine towards the road. It soon became clear that Jon was right because as he flared the helicopter into the hover, they lost sight of the Range Rover on the other side of the hill. As soon as the wheels were on the ground, Jon leapt out and ran to the side of the road and threw himself behind a large gorse bush. Meanwhile, Brian shut down the aircraft.

Just as the rotors were slowing to a halt, the car appeared. It was travelling at quite a speed and all four wheels locked up on the loose surface as it skidded to a halt. Brian was climbing out and turning his back, he ignored the car. He started looking at the engine, prodding at it. Jon immediately realised what he was doing. He started to creep forward being careful to keep behind the gorse bush. As he did so, the car door opened and an angry man stalked out. He reached inside and pulled out a rifle and turned. Jon's heart leapt. It was their quarry.

The sight of the helicopter stopped on the road took Peter Johnson completely by surprise. The last thing he had seen of it, it was flying away to the north and once inside the car he was too busy concentrating on driving. He slammed on the brakes and came to a skidding halt, swearing under his breath. *'What the fucking hell was the pilot up to?'* he thought angrily. He jumped out, remembering to grab the rifle. Something about this just didn't smell right.

Amazingly the pilot was ignoring him and fiddling about with something at the rear of the aircraft. 'Just what the hell are you doing?' he called out loudly. 'You can't land here. Its private property and you're blocking the damned road.'

The pilot looked around. He was wearing a military flying helmet with the visor down so Peter couldn't see most of his face which was odd. 'Sorry about that but I've got a major problem with the engine. There's no way I can take off again I'm afraid,' he said in a strange Irish accent.

'What? Don't be so bloody silly. Look, I own this estate and I've an urgent appointment to keep.'

The pilot didn't look concerned. 'I've said I'm sorry but the engine almost packed up on me. I had no choice but to land.'

'So, how the hell do I get past?'

'Err, I guess you can't old chap. Is there another route you can use?'

Peter was starting to get really angry now, this whole situation stank. 'No, there bloody well isn't and who the hell are you anyway? You shouldn't be flying an old wreck like this if it isn't airworthy.'

The pilot didn't seem put out in the least. 'Yes, well, it's got all the clearances you know. Things do go wrong with aircraft occasionally.' Suddenly his accent changed. 'If you were a pilot you would know that. Oh sorry, you are one, so you probably do. My name is Brian Pearce,' and he pulled up the visor.

Peter stared in amazement and shock. Before he could think further, he caught movement out of the corner of his eye and he whirled around just in time to see someone swinging a large lump of

Retribution

wood at his head. He ducked down and it shot past him and crashed noisily on the front wing of the car. Realising what was now going on, he instinctively whirled around and pulled the trigger of the rifle. The crash was incredibly loud without the normal ear protection but he saw Pearce stagger. His assailant must still be behind him but he wasn't waiting to find out. With his heart racing, he leapt the ditch at the side of the track and started running. He could still get to the main road and flag down a car. There was still time, there was still hope.

Retribution

Chapter 49

Jon was going to take another swing at Johnson when the gun went off and everything changed. Brian was flung backwards onto the road. All thought of continuing his attack fled. All he could think of now was getting to his friend. In his periphery, he noticed Johnson starting to run but ignored the man. He was no longer his priority.

Brian was lying in the road. He seemed to be conscious when Jon got to him. He could see a large red stain appearing on his upper left leg.

'Brian,' he called urgently as he knelt down alongside his friend. 'He seems to have hit you in the leg. I'm going to have a look.'

Brian's eyes were shut but he looked up and opened them at Jon's voice. 'Sorry mate, I think I might have given you away there.'

'Don't be so fucking silly Brian, does it hurt?'

'Nope, just feels numb.'

'Believe me, this is going to start hurting and very soon.' Jon undid Brian's trouser belt and buttons and carefully pulled down his trousers.

'Careful Jon, we don't want people seeing you doing that, now do we?'

'Shut up you silly ass. I need to see what's going on. Bloody hell, this is the second time in a week I've had to do something like this.'

It was immediately clear that the round had gone clean through Brian's upper thigh. There was a small hole at the front and nasty great tear at the back which was bleeding profusely. Jon remembered that there was a small first aid kit in the helicopter and ran over to get it. Luckily, one of the main contents was a military shell dressing. He ripped it open and put the large pad on the exit wound then tied the bandages tightly around the leg. The bleeding seemed to stop as the pressure was applied. He was just wondering what to do when a female voice broke his train of thought.

'Jon, is that you? And Brian, good God. What are you doing here and oh, goodness Brian, have you been shot? I heard the helicopter and came to investigate and then heard the gun.' It was Inga, Johnson's wife and Jon's old girlfriend.

Retribution

With the immediate threat to Brian's life under control, Jon's thoughts were turning to his primary objective.

'Inga, do you trust me?' Jon asked looking up at her.

'What do you mean Jon? Of course I do. You know that.'

'Even if I tell you that we flew up here to arrest your husband as a traitor?' Jon asked, looking hard at her.

A strange look passed over Inga's face. 'Is this something to do with why we came up here so urgently last night? He wouldn't tell me anything and must have left the house very early this morning.'

'Almost certainly. Look, I haven't got much time. Can you look after Brian and call for the police and an ambulance. I need to get after your husband.' Jon noticed an old Land Rover parked behind the Wasp. It must have been what Inga had arrived in.

'Yes, of course. What are you going to do?'

'I'm not sure yet but help me get Brian into your car and then I can get after him.'

The two of them, with some help from Brian himself managed to get the large man into the passenger seat of the Land Rover.

Jon looked at the two of them. 'I'm taking Wanda and I'm going to get him. Brian, get Inga to take you to the house and wait for an ambulance and the police OK? Inga, Brian will tell you what's going on. Now scoot, I need to get on with this,'

Jon didn't wait for an answer. He ran back to the helicopter and jumped in. Within minutes he was lifting into the hover. He knew the direction Johnson had gone and accelerated that way. There was a public road about a mile in the distance and that was probably where he was headed. The ground was mainly covered in heather. It was not going to be easy for a man to move fast through it. Sure enough, Jon quickly spotted his quarry wading through a large stand of undergrowth. Without conscious thought, he dived the little helicopter at the man. He flew as low as he dared and roared over the top of him. As he pulled the aircraft's nose up and turned to look back, he saw Johnson picking himself up from where he had thrown himself flat and doing something to his rifle. Jon immediately realised two things. Firstly, attempting to hit someone with a low flying aircraft might seem feasible in Hollywood but in reality it was just about impossible and secondly doing it to a man with a hunting rifle was even more stupid.

There was a flash from the muzzle of the rifle but there was no indication that it had hit the helicopter. Jon had an idea. While Johnson was struggling to reload, he flung the machine back down but came to the hover almost directly over him. As he got close, he pulled the emergency wire by his pilot's door. It was designed to jettison the door in the event of an emergency landing. Jon was using it as a weapon. Johnson had thrown himself flat again clearly expecting another low pass. He certainly wasn't expecting a large aluminium and Perspex door to come slamming down within feet of his head.

Cursing that he had missed, Jon was about to back off when Johnson scrambled to his feet again and started running. This time he had left the rifle lying on the ground.

'Got you, you bastard,' Jon said to himself as he followed in a hover taxi. However, Johnson wasn't about to give up and seemed to be ignoring the helicopter presumably he was assuming that there was nothing else Jon could do. Jon had other ideas. He remembered a story from a friend of his who had done an exchange job with the Australian Army. Apparently, if you chased a kangaroo in a similar manner, it kept looking over its shoulder until it tripped over its own feet. Funny but cruel. In this case it was just the right idea. What Jon could see from ten feet up and Johnson couldn't, was that just to the right of where he was half running, half staggering was a steep gully with a brook running through it. Jon moved the helicopter over to Johnson's left and forced the running man to slightly change direction. Every time he tried to head back directly towards the road, which was now getting quite close, Jon forced him to keep going the way he wanted. It probably wasn't that obvious to the panicked man on the ground as the changes of direction were quite small. Suddenly, he was at the edge of the gully and just to make sure, Jon flew directly at him getting extremely close with his starboard undercarriage leg. Johnson was looking at that as he lost his footing and, with a soundless cry, fell backwards into the gully.

Jon backed off and came around to look. The body was immobile, face down, next to the shallow water. He looked for a place to land. It wasn't going to be easy. In the end, he picked a spot only a few yards from the prone body and dumped the helicopter down hard, shutting down the engine as soon as the oleos made contact. Wanda leaned over at an awkward angle but stayed upright. For just a second, Jon wondered how on earth they would get her out of there but he had other priorities. As soon as he could, he pulled on the rotor brake and stopped the rotors. He had already undone his straps and he jumped out and ran to Johnson.

The body was lying still. Jon pulled him over and checked his breathing. There was a nasty lump on his forehead and it looked like one of his legs was broken but he was definitely still alive.

Despite all the previous promises he had made to himself and despite all the things the bloody man had done, Jon knew he couldn't kill him even though no one would ever know. All he would have to do was turn him over again and put his head in the water. He just couldn't do it. Anyway, having to spend the rest of his life in prison was a more fitting punishment for the murdering traitor than any Jon could devise. So he made sure he was in a safe position and sat back next to the prone body. Just for a second, he thought he heard a girl's voice, one he recognised, saying *'well done darling'* or maybe it was just the wind in the gorse and heather.

The adrenalin rush was gone. There was nothing more he could do. He was dog tired. The events of the previous weeks had completely drained him. He had done enough.

So he simply sat and waited.

Ten minutes later, he saw blue flashing lights appear on the distant road.

Epilogue

'Captain Hunt, Sir, the First Sea Lord will see you now.' The naval Commander who was Admiral Arthur's Military Assistant stood and opened the door for him.

Jon entered the room. He wasn't worried, although maybe he thought that he should be. Johnson was under arrest and Brian was recovering in hospital and would be out in a few more days. Not only that but MI6 had gathered enough evidence against the civil servant who had aided Johnson to place him under arrest as well. Rupert was certain that, at last, all the old guard of the Soviet days had been accounted for. The navy had offered to salvage Wanda and she was now back at Yeovilton undergoing some precautionary maintenance. That only left Jon's career.

The First Sea Lord stayed sitting behind his desk when Jon entered and the MA closed the door behind them. Not a good sign.

'Take a seat Jon,' the great man said and once Jon was comfortable he continued. 'I really don't know what to do with you Jon,' he said, looking hard at him over the acreage of his desk. 'You've had some interesting episodes in your past but this one takes the biscuit. I've got half the military UN staff screaming for your court martial and other half wanting to give you a medal. The French are going to give you one anyway. They apparently want to award you their Croix de Guerre for rescuing their pilot. The Serbs want you extradited but they have been told in no uncertain terms to sod off. The Croatians want to give you a medal as well although they don't actually have any relevant ones at the moment. The police are hacked off because you didn't wait to be interviewed even though their reasons for doing so were crap and MI bloody Six want you to have another bloody medal. Jesus, you go off to do a simple short term UN job and once again turn it into a circus. What have you got to say for yourself?'

Only a few years ago, Jon would have felt intimidated to spoken to like that by such a senior officer. Today, he didn't give a damn and anyway he knew his man and that most of it was bluster. 'Quite simple Sir, if I had to, I would do exactly the same things all over again. I helped save lives, I helped expose the fucking awful crimes against humanity that are going on in the Balkans as we speak and I nailed the bastard who killed my wife. Why should you or I have a problem with any of that?'

The Admiral roared with laughter at Jon's reply and stood up from behind his desk. He held out his hand. 'Good answer Jon and I don't have any problem with any of it. If it's of any interest to you, I think you did bloody well. But we have a problem or rather I do.'

'Yes Sir.'

'I can't really give you a medal as you were either on seconded service or acting effectively as a private individual. So, what the hell am I going to do with you now? I think I need to get you back to sea where you might just have a normal appointment for once. At least it will be somewhere away from the UN and spies and the like.'

Jon's ears perked up but he didn't say anything, even though his pulse had just quickened.

'You said you wanted her, well she's yours. Bloody well look after her. I'm giving you Formidable.'

Retribution

Author's notes

We have short memories in the West but the fact that a country that hosted the Winter Olympics could descend into such a pit of horror only a few years later is now largely forgotten. The Serbs must take the lion's share of the blame. It's reckoned they were responsible for over 90% of all war crimes. Their behaviour was absolutely disgusting. Anyone who thinks I have exaggerated what went on – just go on-line and look for yourselves. If anything I've been quite mild in my narrative.

The terms of reference for the UNPROFOR were exactly as I describe, as was how they were interpreted. Although some NATO air support had been given earlier, it was the atrocities of the summer of 1995 that really brought the war to an end when NATO were finally allowed to go in. To me, it's tragic that this had to happen to get everyone off their collective arses, especially as it was well known what was really going on. My little addition of the filming of the 'party' is of course fiction but there is at least one house in a small village near the Serbian border where that sort of thing really went on.

UNPROFOR was made up of troops from many countries including Russia. However, it's also true that Russia did a great deal behind the scenes to support Serbia – just like they did in 1914 which caused Germany to start hostilities in the Great War.

There were several NATO aircraft shot down during the conflict and the stories of how the pilots were recovered are well documented. In the case of one French pilot who was captured by the Serbs, he reported that he was well treated. The others escaped and didn't have to find out. Of course, Hollywood had to make a film about the American pilot and his escape……….

In 1995, I was a Commander in the MOD and given a short term appointment on a tri-service team looking at the support of helicopters in all three services. We worked for nine months and even on the day we were finalising our report, we still hadn't got a complete listing of exactly how many helicopters were in the military inventory. So, finding that one Wasp had been overlooked is quite possible. It's not unusual for ex-military aircraft to be put into civilian use, there are several Scouts and Wasps in private hands today. The Fly Navy Heritage trust works hard to keep many flying under the auspices of the Naval Historic Flight at Yeovilton.

A Wasp will happily run on commercial diesel amongst quite a long list of fuels. I stand to be corrected but I've never actually heard of one stopping at a service station for a top up.

I'm sorry to say that chasing Kangaroos by helicopter does often make them trip over their own feet but apparently when you fly over Penguins, the story that they watch the helicopter so much that they fall over backwards isn't.

Nowadays, people understand mobile phones and what they can do. I remember getting my first one in 1995 and it did one thing – it made phone calls and was the size of half a brick. In this story I've tried to go back to the technology of the day and the fact that they were still relatively uncommon. Hopefully, I got it reasonably right but as things were moving so fast then, please don't get cross with me if I described some of it out of time.

Jon and Brian will sail again:

FORMIDABLE

HMS Formidable is the Royal Navy's newest aircraft carrier. Captain Jonathon Hunt has been given command. He faces the uphill struggle of getting a new and untried machine of war into service and then is almost immediately faced with a major crisis. A massive mineral discovery in a small African republic has led to a potential confrontation. With both Navy and Air Force Harriers embarked, Jon and his new ship are the only hope for a group of innocent hostages.